*Chasing Jillian*

**Also by Julie Brannagh**

# *Chasing Jillian*

## A LOVE AND FOOTBALL NOVEL

## JULIE BRANNAGH

AVONIMPULSE

*An Imprint of HarperCollinsPublishers*

*Chasing Jillian*

A LOVE AND FOOTBALL NOVEL

Excerpt from *Heart's Desire* copyright © 2015 by Tina Klinesmith.
Excerpt from *Desire Me Now* copyright © 2015 by Tiffany Clare.
Excerpt from *The Wedding Gift* copyright © 2015 by Lisa Connelly.
Excerpt from *When Love Happens* copyright © 2015 by Darcy Burke.

dition JULY 2015 ISBN: 9780062363886

n ISBN: 9780062363893

6 5 4 3 2 1

To Jessi Gage and Amy Raby,
my critique partners and my friends.
Thank you for your kindness,
your encouragement, and your honesty.
Thank you for making a safe space for me.

## Acknowledgments

I WOULD LIKE to thank my editor, Amanda Bergeron, and my agent, Sarah Younger of Nancy Yost Literary Agency. I have said thank you to them over and over again, but I could never say it enough. Thank you so much for your patience and for going above and beyond. I am so lucky to work with you.

Thank you to Avon's art department, and an extra-special shout-out to Beverly of the copy editing department, who makes sure the atrocities I commit against grammar and punctuation remain a closely held secret.

Thank you to my husband, Eric, for putting up with deadlines and cooking dinner and everything else he does for us every day.

Thank you to Susan Mallery, who's ultimately responsible for all of this.

Thank you to our aunt Suzie Davenport Moore, who has been advocating for and placing foster kids in homes for years now. We are proud you are our aunt, and we love you.

Thank you to Seattle's Treehouse for being a beacon of light and hope.

Thank you to Gary Hopkins of Brotherton Cadillac in Renton, Washington, for answering my questions about Cadillac Escalades.

Thank you to Nordstrom. I have been dressing the characters in my books from your website for quite some time now. When that's not happening, I hate to shop, but I'll always love you!

Thank you to the Seattle Seahawks for giving interviews in multiple forms of media that are always helpful to my research. And I'd like to thank Michael Bennett for his NSFW sack dances.

Last but not least, THANK YOU for buying this book. I hope you'll love it! I also love to hear from readers. I'm on Twitter at @julieinduvall, on Facebook, and I have a website: http://www.juliebrannagh.com.

Go Sharks!

# Chapter One

ALL SHE HAD to do was not get caught.

Jillian Miller let herself into the Sharks' silent weight room. The coaches, players, and other front-office personnel had all gone home for the evening; it was just her and an exercise DVD. She couldn't afford a gym membership on her salary. John, the owner of the Sharks, was a great guy to work for, but she was in her first year here. She wouldn't get a raise for another six months at least.

She wasn't sure about the rules involved in using the team's weight room, but she was fairly sure it might be frowned upon. "It's easier to ask for forgiveness than permission," she muttered.

The Sharks' weight room was approximately the size of an airport hangar. One wall was mirrored; the opposite wall consisted of a garage-style glass-and-metal door opening onto the practice field. The room was filled with what Jillian imagined must be hundreds of thousands of dollars of state-of-the-art exercise equipment and smelled surprisingly good for a place seventy guys spent hours each day in working up a significant amount of sweat. She didn't spend a lot of time working out, let alone hanging around in any gym. She was unsure what she should expect, besides feeling like she'd landed on another planet.

The last straw for her had been such a little thing, in retrospect. A tall, thin, perfectly groomed woman had eyed the contents of Jillian's shopping cart at the grocery store yesterday. Two pints of Ben & Jerry's Late Night Snack, a large bag of dark chocolate M&M's, and a stack of low-calorie microwave meals. She'd caught Jillian's eye, shaken her head, and walked away. It had happened before, but the memory still made her flinch.

Jillian didn't want to be a supermodel or a size two. Mostly, she'd like to feel more comfortable in her own body, and the feeling had been building for quite some time before yesterday's incident in the grocery store. She also knew most people spent their weekends in active outdoor pursuits, especially in the Seattle area. She'd never been a big fan of exercise, but she'd like to meet some new people. Even more, she'd like to meet a guy. She'd like to fall in love, and she'd like to have a family. She wasn't going to accomplish this by spending most of her weekend evenings on her own. A little exercise (and trying some new pastimes) couldn't hurt.

She pulled out the DVD she'd brought with her and popped it into the player. An impossibly fit woman began barking instructions, and Jillian tried to follow along.

The woman in question, though, weighed a lot less than Jillian did. She wasn't winded at all. She looked like the professional cheerleaders that passed Jillian's desk on a daily basis—thin, toned, and perfect.

Jillian was already dripping. She glanced at her watch. Five minutes? That was it? Surely the United Nations would classify this as torture. The DVD woman was jumping around like a lipsticked chimp on Red Bull. Besides being relentlessly, annoyingly cheerful, she barked out a count only the Energizer Bunny could hope to keep up with. It couldn't be good to sweat this much. Obviously, sweating was part of working out, but it seemed a little excessive. She needed to breathe too. Maybe some water would help.

Just a few minutes more. She could do it. Sure she could: All she needed was a transfusion and an amphetamine drip.

SETH TAYLOR PUSHED his way through the front doors of the practice facility. He needed to work out like some guys needed to get drunk to forget. He'd just had the last fight with his girlfriend. Two years of her jealous rages— her baseless, jealous rages—were more than enough. Seth had finally told her it was over, shortly before he flung his cell phone against the passenger door of his car in utter frustration. The screen shattered on impact. It was the last thing he'd lose to Kim, besides the chunks of his soul she'd already taken. She was the most beautiful woman he'd ever met, but he couldn't take it another day.

If he was brutally honest, the problems with Kim were a symptom of what was really going on with him. He was restless. Despite the fact he already had more in life than most, he wanted even more. His inner struggle had nothing to do with wealth or fame. He wanted meaning. He wanted to find something to do in his spare time that made him feel like he'd made a difference in his world, besides attaining the high score on the latest video game. Right after that, he'd like to find a woman who wanted those same things and didn't make him want to shatter a six-hundred-dollar cell phone against his car door any time soon.

At least the place would be long deserted. He would lock himself in the weight room, turn the sound system up to the pain level, and sweat Kim out of his system. She was out of his life, and he could concentrate on things that made him happy for a change.

He strode to the weight room door and stopped. Someone was in there.

JILLIAN HEARD A loud, angry male voice behind her.

"Who are you, and what are you doing here?"

All she saw was a tall, dark-haired man with dark, intense eyes. It was hard to respond to him while she was huffing and puffing. Her heart pounded with a combination of exertion and the rushing adrenaline of fear. She knew he was one of the Sharks, but she didn't know enough about him to know whether or not he would freak out. Her embarrassment took a temporary backseat to her alarm.

"I'm Jillian." It seemed fairly self-explanatory what she was doing, at least to her. "I work here."

"I haven't seen you before." He moved even closer, blocking her against another wall, next to a huge white board, with his height and much-larger, rock-hard body. His muscles had muscles. "Who are you?"

"I work for John Campbell. What are you doing?"

She frantically looked around for an escape. She could make it out the weight room doors if she had to. She couldn't outrun him, but her fingers wrapped around the cell phone in her pocket. She'd hit 911 and scream at the top of her lungs. She stepped away from him. Surprisingly enough, he stayed where he was.

"Don't we all? So, who exactly are you?" he asked.

"I'm John's assistant."

He rested his hands on his hips as he studied her. His brows knit together. "Why are you here?"

"I'm doing my taxes. What do you think?"

Jillian was still a bit scared. Obviously, she'd startled him. He had startled her too. The only thing left to do, though, was stand her ground. She didn't owe Godzilla an explanation, and she took another shallow breath. Her heart was still pounding, but the panic and jitters of surging adrenaline were replaced with dismay. What would happen when her boss heard about this?

The guy reached out and tried to grab the remote from her; she put it behind her back. She turned to extract the DVD from the player, picked up the case, and shut off the TV.

"There you go. I'm leaving. You'll have the place all to yourself," she said.

"Wait!" he said, the word bursting out. "Where are you going?"

"Home." She swallowed hard. "I…I thought everyone was done for the day. I hoped this wouldn't be a problem." She flipped the long, damp blonde ponytail over her shoulder and turned toward the door. He reached out to take her elbow. His touch was surprisingly gentle.

"Hey. Let's give this another try," he told her. "I'm Seth. What's your name again?"

"I'm Jillian. I know I'm probably not supposed to be in here, so maybe I should just leave." The flash of irritation she felt at the fact he'd forgotten her name was superseded by dread. "Please don't tell John. I need this job."

Seth took the DVD case out of her fingers. She grabbed at air, but he flipped it over to take a look. "*Cardio Burn*? Listen, Jennifer—"

"Jillian," she reminded him.

"Yeah. Jill. The treadmill is a lot more effective than this DVD. You also won't be as prone to injury. How about it?" He took her elbow in his fingertips and steered her in the direction of the treadmills.

"I have to go…"

He still held her elbow. A teasing smile moved over his mouth. "Are you sure about that? Let's walk a little. You know how to use a treadmill, don't you?"

She hadn't been on a treadmill in so long, she wasn't exactly sure what to do. Surely she could figure it out. She glanced at the control panel, which seemed to have a lot in common with the flight deck of a commercial airliner. She wondered if anyone actually used all of the readouts available.

"It seems more complicated than I remember," she said.

Seth helped her step onto the machine and reached out to punch buttons on the display. "You can handle it," he said. "How tall are you, Jill?"

"Five-foot-four. And my name is Jillian." She looked down at her feet. Godzilla's eyes were about a thousand shades of brown.

"Short, huh?" Her head shot up. She narrowed her eyes at him, but she saw the flash of another smile, and she had to smile too. He had a dimple in his chin. His eyes sparkled. For a moment, she wondered what it would be like to see his smile more often. "So, I need your weight."

"Don't worry about that. I'll just go home." Jillian stepped off the treadmill.

"Luckily, there's a scale right here," he said. "No big deal."

She wasn't fond of any activity involving a scale…He cupped her biceps in both of his hands and guided her onto the flat piece of metal.

"Don't look," she said, but she was too late.

Seconds later he said, "Got it. Come on."

Tears of shame and frustration rose in her eyes. It wasn't bad enough that she'd gotten caught red-handed in the workout room after hours. He also knew how much she weighed! She knew she needed to lose weight, but she'd prefer to keep that number to herself.

Her face felt like it was on fire with embarrassment. He glanced over at her and said, "Don't worry about it." He didn't seem to care about seeing the number that was going to haunt her.

"But I—"

"Next time, you'll know exactly how to program this," he reassured her. He punched a few more buttons on the treadmill readout, clipped the emergency shut-off to her T-shirt, and directed her onto the treadmill. "Ready?"

"I don't want to bother you. Maybe I should go."

"You're not bugging me. Come on. Do fifteen minutes with me," he coaxed. "You can handle it."

He hit the "Start" button, and he grabbed her around the waist so she wouldn't fall when the moving belt started. "Go ahead. Try it."

Jillian felt his fingers sink into the softness. She glanced up at him. He didn't seem to be disgusted. She was horrified, however. He knew how much she weighed, and he'd touched her...Oh, God.

Jillian's feet started to move, and he let go. He stepped away from the treadmill, picked up the water bottle she'd brought in with her, and put it in the cup holder on the machine. He walked over, grabbed some free weights off the rack, and did butterflies while he watched.

"You're doing just fine."

She appreciated his encouragement, but she really wasn't sure she wanted a workout buddy at the moment. Every little humiliation, every awkward moment she'd ever had as the girl nobody noticed rolled into the tall, dark-haired, handsome man standing only feet from her. He moved closer to the treadmill as he watched her. It would have been endearing if it wasn't slightly annoying.

The display read eight more minutes. She could accomplish this.

"I can do it myself," she insisted as he edged closer while she glanced in his direction. It was like a kitten staring down a Great Dane. He didn't look worried. He actually looked like he was about to laugh.

"Sure you can. That's why you chose a workout DVD that I'd have a hard time with."

"Maybe you should work out more, then," she said.

He let out a snort. "Sassy, aren't you?"

He did a few more curls with the free weights as his mouth twitched with repressed laughter.

"Why, yes, I am."

"So, when's the last time you went to the gym?"

"What do you think?" she said. She continued a little longer in silence. Seth set the weights back down on the rack and grabbed a set of lighter ones. He was still standing in front of the treadmill. He didn't seem to want to leave. She could only imagine how much he'd laugh at her if she told him she'd avoided the whole working-out thing since she was in college. "It wasn't a priority." She stifled a sigh.

"How long have you worked here?"

She was studying the treadmill's readout. It took her a few seconds to answer him. "I don't get it." She'd only burned two hundred calories or so. Maybe the readout was broken.

"Again, how long have you worked here? It seems pretty self-explanatory to me."

She regarded him for a moment. "Two months."

"I got here two weeks ago."

"Uh-huh." She pretended like she wasn't hanging on his every word. He was really cute, his body was even better, and it was all she could do to keep herself from drooling. Breathing was also a priority, and his nearness left her a bit breathless.

"Southern California's traffic sucks, but this may be worse. Is the 405 always a mess?"

He was referring to the freeway that most of the Sharks traveled to get to the practice facility. Jillian had to smile. He looked forlorn.

"Yes. It is. Don't you come here in the late morning, though?" she said.

"Not always. Sometimes I have to be here early because we have meetings. I can't believe the traffic."

"If you carpool with someone, it's a faster trip. Isn't there anyone on the team who lives close to you?"

"I'm not sure. I moved into my house in Bellevue about a week ago. I'll have to ask around." The treadmill shut off. He reached out to grab Jillian's elbow as she teetered. "Easy."

"Thanks." She hopped off, picked up her water bottle, and took a long swallow. He was watching her, but he was trying to pretend he wasn't. She wondered what he was thinking. Then again, her short acquaintance with Seth had already proven he would have blurted it out. "It's late, and I should go. Are you staying?"

"Hell yeah."

"Would you please lock up when you're done?" She gathered up the DVD case and the water bottle and picked up her purse (and tote bag full of office clothes) off the floor by the television set.

"I'll do that."

Jillian took a few more steps toward the door. She wasn't sure what to say to him. Finally, she turned toward him once more. "Thank you, Seth. It was nice to meet you."

He lifted an eyebrow and nodded once at her. "It was nice to meet you too. Maybe I'll see you around." He gave her a big grin.

"That…that would be great," she stammered and smiled in return.

"Have a nice evening. Drive safely," he said. He gave her another nod.

He punched the "Power" button on the sound system. AC/DC blasted over the speakers. He jumped onto the treadmill she'd been using minutes before, hit "Start," and began to run.

ANOTHER FRIDAY NIGHT, but Jillian's date remained the same. As always, a puffball of ginger fur named Crème Brulee, or CB for short, curled up next to her on the couch. She'd gotten Crème Brulee from someone giving away kittens in front of the grocery store a couple of months ago. Her apartment was cozier with the cat. Plus, she'd always wanted a kitten. It was beyond Jillian why this should be different from any other Friday night, but somehow, it felt like it should be. Everything was somewhat normal for her. Well, except for the part where she'd met the most gorgeous guy to have spoken to her in years. Maybe she'd see him again on Monday when she went to work. Surely he was just being polite when he told her he'd see her around. He couldn't really mean it, right?

She let out a groan and covered her face with her hands, though, when she remembered that he knew how much she weighed. She'd awoken the puffball with an unexpected noise. CB batted at her with one small paw.

CB let out an injured mew, hopped off the couch, and scampered away. Jillian knew she'd find the kitten asleep on her pillow later.

She hurried over to the laptop on the little desk in the kitchen, pulled up Google, and searched on Seth's name. She sank into a chair while she read. He was six-foot-four, and she weighed practically as much as he did. Well, not quite, but still…She let out a long sigh. He was two years younger than she was. It also seemed Seth had been busy. He was single. "Very single," according to one of the most recent fan websites she looked at. In Google Images, she found a series of photos of him with multiple tall, dark-haired women, each more gorgeous than the last.

Irritated, Jillian shut the laptop lid with a click, got up from her chair, and hurried into the bathroom. She'd stood in front of a full-length mirror so many times, but it always showed her the same thing. She wasn't unattractive, but she could use a little more self-confidence and a lot more toning. She wasn't asking for physical perfection, but she'd like to make some changes. If she made a plan, started slowly, and kept at it, she'd see a difference. The biggest changes needed to start on the inside, though. Maybe if she got out a little more, she might meet a guy who was interested in her. Seth was gorgeous, but he wasn't really in her universe. Jillian went into the kitchen, grabbed a frozen low-calorie dinner out of the freezer, ripped off the cardboard lid, and shoved it into the microwave. Dinner would taste a whole lot better if it was accompanied by half a bag of chips and some ranch dip. But that wasn't an option right now. She opened the refrigerator door to look for some type of fresh vegetable.

She pushed the fridge door shut after a fruitless search and rummaged around in her apartment's tiny pantry. She located a can of peas. Peas were good. Plus, there weren't many calories in peas. Maybe she could fill up on them if the diet dinner didn't cut it.

Jillian's love/hate relationship with her body and food had started when she was little. Most of the time, there wasn't enough to eat. She ended up in a foster home at three years old after her mother died in a car wreck, and she was moved a few times before she entered elementary school. Things got a little better for Jillian when she was placed in a more permanent foster home, but she was still so hungry. No matter how much she ate, she wanted more. When she was old enough to make her own money, she made sure there was more than enough food, and that's when the problems began. Even more than a diet or a new workout regime, she needed to focus on the great things in her life. She'd build a healthier lifestyle as a result. Change from the inside would last a lot longer. She wanted to build on the goals she'd already achieved and reach out for more of the things she wanted in life: a husband. A family. To belong.

SETH FELL INTO bed later in his new house, tossing and turning for a few minutes as he waited to fall asleep. It had been a long and frustrating day. He could only imagine what waited for him on voice mail from Kim. If he'd made her so unhappy, maybe she should be relieved to be rid of him, but he knew she'd never see it that way.

He'd rummaged around in the storage room at the team headquarters a little before he'd left; he found an Under Armour T-shirt and shorts that looked like they would fit Jillian. She had some cross-trainers, but she'd need better ones. He wasn't sure why he even gave a shit. But his actions showed he did.

The women in his world were physically perfect. They were all beautiful, long-legged, and willing to do just about anything to spend time with a pro athlete. The older he got, though, the more he realized the party was over, at least for him. Kim was the third woman in four years who had looked great from the outside but turned out to be a nightmare when he'd looked any deeper. If he was truthful, he'd say she was a placeholder, which made him a real asshole too. He knew he didn't want to marry her. He should have ended things a long time ago. It was an excuse, but he didn't want to be alone. He'd jumped at the opportunity to be traded to Seattle. He'd enjoyed San Diego, but it was time to leave. Seattle offered opportunities he'd never get there: a championship. More money. A different atmosphere. His agents had put out the lure; Seattle bit, and here he was.

He'd told Jillian he'd see her around. Mostly, he wanted to find out if she was as funny and sweet as she seemed. Something about her touched something inside of him too. She was different than the women with whom he typically spent time, and he was curious. Maybe he could arrange to run into her on Monday at the facility.

Minutes later, Seth was dreaming about Jillian. Actually, he was dreaming of her eyes: big, as blue as the forget-me-nots his mom had in her garden, and flashing with irritation. He'd seen tears in those eyes too and sincere amusement when she smiled at him. He wondered what he'd see in her eyes if he stripped her clothes off and laid her down in his bed. Were her nipples the same shade of pink as the subtle flush that spread over her cheeks when she was embarrassed? What did she taste like? She'd probably knee him or something if he came on to her. Then again, in his dream, she slowly took his clothes off and pushed him down instead. She climbed on top of him, and she unhurriedly sank onto him. She felt so good. She was tight and hot, and she was saying his name...

"Seth. Seth. What the hell is going on?"

He awoke with a start. His kid sister, Lauren, was standing over him. He'd had the house for a week, but he'd been dumb enough to give her a key. He thought the drop-ins would slow down when she finally moved into her sorority house at the University of Washington—apparently not.

"You were groaning. Did you just get home?" she said.

"Huh?" He wanted to go back to sleep, but Lauren wasn't letting that happen, at least not right now.

"I came over here because you didn't answer your freaking cell phone."

"It's broken. What the hell do you want?"

"I wanted to make sure you were okay. I'll leave."

"No." He sat up. Even in the darkness, he grabbed a pillow to put over his crotch. Shit. What a dream. He'd have to spend some time later figuring out why he was dreaming about a woman he'd just met, but there wasn't time to delve into the depths of his psyche (or his hard dick) right now. "Did you want to talk to me or something?"

"I'm fine. I wanted to get out of the sorority house for a little while, so it wasn't all bad." Lauren threw herself down on the corner of the bed. "Mom called. She thought you'd been eaten by wolves."

He saw her swallow hard in the illumination filtering into his room from the hallway light and watched her fingers pluck at the fabric of the comforter on his bed. Lauren and his mom had panicked. He stifled a long sigh. He wondered how many years it would be before any member of his family wouldn't imagine the worst every time he wasn't immediately reachable.

He worried about them too, despite pretending that he didn't.

He attempted to sound irritated. "What time is it?" he said.

"A little after ten. Don't tell me you're getting old, Seth. You're in bed and asleep at this time on a Friday night? That's tragic."

"You should try it." He sat up a bit more and surreptitiously adjusted himself beneath the pillow.

"Yeah, right." Lauren reached out to flip on the bedside lamp. "Have you eaten?"

"Hours ago. Are you hungry?"

"A little." She fiddled with the base of the lamp for some unknown reason.

He suppressed a groan and got out of bed. "Pizza?"

"Okay." She scampered after him. "Vegetarian?"

"Fine."

## Chapter Two

JILLIAN PULLED HERSELF out of bed on Monday morning to a screeching alarm clock and a very active kitten. CB chased her as she hurried to the shower. He wasn't too interested in the water, but he did like sitting on the side of the tub. She quickly dressed, brushed her hair, and for once, she applied a bit of mascara, a swipe of blush, and some lip gloss. This was not for Seth, she sternly told herself. This was for her. She always felt more confident when she looked nice.

As she walked over the threshold of the front office, she moved toward her desk. She was a little early, but her boss was already in.

"Hey, Jillian," she heard her boss, John, call out. "Will you come in here for a minute?"

She hoped Seth hadn't told on her using the weight room over the weekend. That would be a disaster. "I'll be right there."

She tried to still the butterflies in her stomach as she walked into John's office. He was usually fairly unflappable, but she had seen what happened when he was angry with someone. She'd like to avoid ever being that someone.

He indicated one of the chairs in front of his desk. "Hey. Sit down." Oh no. She must be in trouble. He tapped away on his laptop for a few more seconds, clicked the mouse, and glanced up from his work. "I was wondering if you could help me out with something."

"Sure."

"My girlfriend's birthday is next week. I'm a little torn about what to get for her." He gave Jillian a wry smile. "I don't want her to think that I just raced out and bought something at the last minute, but I'm not sure what she's going to want. She likes clothing, but I always choose the wrong things. There's only so much jewelry one woman can wear too. What would you suggest?"

Jillian tried to imagine a world in which there was only so much jewelry a woman could wear. She couldn't. "Why don't you take her somewhere overnight, even if you stay in town? I know she likes spending time with you."

"Jillian, you're good for my ego. Remind me you need a raise." She had to grin. "So, where do you think I should take her?"

"There are lots of places you could go. Would you like to go wine tasting? Does she like to dance?"

"We haven't been dancing together for a while." He looked a little helpless. "Could you check this out for me? I'll make the reservations and stuff, but I know you're great at putting information together so I can decide at a glance."

"I'll get right on it, John."

"Thanks." Jillian got up to walk out of the office, but she heard John's voice once more. "Seriously. Thank you. And if I haven't said so lately, I really appreciate all the extra stuff you do around here to make things easier for me."

"I'm happy to do it." She sank into a chair at her desk, John's compliments still ringing in her ears. She'd work even harder.

A couple of hours later, Jillian had selected three hotels for John's getaway with Sophie, worked on some business correspondence, answered a flurry of phone calls, and tried to push any thoughts of Seth completely out of her mind. John had left the office for a luncheon meeting and wouldn't be back until late afternoon.

No matter how many times she'd told herself over the weekend that Seth wasn't counting the minutes until he saw her again, that his "See you around" when she'd left the other night was right up there with every guy who told a woman "I'll call you" but didn't, she wished he was. She knew he was probably in the weight room or on the practice field with his teammates; there was little to no chance she'd run into him again during her work hours. She stifled the resulting sigh.

She glanced at the clock on her computer monitor: only a few more minutes until lunchtime. She slipped off her dress shoes and reached into her desk drawer for the pair of cross-trainers she'd brought to work today. She'd go for a short walk outside in the sunshine. A few minutes after that, she'd reheat the leftovers she'd brought for lunch and eat at her desk while her coworker Vivian took her own lunch hour.

Jillian jammed her feet into the cross-trainers. She stood up from her desk as the clock struck twelve.

"I'll be back in an hour, Vivian," she called out.

"I'm guessing you're going for a walk. It's nice out there," Vivian said and grabbed the receiver of her desk phone as it rang.

Jillian pocketed her cell phone and let herself out the front door of the facility. She breathed in fresh air; it had the slight tang of falling leaves and the underlying chill of oncoming fall. Bright sunshine and blue skies beckoned. The street in front of the Sharks' practice facility was deserted. She couldn't hear the typical practice noises from the field, so the players must have had something else to do. She had the sidewalk to herself.

Even a confirmed exercise-hater could enjoy a walk during September in Seattle. Birds sang. A squirrel darted across the street in search of food. The distant hum of traffic was almost soothing. She concentrated on breathing deeply as she set a slow but steady pace.

Minutes later, she heard the unmistakable "slap, slap" of the soles of someone's shoes hitting the pavement behind her. She heard a newly familiar voice as she turned to look.

"Hey, it's me," Seth said as he stopped a couple of feet away from her, running in place. "What's up, exercise warrior?"

She told herself to remain calm while she resisted the urge to jump up and down like a nut. "Not a lot," she said. "How are you?"

"Doing well," he said. "I thought I'd get a little running in before I knock off for the day. Want some company?" He nodded at the deserted road in front of them.

"I'd enjoy that." She tried to keep her voice casual. He grinned at her again. The beautiful day paled in comparison to his smile. Maybe she should pinch herself; she had to be dreaming.

"I'll try to keep it under a hundred," he teased.

"You do that," she said.

Of course, he laughed and took off like someone was chasing him. He wasn't even breathing hard.

Jillian attempted to keep up with him, but his legs were so long that she had to take two steps for each one of his. His idea of a "walk" could incapacitate a normal person. She made it about half a block before bending over at the waist and trying to catch her breath. He doubled back, reached out for Jillian's wrist, and felt for her pulse. She wondered how much of her heart rate was due to exertion and how much was Seth standing less than a foot from her.

"Okay. I'll slow down, Shorty," he said. "Breathe."

"Right." She took great gulps of air. Maybe she should trip him—if she lived through the next thirty seconds or so. That might slow him down.

Her heart rate was returning somewhat to normal. She might live. She straightened up again.

"You okay?" he asked.

"I'm fine. Yeah. Let's go." She told herself to stop nodding like a bobblehead. The women he dated were probably used to attention from guys like him. She wasn't. Maybe she should try treating him like anyone else; she might forget her nervousness around him as a result.

"I'll take it easy," he assured her. "I sometimes forget that everyone else doesn't run wind sprints on a daily basis."

She took another deep breath as he switched to a walk. She couldn't imagine what kind of hell a "wind sprint" was.

"You can outrun me, but I bet I can type faster than you can," she blurted out.

He burst out laughing. "I'll bet you can too, Jill." He swung his arms as she struggled to keep up with him. "By the way, I found a T-shirt and a pair of shorts you might like. They're back at the building," he said. He gestured at her cross-trainers. "There's some new cross-trainers in the equipment closet too."

Any shoes available in the Sharks' equipment closet were top of the line—with a price tag to match.

"I'll think about it," she said as she glanced up at him.

"Hey. The best part is the price. It's all free."

He did lunges as she attempted to keep up.

"It's nice of you to offer," she said. "Thanks."

"Let's just say I like company when I'm getting in another couple of miles in the afternoon," he said. His voice dropped. "I'm actually kind of a selfish bastard, so it's good to share the pain. And the stuff from the equipment closet."

She had to laugh. "Your generosity is overwhelming."

"That's right. I'm a giver. Plus, I just moved here. I don't know anyone in the Seattle area besides my family. I love them, but I've had enough of them for a while. I thought we could help each other out. You show me some of the places you like to go or stuff you like to do, and I can offer my training expertise." He gave her a nod. "I'm already broadening my horizons. This is the first time I've been out of the building since I got here."

Jillian stopped in the middle of the sidewalk. She really wanted to spend more time with him, but she didn't want to feel like he felt sorry for her or whatever. "It's really nice of you to think of me, but don't worry about it. Don't you have some supermodel to take to lunch or something?"

Seth turned to glance at her. "Unless Vivian's a supermodel in her spare time, I'm fresh out of them." His mouth curved into a smile. "Right now, you're getting all my attention." Jillian's mouth opened, but he interrupted her. "Do you know how much I could charge as a personal trainer?" he teased.

"Whatever it is, I can't afford it. Plus, I know you don't need the money. I saw your contract information."

"Don't be a hater," he said.

She couldn't stop the laughter that rolled out of her.

"Forty-five million dollars for four years, twenty-seven guaranteed? It's like Monopoly money. I can't imagine it." She stifled a sigh. "You really want me to show you around? I hope you're not expecting the same level of expertise in my tour guide skills," she said. "I've lived here all my life and I still get lost."

"There's GPS on my phone. We'll figure it out," he said.

He reached out to take her elbow in his fingertips as they approached a busy intersection. Exercise had never been her favorite pastime, but she had to admit it wasn't so terrible right now. They walked in silence for a few minutes after crossing the street. Jillian noted he'd slowed his steps to keep up with her, and he hadn't dropped her arm. She wanted to know more about him. Maybe she should ask him some questions about himself.

"You said your family lives here?" she blurted out.

"They do. My parents live in Issaquah, and my kid sister is at the University of Washington."

"Did they come to your games when you played in San Diego?"

"You're turning into a regular chatterbox, aren't you?" He did a few more lunges as they paused. "Sometimes they did. My sister hung out at my house for most of last summer. She took care of things while I was in training camp." He waited for the signal to change at another crosswalk and glanced at his watch. "They liked it when we'd play the Sharks. Now I'll be in the stadium all season, so they don't have to fly so often to see me." He glanced over at her. "How are you doing?"

"Huh?"

"You okay? Want to turn around?"

"Maybe a few minutes more," she said.

"Gotcha. So, Jillian..." She laughed at the exaggerated expression on his face. "More about you. How long have you lived here? What do you like to do when you're not at work? Who's your favorite pro football player?"

"Seriously? Weren't you just objecting to all of my questions?"

"I have to answer questions as part of my job. Let's see how you do with it," he said.

She slowed down a little so she could catch her breath, and he slowed his steps to match hers. "I'm a native."

"Does your family live here too?"

She really didn't want to answer that question. Maybe she could get him talking about something else. "Let me answer the questions you asked first," she said.

"Nice," he said. "I'll have to remember that the next time a reporter asks me fifteen questions and keeps asking more as I'm trying to answer the first set. So, go on."

"When I'm not at work, I do stuff like read, go to the movies, or hang around with my friend Kari. I also have a kitten. She's fun to play with." She pulled in some breath. "I do the same stuff everyone else does."

They walked through the parking lot in front of the facility, and he opened the door for her as they stepped inside.

"Not necessarily the same stuff, Jill. I don't have a kitty," he said.

"You could get one," she teased.

He let out a loud laugh. "I don't think so," he said. "I'm more of a dog guy. Maybe I should visit with yours instead."

JILLIAN SLUMPED INTO a chair at her desk a few minutes after she and Seth arrived back at the facility. Her face was sweaty, her hair was matted to her head, her clothes were a mess, and her feet were aching too. Next time, she'd make sure she was better prepared. Right now, though, she wondered how she'd get through the rest of the afternoon. She pulled her lunch sack out of the drawer and dropped it on her desk.

"What happened to you?" Vivian called across the room.

"I went for a walk, remember?"

She was exhausted, but she had too much work to do to dwell on how she felt—or what she looked like—at the moment. She tried to wipe the sweat from her forehead with a tissue or two. Her office clothes would need laundering ASAP.

Seth reappeared with a plastic shopping bag and set it down on her desk. "Here's the swag I mentioned earlier. Maybe I'll see you tomorrow."

"That would be nice," she said. "Thanks for the stuff." She would have preferred flowers or fine jewelry, but it was kind of cute he'd thought about her.

"Happy to help." He winked at her and moved away, calling out to Vivian, "So, gorgeous, want to have lunch with me? There's a hole in my schedule." Jillian saw him wink at her. "It's split-pea soup day. You know I love that stuff."

"You can't be serious." Vivian was blushing again.

"Oh, I am. Come on. Think how jealous the other guys will be that I have a date and they don't."

"Seth, does your mother know you're flirting with me?"

"Oh, she'd want me to." The two of them walked away, and Jillian took a bite of her reheated leftovers. The phones were quiet. Hopefully, she could eat before she had to start in on the afternoon's work.

Vivian arrived back at her desk an hour later, glowing with happiness.

"Did you have fun?" Jillian called out.

"Absolutely. Those boys are good for my self-esteem. What a bunch of flirts!" She fanned herself. "That Deion wants to take me out for a drink. I had to tell him no. Wait until I tell my husband about this. He won't let me out of the house by myself!" She patted her hair and laughed. "Did you know that Seth just broke up with his girlfriend?"

"He did?" Jillian was not going to bring up her Friday night Google search. Nope. Not going to bring that up.

"Oh yes. They were together for two years. He said that she's very jealous, and he'd finally had enough. He also said his younger sister is relieved. Can you imagine?"

"His sister didn't like the girlfriend?"

"Oh no. Seth says he's single again, so of course the other guys at the table were insisting they'd 'hook him up.' There was some name-calling, and I had to threaten to wash someone's mouth out with soap."

Jillian heard the telephone ring, and Vivian picked it up.

Just the thought that the guys were going to "hook up" Seth with anyone else made Jillian want to smash her coffee mug against her desk. He wasn't a possibility for her by any stretch of the imagination, but she could still dream, couldn't she?

## *Chapter Three*

JILLIAN'S WEEK SPED by after another lunchtime walk with Seth. She'd given him her number during their last walk, and he was going to text her when he could do another. She pretended like giving her number to a guy she was insanely attracted to happened every day of the week, but when she got home from work that night, she danced around her living room with glee.

The team wasn't playing until Monday night, which meant Seth was getting ready for the team's flight to San Francisco today.

She pulled up to the back door of a warehouse in Seattle on Saturday morning. The warehouse was part of the headquarters of Treehouse, a local charity that helped foster children have a childhood. Jillian had been volunteering with them for many years. She was digging into the pile of kids' hats and mittens she'd bought a few days ago at Costco. She'd bought as much as she could afford. They'd go great with the five kids' winter coats she'd bought last month. She made a good salary with the Sharks, but after paying her bills and putting money in savings and donations, there wasn't a lot of room for frills.

She kept coming back to Treehouse because she felt needed. After all, she wanted to be like everyone else, and that was tough to do when others found out the thing they took for granted—a loving family—was something completely foreign to her. She did her best to keep her chin up every day, but it was a relief to be anywhere that there were others who had the same problems in life.

A staff member hurried past the doorway but doubled back when he saw her.

"Hey, Jillian. You bought more stuff? Do you spend any of your paycheck on yourself?" he joked.

"I found a sale." She held up one of the winter coats. "These are great, aren't they?"

"They are. I really like the white hat and gloves set with the sparkly pony on the side," he said.

"I'm kind of into the pink one with the flowers myself," she said.

"Need some help?"

"Nope, I'm good," she said.

He gave her a nod and vanished into the building. Everyone here was busy and sometimes overwhelmed, but they did it because they loved the fact they could make a difference.

Jillian gathered up her donations in both arms, snagged her purse, and hip-checked her car door to shut it.

Most single women spent their weekends with friends, dancing at clubs, or out on dates. Jillian's weekends were typically spent supervising other volunteers or chatting with teens who were ready to age out of the system when they visited headquarters. She did whatever she could to be helpful. Some days were heartbreaking. She knew from experience that one person could make the difference between a teenager who believed his or her life could be different and one who just gave up.

Her former foster parents weren't the warmest, but they kept her housed, fed, and clothed. Instead of getting a part-time job when she was in school, they'd urged her to study. Jillian's excellent grades translated into a scholarship to the University of Washington. It took her almost ten years to pay off her student loans when she graduated with a business degree, but even the ability to make the payments was a cause of pride to her. She'd beaten the odds. She was one of the 3 percent of former foster children who graduated from college.

She didn't see her foster parents anymore. She sent them a Christmas card each year, but she didn't receive any invitations to their holiday celebrations in return. Her foster parents had done their best to make sure she had the tools she needed to succeed on her own when she was out of foster care. Unfortunately, their biological children were hostile to her, at best. She wasn't sure how to salvage a relationship that never happened in the first place. But she was still thankful for the family's help.

Everything was quiet so far. It would get a lot crazier at ten AM, when children and their foster parents were allowed into the donations area for "shopping." Most people had no idea that foster kids received $150 per year from the state of Washington for all grooming needs. It wasn't enough. Clothing could eat up that $150 in one shopping trip. There were so many things foster children struggled with, even if they had loving and supportive foster parents. Mostly, they wanted to fit in and belong.

Jillian hung up the five winter coats on a department store rack donated to Treehouse for clothing display. She piled the hats and mittens on another table covered in additional winter wear. After that, she hurried to a multipurpose room where she knew her latest "client" would be waiting. Treehouse had staff members with appropriate training who worked with the kids who were going to college. Jillian didn't have that training, but she could act as a mentor. She enjoyed any opportunity to help with filling out scholarship and college applications or talking about the future plans of the teens she met. Plus, sometimes the most important skill she possessed was the ability to listen.

A young woman named Chastity sat at one of the long folding tables shoved up against a wall. She glanced around and grinned as Jillian hurried in.

"Hey. Sorry, I'm late," Jillian called out. "Would you like a cup of coffee?"

"No, thanks." Chastity brushed long black curls out of her eyes. "It's good to see you."

"Good to see you too."

Jillian poured herself coffee, splashed in a little nondairy creamer, and took a seat next to Chastity. Chastity was one of the lucky ones—she lived in her cousin's house. She wouldn't be asked to leave on her eighteenth birthday when the money stopped coming. She'd have to get a job and earn her way, but she had a roof over her head. At the same time, she longed to go to school, but there wasn't any money for that right now.

"How are you doing?" Jillian asked.

"I'm okay. I filled out the scholarship paperwork and applications for school. There's just one problem." Chastity tried to peel off some chipped nail polish with her thumbnail.

"What's that?"

"Application fees," Charity said. "I hope I'll get at least one scholarship. My grades are good, but…" She studied the ceiling. "I wonder if I should go to a voc-tech instead."

"Why?"

"The programs are shorter. I'll get out with a skill."

"Didn't you tell me you wanted to be a clothing designer?" Jillian said.

"Yeah, but it…I want something I can find a job at right away. Maybe I can work on that in my spare time." She wasn't looking at Jillian. It was hard to look into someone else's eyes and know you were failing, and you hadn't even had a chance to try.

"What would you like to do instead?"

Chastity folded her arms over her chest. "I was thinking about the food service program."

"Do you like food service?"

"It's okay." She looked at the floor and bit her lower lip. "I could do it."

"But you'd hate it."

"I'd be making money."

Jillian took a sip of coffee. Chastity had shown her some of the designs she'd done and a few of the outfits she'd made on an old sewing machine her foster mother had bought at a thrift shop for twenty dollars. Jillian was amazed at what seemed to be a surprising amount of talent.

Chastity dressed herself out of donations and thrift-store finds; she seemed to know what went with what and why. She made other people's castoffs look fresh and new.

"Okay. If you really want to apply to the voc-tech, I believe Treehouse can cover the application fee. I want you to apply to the School of Apparel Design and Development at Seattle Central Community College, though. If you'll apply, I'll pay your application fee."

Chastity's eyebrows shot up. "You would?"

"Yeah. When you're a famous designer, you can pay someone else's fee."

Chastity seemed like she didn't know what to say but then blurted out, "Absolutely. Thank you."

Jillian pulled her checkbook out of her purse, wrote a check for the amount payable to the community college, and handed it to Chastity. "That should cover it, but if you need additional application fees, please let me know." Jillian noted the check and the amount in her check register and glanced up at Chastity again. "How's everything else going?"

"My cousin has a new boyfriend." She wrapped her arms around her midsection. "He wants me to move out."

"What does your cousin say?"

"She says I can stay, but she's not going to let me stay if he says he'll leave."

This was the hardest part of the work for Jillian. She couldn't take anyone else into her five-hundred-square-foot apartment. She knew she couldn't offer everyone a home, everything they needed, or even a sense of belonging, but that didn't prevent her from wanting to. The worst thing about being a foster child wasn't the fact that you didn't have a lot. You got used to that. It was the fact that no matter how hard you tried, every bit of security you'd worked so hard for could be ripped away in a matter of moments.

To this day, Jillian had a change of clothing and some emergency money in a backpack in her bedroom closet, just in case. She realized a therapist would have a field day with her reasons for doing this, and she wondered how long it would be before she could unpack that change of clothes and put the money back in her checking account. Other people had someone to rely on—a family member, a friend, a spouse. She had nobody but herself. Well, she had her friend, Kari, who would try to help if Jillian needed her. Ultimately, though, Jillian was on her own.

Chastity wrapped her arms more tightly around herself, and Jillian felt her own stomach knot in fear. If Chastity could stay at her cousin's for a while longer, she could go to school. Her chances for a somewhat successful adulthood would only increase with education and a stable living environment. Jillian pulled in a breath, despite wondering if her lungs would let her do so.

"Your cousin knows you need a place to live. She wouldn't kick you out over some guy," Jillian reassured her.

They both knew the truth, but sometimes it was easier to lie—Chastity's cousin wouldn't kick her out. Nobody's family member would ever decline to take them in or steal what little any foster kids had or abuse them. They'd all grow up to be healthy and successful adults. It was the lie they told themselves to get through another day, another foster home, another reminder that they didn't fit in.

Jillian patted Chastity's upper arm. "Everything's going to be fine."

Chastity glanced up from a long examination of her chipped fingernail polish. "Yeah."

Jillian picked up the forms. "Let's get these into some envelopes, and I'll mail them on my way home. Want a cookie or something?"

"I'd like that." Chastity and Jillian headed off down another long hallway to the office area.

## Chapter Four

THE EARLY SEPTEMBER sun was sinking on the horizon as Seth walked through the front door of his parents' house a day after he arrived home from San Francisco. The Sharks had annihilated the Miners in their season opener, so he had today off.

He liked not grabbing for his keys when he stopped by to visit, but he wasn't so sure his mom's front-door-unlocked policy was a great idea these days. The vast majority of Sharks fans were nice people. There was always a small percentage, though, who would think it was cool to pay an uninvited visit to one of his family members. Hopefully, those individuals had no idea where his parents lived.

"Hey, Ma," he called out. He heard running feet, and his mother, Nancy, emerged from the living room, all five-foot-nothing of her. It never ceased to amaze him that someone so slight could have given birth to a giant like him.

"Honey! How are you?" She threw her arms exuberantly around his neck. "It's great to see you. How have you been?"

"Ma, you talked to me yesterday. What's up?"

His mom was acting a little weird, but she grinned up at him. The uneasiness he felt drained away as she released him and smoothed the wrinkles out of her blouse. She patted her short dark hair as she pushed it off of her face. He glanced into the living room at the temporarily abandoned vacuum, dust rags, and can of furniture polish she must have been using. She always managed to keep herself busy at home, but he knew she wouldn't mind a few minutes' break.

"Well, your dad and I haven't seen you for a few days, and we were wondering if something was wrong."

"Things are fine. Well, they're fine now." He looped an arm around her shoulders. "Something happened, and I thought you should probably hear it from me before you heard it on *Sports Center*." He walked her toward the kitchen. "Let's sit down."

Of course, this was her cue to start fussing over him. He tried to pretend like he didn't like it, which made him a damn liar. No matter how old he was or how long he'd been on his own, he still liked it when his mom made a big deal about him.

"Do you want something to drink? You must be hungry. Let me fix you something," she urged.

"No. I'm fine. I can get something out of the fridge if I'm thirsty." He guided her into a chair at the kitchen table and sat down opposite her. "Relax."

"Did something happen?"

He stifled a long sigh. "Yeah, it did. It's been coming for a while, but I broke up with Kim last week. She's been pushing me to take our relationship to the 'next level,' and she wanted me to move her up here. At the same time, she accused me of dating other women, and then she wanted to know when I was going to give her a ring…" He felt his hands form into fists, and he hauled in a breath to calm down a little. Even talking about the fight he'd had with Kim pissed him off all over again. "I wasn't seeing anyone else. I wasn't interested. I don't know where she got this crap." He felt anger and hurt surging through him again. He knew things with Kim hadn't been going well for quite some time, and he shared in the blame. Instead of breaking it off like adults, she wanted to make accusations, and he wanted to get as far away from her as possible instead of dealing with what went wrong.

"Of course you wouldn't do something like that," his mom said. "If she thought you would cheat on her, she didn't know you very well, did she?"

"I've had enough of the wall-to-wall drama." He bit his tongue as he remembered his mom probably wouldn't appreciate his observation that the sex wasn't worth it either. Maybe it was time to wrap up this whole discussion. "Anyway, I had my assistant pack her stuff and changed the locks on the San Diego house this morning. If that doesn't convince her we're done, I don't know what will."

His mom's lips twitched a bit as she struggled to conceal a smile. She had never liked Kim, but Seth knew she was smart enough to listen instead of getting in his face about it. She took his hand in both of hers. "Are you okay? Is there anything we can do?"

"No. I'm fine, but thanks." He sat back in the chair and sighed heavily. "Kim's called several times already today, but there's voice mail for that."

"Does your sister know?"

"Yeah."

She held his hand. Obviously, he was a grown man. He didn't need his mommy to fix things for him. At the same time, it was comforting for him to be here with her. He didn't come to his parents for a lot of advice anymore. Most of the time, he could handle it himself. He'd had the urge to talk with his mom, though. He wondered if this made him a candy-ass or something.

"I'm not going to lie to you," she said. "I'm relieved. Kim never liked us."

"Most of the time, I didn't think she liked me either." He stretched out his legs and crossed them at the ankles as he leaned back in his chair. "Ma, this is the thing I can't get past. Why did she date me for so long? She didn't love me. I don't think she ever did. Was it the money?"

He knew why he'd dated Kim for as long as he had: apathy. It was easier to deal with what he already knew than to start all over again. He'd never been a big fan of change. He told himself he was too busy to break up with her and find someone new. Mostly, he was worried about his picker. He knew the definition of insanity was doing the same thing over and over and expecting a different result, but he kept dating the same kinds of women and expecting someone different than who she turned out to be. He'd like to think he had the smarts to find a woman who was a better choice, but maybe he didn't. He folded his arms across his chest. Maybe the problem was him.

His mom thought about his question for a few moments. "We may never know."

"But what does that say about me? One thing's for sure—it makes me look damn stupid. You'd think I'd choose someone who'd treat me and my family well. Evidently not. I made a bad choice."

"Why would you think it was all your fault? You got involved with a woman; it didn't work out, and now you're going to meet someone else. That's the way things go." She squeezed his hand. "What about that friend of Lauren's? She's always liked you."

Seth was shocked. He regarded his mom with outrage. "She's a baby!"

"She's twenty-two now." His mother was laughing, though. He hoped she wasn't serious.

"Too young for me." He shifted in his chair. College girls weren't his preference these days either. "Actually, I met someone at work, but I don't think it's going anywhere."

"Why not?"

"She works for the big boss. She's off limits." He shrugged one shoulder. "She's different."

"What's she like?"

Seth rubbed his face with his hand. "Well, I think we're about the same age. She's funny and feisty. She doesn't seem to give a shit what I do."

"Seth Joseph—"

"Okay, Ma, I'll try to can it with the swearing." He grinned at her. "I know you don't like it, but you ought to hear the locker room."

"We see how it is when you guys play."

"Yeah." It always made him laugh when his mom would climb on him about his language. At least she wasn't threatening to wash his mouth out with soap anymore. It wouldn't kill him to try to keep it a little clean when she was around. "Here's the deal with Jillian, though."

"Jillian?"

"The woman at the office."

"Oh. Okay."

His mother busied herself straightening the paper napkins in the holder that had been on the kitchen table since he was a little boy. She aligned the matching salt and pepper shakers too.

"She's different from the women I've dated before."

His mother's head snapped up. "What do you mean?"

"She's…she's normal," he stammered. "Not a model or whatever. She's short and curvy." Seth made hand motions in the air to demonstrate Jillian's shape. It didn't explain how her hips swayed when she walked, though, or the laughter in her voice or the softness of her skin beneath his fingers. He could never explain to anyone else how remembering the stuff she'd said to him made him smile when she was nowhere around.

Nancy raised an eyebrow and gave Seth a slight head shake but said nothing.

"I like her. She's fun to talk with." He glanced away from his mom's probing eyes. "I met her when she snuck into the weight room. She was working out to a DVD the other night," he said.

"What happened?"

"I showed her how to use the treadmill, and we've gone for some walks at her lunchtime. We've talked a little." He didn't tell his mom that spending time with Jillian was the highlight of his day or the fact he was still having brain-melting wet dreams about her. Maybe her perfume was some kind of aphrodisiac.

Nancy's hands went to her hips, and she narrowed her eyes. "And this was her idea? You're not telling her what to do?"

Seth's eyebrows shot up. "Of course not. Why would you think I would?"

His mom studied him for a moment. "You forget that I've known you for a while." She crossed her arms in front of her. "When did you decide you needed an exercise buddy?"

"It's not a formal thing. I give her some exercise tips, and she said she'd show me around town a little in return."

Seth knew he probably should explain to his mother that despite the fact he hated change, he needed some—and fast. Right now, though, he didn't want to get into it with anyone else, even someone he knew loved him. He'd agreed to come to Seattle because he thought he'd get back the burning hunger in his gut that drove him to achieve from the time he'd walked onto a football field for the first time. He still loved the game. He'd always love the game. He needed more than three hours on a Sunday afternoon sixteen weeks a year, however, and he needed to figure out what that "something more" might be for him.

His personal life wasn't all it could be either. Part of the reason he'd agreed to the trade was that he wanted to be closer to his parents. They were getting older. His kid sister couldn't handle their parents all by herself. He also couldn't handle the nagging thought that spending time with Jillian seemed to be a hell of a lot more important to him than it was to her. She wasn't sneaking around the building, trying to figure out ways to run into him.

Nancy shook her head. Her lips twitched with repressed laughter. "'Show you around town'? You've been making trips to see us for years now. What's really going on here?"

"Ma. Nothing's going on. It's not a big deal."

JILLIAN ARRIVED HOME from the office, fed CB, and stripped off her office clothes. She didn't smell daisy-fresh. She'd actually have to use the T-shirt and shorts Seth had dropped on her desk last week if she kept walking at lunchtime. She tore the cardboard lid off a frozen dinner, shoved it into the microwave, and hit a few buttons. She needed to relax a little. It hadn't been that bad of a day, but she had had another encounter with Seth when he stopped by the facility to pick up some things on his day off, and it had taken the rest of the afternoon to stop thinking about him.

He wasn't in her world. The best thing she could do was to pretend that he wasn't there and put a stop to his dropping by her desk. She hurried into the bathroom, stripped off what was left of her clothes, and flipped on the shower. If she really hurried, she'd have time to catch a movie tonight before bed. Maybe she should call Kari. She and Kari had been friends since childhood. Kari had grown up and gotten married, but her husband traveled for work. She might have time for an evening out.

The phone rang while Jillian was drying her hair. The caller ID indicated it was Kari. Jillian laughed as she grabbed up her phone. "You must have known I was thinking about you."

"So, what are you up to tonight?" Kari said.

"I was going to ask if you wanted to go to the movies. I need to get out of the house."

"That bad, huh?"

"No. I just need to see something besides the television and the kitty. How are you doing?"

"Oh, work's stressful, but I can deal. Patrick's on a trip to London. He'll be back the day after tomorrow."

"You must miss him."

"I do, but it's a great time for us to catch up with each other," Kari said. "Want to come over? I'm not sure I'm up to the movies tonight because I don't have a sitter lined up, but I'd love a chat. The baby's asleep for the night already. Have you had dinner yet?"

"I'm making one of those frozen dinners—"

"Dump it. I've got stir-fry," Kari told her. "Get in your car and get over here. Don't forget your overnight bag."

An hour later, Kari and Jillian brought bowls of chicken and veggies and a bottle of wine to the family room table in Kari's house. Jillian had kept up her friendship with Kari through Jillian's many moves over the years. Kari's house was as welcoming and familiar to her as her own.

"So, Jill, tell me everything. How are all those gorgeous guys you work with? How's your boss?"

Jillian had to laugh. Kari was happily married, but like many other women in the Seattle area, she was pretty interested in the exploits of the local pro football team. They'd had this conversation multiple times already, but it never got old, at least not for Kari.

"Well, let's see here. One of the defensive guys came through the front office the other day in nothing but a pair of football pants. He wanted to talk to John, and John wasn't in. It's always weird to have a half-naked guy hanging out in the office."

"It's not bad if the guy in question has a body to die for."

"No, it wasn't bad at all," Jillian told her. "He didn't have a lot to say to me. He vanished fairly quickly when I told him John would talk with him the next morning." She settled back against the couch. "The linebacker we got from San Diego caught me in the weight room after hours a couple of weeks ago."

Kari's eyes got huge. "What happened? I can't believe you didn't tell me this the minute you got here!"

"It's a little embarrassing—"

"Come on!" Kari took a long swallow from her wineglass. "That's Seth Taylor, right? God, he's gorgeous. I saw his pics in the *ESPN The Magazine* body issue." She let out a sigh. "His body is unreal."

Jillian had seen him up close. "Unreal" didn't explain it.

Jillian nodded. "He's handsome, and he towers over me. He was pretty mad when he walked in there. I was a little scared."

"What did you do?"

"I was doing a workout DVD. He came in to lift weights, and there I was. I wasn't sure what to do. I was afraid I'd get in trouble with John."

"John won't care. He likes you, doesn't he?"

"It's going well so far, but I don't want to push it." She pulled a throw over herself. "I haven't been there that long, and I wasn't sure it was okay to venture into the players' area."

Kari waved off her concerns. "So, did you talk to him?"

"John or Seth?"

"Who do you think? Out with it! You're blushing. I know something happened!"

Jillian took a deep breath. How was she going to explain to her friend what had happened? She wasn't sure herself.

"Like I said, Seth seemed kind of mad. He asked me why I was there, and I told him I worked for John. He said he didn't remember me." She studied her hands clasped in her lap for a moment. "I guess that's the way it is, but it hurt. He'd talked to me in the office before...but he didn't remember me."

"I don't think he'll forget you now," Kari said. She reached over and patted Jillian's hands. "What happened then?"

"Oh, it gets even more embarrassing." Jillian let out a long sigh as she told Kari about her first encounter with Seth. "I thought he'd think I was a weirdo or something, but I've run into him a few times when I've gone for a walk at lunchtime." She took a sip of wine. "He even brought me some workout stuff and shoes from the team's equipment closet."

"Sounds like he's interested, Jillian."

"No. He just broke up with his girlfriend. He said he'd give me some exercise pointers and asked if I'd show him around town."

"I'll bet. 'Show him around,' huh?" Kari laughed.

"Kari, he's not into me."

"Guys who aren't into you wouldn't go out of their way to spend time with you. Something's going on with him."

"I don't know." Jillian picked at a loose thread in the throw. "Have you seen his ex-girlfriend? I'd have to be insane to think I had a chance with him."

"How old is he?"

"He's almost twenty-nine, evidently."

"Ahh. A younger man." Kari tucked her feet up underneath her. "How do you feel about this?"

"What do you mean? I'm thirty. He's not that much younger."

"You know what I mean. Are you interested?"

Jillian could feel the heat rising in her face. She'd have to be dead to be uninterested, but this was not a conversation she was having, even with her best friend.

"It wouldn't be realistic. The guy dates these fashion-model types. Plus, Kari, he's great to look at, but I don't know how I feel about any guy who works out eight hours a day."

Kari leaned forward again. "Stop putting yourself down. Maybe he likes the fact that you're pretty, you're easy to talk to, you're funny, and you're nice. Why can't you believe that maybe he'd like to spend time with you?"

"Is this the part where you tell me that I should be doing affirmations and practicing better self-love?" Jillian rolled her eyes.

"God, Jill!" Now they were both laughing. "Listen. Give the guy a chance. Maybe he sees something in you that you don't realize."

"He practically picked me up to help me onto the treadmill the other night," Jillian said.

"Oh, really? How'd that go?"

"He's strong." Jillian took a breath. "He smells good."

"Cologne?"

"No. Just him. Clean and nice. His eyes are really beautiful too."

"They are, huh?"

"You can stop this at any time. It's really not going to happen. Ever." Even if Jillian wished it would with all of her heart.

Kari grinned at her. "Okay. I can take a hint. Let's just watch a movie, okay?"

## Chapter Five

DESPITE ANOTHER LATE-NIGHT pizza fest with his kid sister, Seth pulled his ass out of bed a little after six o'clock on Saturday morning. It was time to go for a run before he was due to practice. He also needed to burn off a little pent-up energy because he'd had another sexy-as-hell dream about a feisty blonde named Jillian, but that was beside the point.

He tiptoed past his little sister's room. Lauren lived in her sorority house at UW most of the time, but when he'd bought his house, he made sure there was a room for her so she had somewhere else to go. She migrated back and forth between her sorority and his place. Something about family staying with him made him happy. He had to admit she livened up his too-quiet house most of the time—even if, at times, she bugged the crap out of him.

A few stretches later, he let himself out of the house, locked the front door, and broke into an easy jog. The development he'd moved into was full of young families, but at this time of day, nobody else was out—well, nobody but a couple of his teammates. He'd asked around a little and found out that a bunch of them lived in his new neighborhood. He fell in beside them.

"Morning, pussy," Tom said. Tom was the Sharks' quarterback, an All-American, All-Pro gunslinger. His personality was as outsized as his football skills.

"Morning, dickweed," Seth said. Tom laughed loudly.

The other guy, a massive defensive tackle named Zach, grunted in Seth's direction.

"So, ladies, how about a little race this morning?" Zach said.

"C'mon. Let's get a little warm-up here before the games begin." Tom glanced over at Seth. "We'll get to the next block. A few of the other guys should be out too."

Seth gave him a nod. His teammates preferred the proximity to great schools and the practice facility, not to mention the fact the neighbors were fairly protective of their privacy. In exchange, there was an extra effort to take care of things—the kids in this neighborhood got autographed memorabilia, free game tickets, and sideline passes. According to Seth's teammates, the neighbors invited the players to wintertime get-togethers and summertime barbecues.

It was nice to find people who treated them like anybody else.

The group ran in silence until they met up with two other guys from the team, who both had emerged from their houses as well.

"Kids still asleep?" Tom asked Jeff, a wide receiver who'd been traded to Seattle the year before from Atlanta.

"Hell yeah. My wife would be looking for me if I woke them up. It's so nice to sneak down the hall of my own house."

"My kids can hear a pin drop. How did you manage to do that?" Tom asked.

"No shoes, buddy. Works every time. Plus, our master's on the first floor. I can get out the door before they know what happened." Jeff's stealth might also have something to do with the fact he could run a 4.3-second forty-yard dash.

"I don't have kids. My ex-girlfriend would've flipped out if she woke up and I was gone," Seth said.

Zach glanced around. "Good reason to get another girlfriend," he said. "I spent a year and a half doing that. It sucks."

"We were done as of two weeks ago," Seth told him.

"So, the girlfriend in San Diego's officially history?" Tom asked.

"Yeah." Seth didn't expound.

"Want us to fix you up?" Jeff asked. Jeff and Zach glanced at each other and let out a burst of laughter.

"You assholes are so supportive," Seth muttered.

"We give you shit because we care," Zach insisted. Seth had to grin. "Plus, if you aren't getting laid, we have to deal with you, don't we?"

"Oh, go fuck yourselves."

By now, the entire group was laughing. They ran on.

"So, I heard that Jasha was on the coach's shit list this week," Zach said. "I told him that mouthing off to the defensive coordinator about his game planning wasn't the best use of his time."

"He's such a diva. Shit," Tom said, "you'd think he was a wide receiver or something."

Jeff let out a bark of laughter. "Name-call all you want, Reed. I'm all about that action."

"You blew up that DB from Tampa Bay, brah."

Zach made the "boom" hand signal. "He still remembers your name, doesn't he?"

The guys were making one last loop of the neighborhood, and Seth glanced over at Tom.

"Hey. How'd you meet your wife?" Seth asked.

"Are we having a conversation now?"

"Yeah. Where'd you find her?"

"I met her my rookie season. I didn't know how to cook, so I went to the same restaurant every morning for breakfast. She was a waitress there." A soft look moved over Tom's face. "She had no idea who I was or what I did, and she didn't care. I kept asking her out. She kept telling me no."

"How'd you get her to go out with you?"

"I told her that if she went out with me once, I'd never ask her again if she didn't have fun. We had a great time. We've been together ever since."

The other guys were starting to split off as the group passed their houses; Seth would see them at practice later. Tom raised a hand as he ran up his driveway, and Seth continued on to his house.

Seth needed someone like her. Someone who cared for him, not for who he was or the money he earned with bone-jarring practices and a million injuries over the years. He needed someone he could fall in love with every day for the rest of his life.

JILLIAN'S PHONE RANG as she pulled into a space in the Treehouse parking lot. She shut off the car's ignition, grabbing for her phone, which (as always) was lurking at the bottom of her purse. She managed to grab it out just as the call went to voice mail.

She didn't recognize the number. "Oh, hell," she muttered to herself. "Maybe they'll leave a message." She waited a few seconds. The little symbol denoting a brand-new message popped up on the screen. She hit it with a fingertip as she enabled the speaker function.

"Hey, Jill, it's me, Seth." The air whooshed out of her lungs in surprise. She almost hugged the phone. "I was wondering if you had some time today. I need a walk." He chuckled a little. "Or you can take me to your favorite place for lunch. My treat. Call me." She heard the call end.

She let out a squeal and waited for her heart rate to return to normal. The new group of volunteers she was working with would be here in ten minutes. She couldn't blow off her volunteer shift, no matter how badly she wanted to do almost anything Seth suggested. He wanted to have lunch. He wanted to pay for lunch.

Had he just asked her out on a date?

Her finger hovered over the "Return Call" button on her phone. She took the deepest breath she could and told herself to act like this kind of thing happened to her every day. He answered on the first ring.

"It's Taylor."

"Hi, Seth, it's Jillian. You called me."

"I sure did," he said. "What are you up to today? Let's get together."

"I would love to, but I can't."

"Well, that's no good. What's happening?"

"I have this volunteer thing that's going to take up most of the day. I really wish I could hang out. It would be fun." That was the understatement of the year. If he had any idea how much she really wanted to see him, he'd freak out.

"Volunteer thing, huh? Tell me about it."

"I'm at Treehouse in Seattle. We're sorting donations and stuff," she said. "I'll be done later, but don't you have to be at the team hotel by then?"

"Oh, hell yeah. There's meetings and a chapel service before bed check." She could hear the smile in his voice. "Listen. Maybe we can try this lunch thing another time. How about it?"

"I'd like that," she said.

"Good. We'll make it happen, then," he said. "I'll see you Monday, Jill."

They said good-bye; she hung up the phone in a daze and stared at the side of the building as she told herself to breathe. She knew she hadn't imagined it because his number was still in her phone. She impulsively hit "Save" and typed in Seth's name. She dropped her phone back into her purse, grabbed her keys, and got out of the car.

Twenty minutes later, Jillian took a sip of coffee as she regarded the huge pile of clothing that needed to be sorted and hung up for display. She was happy about the donations, but this was going to be some work. Luckily, it would also help take her mind off Seth for a little while as well. One of the new volunteers Jillian was training this weekend glanced at her.

"My mama always said there's no rest for the wicked," she said in a softly accented voice.

"And the good don't need any," a young man whose nametag read SHANNON said.

Jillian put her paper coffee cup down on a nearby table. "Does anyone need something to drink or to visit the facilities before we start?" she asked. The six students fulfilling their school-mandated community-service hours shook their heads.

"We're fine," another young man told her. "Let's get started."

"We're separating the items to make sure everything is clean, gently worn, and in one piece," Jillian said. "We'll get them on hangers or folded as we go. We can throw out stuff that's junk."

"People donate junk?" Shannon asked.

"Yeah. Sometimes." Jillian passed out latex gloves to the group. "Put these on first, okay?"

They plunged into the pile of plastic bags, grabbing a few and sorting through the contents. Some were new clothing or shoes with tags still on and were stacked on another table by type and gender for display. Foster children came to Treehouse to go "shopping" for needed clothing and toiletries. The contrast was jarring between well-dressed teenagers who came from upper-middle-class homes and were donating a few hours of their time, and the kids who worried about obtaining things like a warm winter coat or shoes that didn't have holes. It must have made an impression on the teens, who filled the silence by talking to each other in hushed voices.

"My brother has an almost-new pair of Nikes he grew out of. I wonder if someone here might want them."

"I got a brand-new winter coat. My mom bought me another one before I even cut the tags off it."

"My grandma gave me this heinous sweater that she knitted. She'd be really mad if I donated it, but I have some other stuff another kid might like."

The young woman with a soft Southern accent glanced over at Jillian again. "I have some things at home that I've never worn," she said. "They still have tags on them. May I bring them in? Someone else might like them."

"Of course you can," Jillian said. "Thank you."

They made surprising progress in a few hours. Jillian felt the alarm on the phone in her pocket go off. It was lunchtime, and the teens needed to eat.

"I know everyone's probably hungry, so let's break for lunch. There's a fast-food place across the street. If you want a sandwich or something, there's a grocery store close by too." She pulled in a breath. She hoped some of the kids would stay to get in a few more hours, but she knew they probably would prefer going to the movies or something on a Saturday afternoon. She made her voice casual. "If you'd like me to sign your community hours paperwork before you leave, I can do that. Thank you so much for all your help today. You did a great job."

The six teens glanced at each other. Jillian saw some foot shuffling and fidgeting. Shannon jammed his hands into his jeans pockets. He must have been nominated as the spokesman.

"If you'd like some more help, we'll come back after lunch," he said.

"Yeah," one of the other teens said. "We'll go through the rest of this stuff before we go home."

"Jillian, would you like to have lunch with us?" the young woman with the Southern accent asked. "Maybe some of the other kids at school would like to help out once in a while too."

"That would be great," Jillian said. "Let me grab my purse. I'll be right back."

Even though she'd wanted to have lunch with Seth and wished she hadn't turned him down, she was touched that the teens asked her to join them. She liked chatting with the volunteers.

She dashed around the corner to the desk where she kept her purse, forcing herself to take deep breaths. She realized people might think it was weird that she was so excited others wanted to help out an organization that meant so much to her. Some of the kids who showed up as volunteers weren't a lot of help. They didn't seem to understand why other kids couldn't put a new wardrobe on a charge card, or why some kids couldn't afford stuff like yearbooks or sports fees or ballet lessons. She knew what it was like to do without. She also knew why other people might not. Every volunteer who wanted to come back was one more enlisted in Jillian's personal campaign to improve the lives of foster kids in her area.

She had a great time at lunch with the teenagers, talking and laughing as they told her about starting school and what their plans were for the year. They walked back to the building and started in again. An hour or so later, one of Treehouse's staff members walked into the room where Jillian and the volunteers were working.

"Hey, Jillian. We just got a call from Seth Taylor of the Sharks. Do you know him?"

"A little," she said.

The teenage guys in the room stopped working and stared at each other.

"You know Taylor?" one asked.

"He's the best," another added.

"He's really cute," the girl with the Southern accent said.

"He said he knew you," the staff member said. "He also said he can't sign up for the volunteer orientation until the season's over, but he's pretty interested. He also gave us a ten-thousand-dollar donation."

"That's a lot of money," Jillian said. She could feel the heat of a blush rising in her face, and she couldn't quite look at anybody. She realized that ten thousand dollars wasn't a fortune to someone like Seth, but it meant a lot to her that he would even consider making a donation to an organization she cared about so much.

The staff member reached out to squeeze Jillian's upper arm. "I thought you might want to know. Really nice of him, huh?"

"Yeah. That's great," she said.

The staff member left, and the teenagers went back to work. Well, they went back to work after asking Jillian how she knew Seth Taylor.

"I met him recently. He's a good guy."

"Are you dating him?" the young woman with the Southern accent asked.

"No. He's just a friend."

"Just a friend?" one of the teenage guys teased.

"Just a friend."

A couple of hours later, Jillian threw herself into her car, grabbed her phone out of her bag, and hit "Redial" on Seth's number. She felt a little weird about calling him, but this couldn't wait. She knew he was probably already at the hotel. She wasn't surprised when the call went to voice mail.

"Hi, Seth, this is Jillian. Thank you so much for giving such a generous donation to Treehouse. It means a lot to me. And thanks again for the lunch invite. I'm looking forward to taking you up on it another time," she said. "Have a great game tomorrow. Bye."

Jillian also pushed herself to go for a walk on both Saturday and Sunday. It wasn't bad when she could come home and shower. Maybe she should walk in the mornings before she went to work. That would require getting out of bed, though, and she liked to sleep in a little. Every time she put on the cross-trainers and went outside, she had a better chance of meeting someone new. If she'd never pushed herself to try something different from her daily routine, she never would have gotten to know Seth.

If she concentrated on walking a little farther each day and picking up the pace a bit, she could try hiking or even a 5K. She knew the Sharks' PR department was planning a fund-raising 5K for season-ticket holders in a couple of months. The proceeds would benefit several local charities, including Treehouse. She'd told the PR group that she'd help with on-site registration on race day, but she could only imagine how it would feel to participate in the race and finish, instead of being behind the scenes, as always.

Tomorrow, she'd get out of bed a little early, put her shoes on, and go for another walk.

"No pain, no gain," she muttered to CB, who gave her a quizzical look. Even the cat thought she was nuts. Jillian liked her job, but now, no matter how she tried to pretend it meant nothing to her, she was looking forward to Monday. She'd see Seth.

Her heart beat a bit faster at the thought.

JILLIAN'S DESK PHONE rang at the same time her in-box chimed on Monday morning, alerting her to multiple (urgent) incoming e-mails. She clicked to open the first message marked "911 Urgent" while she answered the ringing phone. Then, the cell phone in her pocket went off with a unique ring she'd given John's calls. She needed a few more hands today.

"Hello, Seattle Sharks. Would you hold, please?"

"It's me," John said. "My nine o'clock appointment is dicking me around again. Would you call him back and tell him we're rescheduling for the last time?"

"Did you just call my cell phone as well?"

"I sure did. Keep me updated, please."

She could hear laughter in John's voice as he hung up.

As she returned to reading the "911 Urgent" e-mail (consisting of John's telling her to cancel his nine AM appointment), a shadow moved across her desk, indicating the arrival of someone tall enough to block out the carefully calibrated spotlights overhead.

"Hey," Seth said. "What's up?" He also winked at her. Her heart skipped a beat in response. Her heart-monitor watch was probably shorting out or something right now.

She glanced up at him. "Hi. Don't you have practice or something?"

"I'm here for the post-game health check." He wasn't going away. "What do you do in the mornings before you have to be in the office?"

She was attempting to talk to Seth while dialing the nine o'clock appointment's cell phone. Of course, he wasn't answering. She grabbed her phone out of her pocket, typed in the guy's e-mail address, and shot him an e-mail marked "Urgent," canceling the meeting.

Her desk phone was ringing again. She really needed to answer it, but she seemed to be frozen in place. "How come?"

"I figured out that if I leave my house earlier in the morning, the traffic isn't quite so bad. Maybe we could grab some coffee or breakfast once in a while."

He braced one hand on her desk as he watched her expectantly. She could answer him, but her mouth had just gone dry. He smelled good. The scent of clean skin and woodsy-smelling soap enveloped them.

"Six works for me," he said. "It'll be fun."

"Six AM? In the morning?"

She was still trying to concentrate on a ringing desk phone and cell phone and shuffled some paperwork on her desk. The last call must have gone to voice mail. If it was John, she was in some trouble. But if it *was* John, he'd be storming out to her desk by now, so she had a minute or so.

"Yeah. Are you busy?"

"Other than the usual showering and dressing for work, not really." She wasn't exactly alert at six AM, either, but maybe he wouldn't really notice.

His smile was enchanting. "I'm guessing you need to have this spelled out. You. Me. Coffee or breakfast. What else is it that you do in the mornings that might prevent that from happening?"

She had to admit that the look on his face when she gave him a hard time was hilarious, and she wasn't quite ready to stop doing it yet. "It's a secret. I'd tell you, but then I'd have to kill you."

Jillian watched the smile move slowly over Seth's mouth.

"What's with all the secrets? You're only as sick as your secrets, you know." He let out a bark of laughter. "Maybe I'll run into you outside at noon."

He marched off toward the players' area of the building, and Jillian let out the breath she'd been holding. Vivian had just walked into the office.

"What was all that about?"

"Oh, he's teasing me. It's nothing."

Vivian gave her a speculative look. "You know John fired his last assistant for getting involved with one of the guys on the team, don't you?"

"He mentioned that."

And he'd asked Jillian if she had a boyfriend during her interview. Jillian needed the job, and she sensed John wanted her to say yes about having a boyfriend, so she'd told Seth the same whopper. If anyone really wanted more information about her alleged "casual thing," she could tell them he traveled a lot or something.

IT WOULD TAKE a bulldozer to shove Seth out of her mind, but she did her best. John had left quite a stack on her desk for this morning. She pulled up her e-mail, and there was even more work. He was trying to keep up with each week's opponents, so there was a ton of printing and collating of lists and spreadsheets for her to get done. John asked for a lot of stuff, but he was pretty easy to work with, as long as she finished the work before he needed it. Then again, the only time she'd blown a big deadline, he'd laughed and said, "You'll get it next time."

There was too much to do to wonder why Seth kept asking her to hang out with him. She was fairly sure that there were thousands of other women in the Seattle area who would be happy to see him at six AM for any reason at all. Mornings were never her favorite time, but maybe she needed to rethink that whole thing if she got some time with him as a reward for pulling herself out of bed.

John blew through the office as he returned from a meeting. "Hello, ladies. Jillian, you got the stuff I left you?"

"Yes, John. I'll finish it as quickly as possible."

"Actually, do you have a minute? Come into my office." She followed him in as he flipped the lights on, hung up his coat, and dropped his briefcase next to his desk. "Sit down." John sat down in his chair, steepled his fingers, and regarded Jillian for a minute. "Remember when I interviewed you for this job?"

"Yes, I do."

"We talked about not getting involved with the players, didn't we?"

Jillian swallowed hard. The hair stood up on the back of her neck. "Yes, John, we did."

"Do you have something you'd like to tell me?" He waited.

"I...I went for a walk at lunchtime a couple of weeks ago with Seth Taylor."

"Why?"

She bowed her head. She twisted her hands in her lap. What should she say? She took a deep breath and said, "It's not what you think."

"What do I think, Jillian? Fill me in." He leaned back in the chair and folded his arms across his chest.

"We're not involved with each other. I...I was trying to work out, and he decided to help."

"Excuse me?"

She let out a sigh. "I bought an exercise DVD. A gym membership isn't in my budget right now. My neighbors get mad if I exercise in my apartment. The walls are thin." She pulled in a breath. "I didn't know how to get started, so I wondered if I could use the gym in the evenings after work. Seth found me with the DVD and offered some exercise pointers. And…well, it's stupid. I'm sorry, John. I know you're probably not happy about this."

"So, you were in the weight room after hours. What else happened?"

"Seth was initially mad at me. I think he thought I'd broken in or something. Then I think he felt bad for me. He said I was doing it all wrong, so he showed me how to use the treadmill. Sometimes he walks with me on the sidewalk outside the facility at lunchtime."

John had leaned forward in his chair and laid his forearms on his desk. "No gym membership, huh?"

"No," Jillian said miserably.

"Taylor called me over the weekend."

"Excuse me?"

"He wanted your address."

Her mouth dropped open. "Seriously?"

Seth didn't seem like some kind of stalker, but this was a bit worrisome. She was a bit confused as to why he'd asked John for her address. They'd talked on the phone, but she couldn't imagine why he wanted to know where she lived.

"He wouldn't tell me why he needed it. I told him that I couldn't give out that information without your permission. He apparently dislikes the word no." Jillian saw John's smirk. "Does this mean I'm going to have to chaperone you? You might want to tell him that you're dating someone else."

She should never have lied to John in the first place. She needed to confess, but maybe that might work out better for her another day.

Her words burst out. "I'll take care of it. He said he didn't mind showing me some exercise stuff, but—"

"You don't need a gym membership," John said. "We have one here. You can use the machines if you'd like when the team isn't in there, but first of all, you need to get checked out by a doctor. We have one of those here too. I'll ask the team doc to take a look at you—draw some blood or whatever."

He gave her an encouraging smile and pulled his desk drawer open and rooted around in it. He passed a pink heart-monitor watch to her across the desk. "We get free stuff from athletic companies all the time. Go in the storage area later and check it out, okay? This is for you. My girlfriend has one, and she really likes hers."

She already had a heart monitor watch, but she wasn't going to refuse his thoughtful gift. Maybe she could donate it to someone else who needed it.

"Thank you," she said.

"Thank you. So, Seth wants to be friends with my assistant."

Jillian shrugged her shoulders.

"Okay. We'll see how it goes. I'll give the doc a call and get things set up. In the meantime, tell Seth he can't flirt with you," John said.

## Chapter Six

SETH PULLED THE overstuffed easy chair in his room closer to the window. He propped his bare feet up on the broad windowsill as he stared at a darkened sky. He saw the faint illumination on the horizon; the pink and yellow rays of a late-summer's dawn would come eventually. He knew he'd feel better if he could get some sleep. He also knew it wasn't going to happen. He glanced over at the clock radio on his nightstand. It was four forty-seven AM.

He'd had more than a few sleepless nights over the past five years. He wondered how many other people were looking at the stars tonight and remembering someone they'd miss for the rest of their lives.

His little brother, Liam, had died five years ago. Five years of grief that lessened (allegedly) as time passed but cut him like broken glass at unexpected moments. He never knew when it was going to happen either. He'd see something or hear something that reminded him of Liam, and he'd be breathless with pain. It was such a senseless loss. Even worse, it wasn't like he was discussing it with anyone outside of his family.

Most days were fine. He didn't dwell on it. He kept busy. He usually slept like a rock. Once in a while, though, he found himself lying awake and remembering.

Seth and Liam had had one last summer together before Seth went to training camp and Liam went into premed. They'd managed to duck Lauren early one morning, heading off to Snoqualmie Falls for a hike and breakfast afterward at one of the cafes in town.

Liam asked the college-aged, pretty blonde waitress who brought their breakfasts to have coffee with him. Seth considered himself fairly confident, but his brother had moves.

She glanced at Liam, raised an eyebrow, and said, "You're a bit young for me, don't you think?"

"Maybe you should date me and find out," Liam said.

She laughed and agreed to meet Liam for coffee after the family returned from Hawaii in two weeks. Eleven days later, Liam was gone.

Seth glanced out the window. The sky was lightening as the sun edged over the horizon. He stood up from the chair, walked into his bathroom, and flipped on the shower. He wanted to visit Snoqualmie Falls again, but he didn't want to do it alone.

JILLIAN OPENED HER eyes on another Saturday morning to CB purring on her chest and someone knocking on her front door. The jolt of adrenaline caused by an unexpected (and evidently urgent) visitor cut through the fog of a steely gray Seattle morning and forced her out of bed. CB let out an aggrieved "meow" and dived into the still-warm blankets.

She didn't have to be at her volunteer shift until later that morning. The extra sleep she was hoping for looked like it wasn't happening.

She pulled on a sweatshirt over her nightgown and hurried to answer the door. Whoever was out there sure was impatient. The doorbell had rung three times now, and the person had knocked twice. She peeked through the keyhole and saw nothing but flesh. Someone's finger was over it.

"Who's there?" she called out.

"It's me, Seth. Open up."

Jillian pulled the door open to stare at a rumpled-looking Seth.

"It's six thirty AM. What on earth are you doing here?"

"You texted me your address last week, silly. Go get your shoes on," he said. "I don't have to be at the facility until later today. I have something I want to show you."

"'Something you want to show me'? Really? Does that usually work for you?" She realized she was babbling, but she couldn't seem to stop talking. He looked like he was about to laugh.

"Shit, yeah." He raised an eyebrow, smirked, and pushed past her into the apartment. CB raced into the living room and came to a dead stop on the top of Seth's foot. "Who's this?" He reached down and scooped the kitten into one big hand.

"That's Crème Brulee, but I call her CB."

"The hell? It's a kitty, not a dessert in a four-star restaurant." He looked into the kitten's eyes. "I can't believe you let her name you that."

CB responded with a purr. Seth cuddled her close to his chest, and she nestled into the crook of his arm. "You know, I usually don't like cats," he said.

"You can leave at any time."

"What if I don't want to?"

"I don't get it. Why are you here?" she said.

He ignored that, crossed the living room, and sat down on the couch with the cat in his arms. "If you'll put some shoes on," he coaxed, "we can get out of here. We'll get to where we're going before the tourists take over the place."

She indicated her current attire with one hand. "Tourists? In my nightgown? And I have to be at Treehouse at eleven AM."

"Whatever floats your boat," he said. He gave CB a scratch behind her ears. "I see your 'casual thing' boyfriend is nowhere to be found."

"He could be in the bathroom."

"Sure, he is," he said. He lifted one eyebrow.

This was her time. She couldn't imagine what in the hell was wrong with him. There must be something else for him to do at the crack of dawn on a Saturday.

"Don't you have a new girlfriend or something?" she said.

"Nope." He settled one ankle over his knee. "Right now, you're my date. Go get dressed, and I might even pay for breakfast. I'll have you back here by ten AM." He held the cat inches from his nose again, looked into her eyes, and said, "Sorry, kitty, you can't go. We'll try to find you a treat." CB let out a pitiful mew. He stared into the kitty's face. "I've dated supermodels. You'll have to try harder than that."

Of course, CB purred some more and head-butted him. What a flirt.

He glanced over at Jillian again. "You've got ten minutes."

"Is this a dress-up thing?"

He looked horrified. "Oh, hell no."

Jillian turned and fled into her bedroom. She wanted to slam the bedroom door, but waking up the neighbors this early on a Saturday would be a disaster. She pulled off her nightgown; brushed her teeth; yanked on a bra, T-shirt, and sweats; covered the T-shirt with a sweatshirt; and jammed on her cross-trainers. She put her front door keys in her pocket. Minutes later, she reappeared in the living room.

He looked like a cover model in messy hair, stubble, a pair of warm-up pants and a long-sleeved T-shirt advertising some NFL event. She didn't even have time to comb her hair.

"Nine minutes and thirty seconds, Jillian? I'm impressed."

"Again. Why are you here?"

He gave her a raised eyebrow and explained in an excruciatingly slow manner. "We're friends. Friends spend time hanging out. I think you'll enjoy what I have planned this morning." One side of his mouth twitched. "Okay?"

"Fine. Let's go," she said, both hands on her hips. "Don't you have to be at the walk-through before tomorrow's game or something?"

"We'll do that shortly before we go to the team hotel late this afternoon." He let her kitten head-butt him again. "Crème Brulee, do you mind if I call you CB?" The kitten meowed. "Your mom is pissed at me," he said.

Jillian steeled herself. She was not going to melt at how cute he was with her kitten or how at home he looked sitting on her couch. "Do you often get out of bed at six thirty on weekends?"

"I was up at five," he said. "I waited an hour."

"You're joking!" she cried out.

"Oh no. I don't joke about stuff like this."

SETH SET THE cat down gently on the couch cushion, unfolded himself, and got to his feet. He wasn't sure what it was with Jillian and why he couldn't seem to stay away from her. He kept inventing reasons to run into her or spend time with her. Maybe it was the fact she didn't fawn over him. She didn't seem to care that he was famous, and she gave him shit about his money. At the same time, he'd seen vulnerability in her when he hadn't expected it.

Jillian kept him on his toes, and he hadn't had that for a long time now. He wondered to himself how many women he'd passed up over the years who might have been a better choice than Kim. One such woman had just let both of them out of her apartment and stuck her house key back in her pocket. He had to admit he was more than a little attracted, even if she was currently trying to incinerate him with her eyes. Her morning crankiness was pretty damn funny.

"So, where are you taking me?" she said.

He gestured toward the apartment house parking lot. "Let's get in my car and you'll find out."

"Am I going to end up as the subject of a *Lifetime* movie?"

"That would be a no."

She stared at his Escalade as he clicked the key fob to disengage the locks. "Nice ride," she said.

A few minutes later he pulled onto I-90, the freeway that led to Snoqualmie Falls, one of the most spectacular sights in western Washington. Hundreds of thousands of tourists visited the falls each year, which were internationally famous due to the television show *Twin Peaks*. When people weren't marveling at the beauty and force of water cascading hundreds of feet, they were visiting the hotel perched at the top of the falls or touring the small town where it all was located.

The sun's rays were peeking through the quickly dissipating cloud cover, exposing blue skies. Autumn was on its way, but the Seattle area still basked in late-summer sunshine and moderate temperatures. There were hardly any cars on the road this morning. Hopefully, he could spend a little time alone with Jillian before someone recognized him.

He pulled into the lower parking lot at Snoqualmie Falls half an hour later. The place was almost deserted. He stifled a sigh of relief. Hopefully, the entire hiking community had decided to attend today's University of Washington football game or other outdoor pursuits. He only had a few hours before he had to get himself to the practice facility and she was due at her appointment. If she liked it here, he'd bring her again, when they could hike from the top of the falls to the observation platform and back.

"Have you been here before?" he asked above the roar of pounding, falling water.

"Not since I was a lot younger." She opened the passenger door and slid out. He walked around the front of the car to join her.

"Gotcha," he said. They took a few steps on the path toward the observation platform that gave a 180-degree view of the falls. "It isn't far to the observation area, but you might need to stretch a little. Try this." He pulled one of his legs up by the heel.

"If I did that, I'd be in the ICU."

"Just try it," he coaxed. "Put your hand on my shoulder."

Jillian bent to try to grab her heel, teetered alarmingly on one foot, and he reached out to steady her before she fell into the brush that lined the pathway. For someone who probably didn't attempt to twist herself into a pretzel on a daily basis, she wasn't doing too badly with the stretching.

"Oh! Oh!" She looked a little panicky as she lost her balance again. "Sorry."

"You're doing fine," he reassured her. "Take it easy. It's a stretch, so it's okay to go slowly."

She wasn't one of the super-fit guys he spent all day with. He saw color rising in her cheeks from embarrassment. She seemed to come to some decision while he still held her upper arm.

"Okay. I'll see if I can pull my leg up a little higher," she said.

Seth took a deep breath. He recognized the slight vanilla scent she always wore. It reminded him of how she felt when he'd touched her arm—warm and soft. Most of the women he knew spent a fortune at the fragrance counter. He'd bought his share of perfume for women he'd been with too, despite the fact he'd never liked it much. He mentally shook himself. He needed to get his head back in the game. She'd run like a scared rabbit if she had any idea he'd had yet another steamy dream about her.

Jillian gave up on stretching one leg; she shifted to the other, and she almost lost her balance again. He caught her around her waist. Her breasts brushed against his forearm, and he felt the shock of static electricity—and an unmistakable stirring in his shorts.

"Oh, God. Oh no! Sorry."

"Don't worry about it." He set her back on her feet, but he didn't let go. "You okay?"

"I'm fine. We should walk."

"Yeah." He dropped his hands to his side and moved away from her reluctantly.

SETH'S HANDS FELT branded into her sides, and she was tingling in more than a few places. Damn! She walked away from him; he caught up to her in a few quick strides.

It was the strangest feeling she'd ever had—he'd caught her, he'd held her close, and her head rested in the middle of his chest. He finally set her back on her feet and walked away from her, but not before she saw something in his eyes that made her wonder.

What was going on with him? He'd sought her out. He'd walked with her. He'd made sure she had exercise clothes and correct shoes. He'd asked her for her address the other day; she gave it to him, but she never dreamed he'd actually use it. He showed up at her apartment very early this morning, inviting her out for a hike. And breakfast.

She concentrated on taking careful steps. The path slanted down; they'd end at a small platform to get the full effect of the falls. Maybe she could take a few pictures or a short video with her cell phone camera.

"So…" Seth said, "did you go out last night?"

"Nope."

"What about the boyfriend?"

"Out of town. No date," she answered. She saw his mouth twitch with repressed laughter. "Did you have a date?"

"The guys were giving me crap about fixing me up, but I told them no." He turned to face her, walking backward. She reached out for his forearm.

"I'm afraid you'll trip."

"No such luck, Jill," he joked. The slight breeze had blown droplets of water over his skin. He grinned at her. "Back to the subject. Why didn't you go out with friends? It would be nice to get out and have some fun."

"Maybe you should 'get out' and 'have some fun' yourself," she told him, complete with air quotes.

"Maybe I should stay home with CB. It's safer there. I'll cat-sit while you go out," he said.

This was the strangest conversation they'd had yet. She knew it was better for both of them if she told him she was dating someone else. After all, those who weren't on the prowl for companionship (so to speak) could be friends with a member of the opposite sex, without all the stickiness involved in unrealistic expectations and feelings that would never go anywhere. Seth probably wasn't sure they were friends yet, but she was. Even if he woke her up at insane hours to go hiking and teased her, she liked him. Well, she liked what she knew of him. He made her laugh. Plus, he was gorgeous.

Seth and Jillian walked along in silence for a few minutes, which eventually proved to be too much for him.

"So, when am I going to meet him?"

"Meet who?"

"Your casual-thing boyfriend."

"Never," she said. "We've only been seeing each other for a short time. I don't need you scaring him off."

"Why not? You're dating someone; I'd like to meet him."

"You wouldn't like him. He hates football," she said. "He's into ballet."

His mouth opened and shut, opened and shut, like an outraged goldfish. Laughter rose in her throat again. It was all she could do to control her mirth. She glanced away from him. It was beautiful out here. After all, most people were still sleeping at seven o' clock on a Saturday morning. She took a deep breath of air newly washed by cascading water. The sound of the falls hitting rocks in the pool below with incredible force was soothing.

"You're shitting me," he said.

"Nope," she said.

"I'd introduce you to someone I was dating," he said.

"Why? That's very nice, but really, it's not necessary—"

"We're friends, aren't we? Friends do those kinds of things for each other," he said.

"When did we become friends?" she teased.

"Oh, we're friends," he said. "We spend time together. I met your kitty. I still can't believe you named her after a dessert, but hell, whatever does it for you."

"Okay—friends. You're going to let me pass judgment on your dates too?"

"Why not?" he said. They stepped onto the observation platform, and he nudged a pebble off of the edge with one foot. The falls looked close enough for them to reach out and touch. The breeze draped her with a veil of water droplets too. "This was worth the drive, wasn't it?"

"Yes. It was." She reached into her pocket to grab her phone.

"It's selfie time," he said and pulled his phone out of his warm-ups pocket. He turned his back to the falls and reached out one arm to pull her into his side.

"Really?"

"Smile," he said.

She probably looked like hell, but his arm slid around her shoulders, and he laid his stubble-covered cheek against her own. She breathed in the woodsy smell of the soap he liked and his shampoo.

"Say cheese," she joked.

He snapped the picture and said, "One more."

She held up her camera too. "I want one."

"You just want to put it up on Instagram," he teased, but he grinned again, and his arm tightened around her shoulders. He jammed his phone back in his warm-ups pocket, and they turned toward the falls once more.

She wasn't sure what to say and was even more unsure of what to do. Maybe she should keep it light and revisit the conversation they'd been having before he actually put his arm around her shoulders. He'd do the same thing with anyone else. She pulled breath into her lungs, hoped her racing heart wasn't visible on her face, and she grinned up at him.

"So, back to the conversation. What if I don't approve of the woman you're dating?" she said.

"Well, then, I'll dump her."

Jillian burst out laughing.

He wagged one finger at her. "I have to make sure you're with a good guy."

"You don't have to do anything. I'm fine," she said. The lack of coffee was catching up with her. She was a little hungry, but if he wanted to stand there all day, she'd do it. "Why would you think you have to check out someone I'm going out with anyway?"

Seth turned to look at her. He held her eyes, and she felt a shiver run up her spine. Despite the roar of the falls, the immense clearing they stood in, birds wheeling overhead, and a million other things to see, smell, and feel, she couldn't concentrate on anything else but his face.

"I just do," he said.

*Chapter Seven*

A FEW DAYS after visiting Snoqualmie Falls with Seth, Jillian arrived home from work and dropped her purse and car keys onto the little built-in desk in her kitchen. She loved fall, but the cooler weather made her want to hibernate. She let out a long sigh as CB raced out of her room with a long piece of TP stuck to one of her hind legs.

"Unrolling the toilet paper roll again?" she asked.

The kitten let out a *prrt* and wound around Jillian's ankles. Jillian could add cleaning up her no-doubt-trashed bathroom to a long list of tonight's household chores. She needed to wash a load of clothes before she was forced to show up commando at the office. She could stand to run the vacuum around, and she could only imagine what waited for her in the bathroom. CB was adorable, but a bored kitten usually meant a mess. It might also be nice if she composed a shopping list before she stepped foot in the grocery store.

She would have preferred spending the evening in a hot bath with a great book or settling in for a long, chatty phone call with Kari. It was the team's day off. She hadn't seen Seth for two days now. She'd stopped reminding herself to quit longing for a glimpse of him; it was pointless. She'd printed off the pic of them she'd snapped with her phone at the falls. She'd stuck it to the front of her refrigerator with a magnet. So much for that whole "forget about him; he's out of your league" thing.

Jillian heard the chirp of a text and grabbed her phone out of her bag. She let out a happy squeal as she realized it was from Seth.

HEY. WHAT ARE YOU DOING RIGHT NOW?

She was sure he'd be dazzled by an evening of housework and grocery shopping.

JUST GOT HOME, she responded. PLAYING WITH CB.

He answered seconds later. LET'S GO DO SOMETHING. I'LL BE THERE SOON.

She reached out to grab the picture of Seth off of the refrigerator door and stuck it into the silverware drawer.

SETH GLANCED AT his phone as another text came in.

WANT TO PLAY GAMES WITH MCCOY AND ME TONIGHT? Derrick Collins wrote.

GOT PLANS. NO CAN DO, Seth responded.

His phone made the sound of another person joining the convo.

MAN UP AND TELL HER YOU'LL SEE HER TOMORROW BRO, Drew McCoy texted.

YOU'RE ABOUT TEN MINUTES TOO LATE, Seth told them.

THE MYSTERY WOMAN AGAIN? Derrick texted. SOUNDS SERIOUS. WHO IS SHE?

Seth grinned down at his phone, shut it off, and stuck it in his jeans pocket. Two minutes later, he was in the car and headed to Jillian's place.

JILLIAN SAW THE headlights of Seth's Escalade through her living room windows as she tried to shove the dirty laundry spilling out of a small alcove in her kitchen behind folding doors. She wasn't having a lot of luck. She'd spent fifteen minutes cleaning up the mess CB had made in her bathroom, with toilet paper dragged into the shower. She'd swapped out her office clothes for jeans, a sweater, and flats, and she thought she could clean up a bit before Seth arrived. It wasn't going to happen.

She heard his knock at the front door. "Come on in," she called out.

CB launched herself at Seth as he closed Jillian's front door behind him. "Hey, kitty," he said. The kitten rubbed her face on his clothes. "Is she always like this?"

"Pretty much," she said. "How are you?"

"Great," he said. "How are you doing?"

"I'm fine." She wished she had something more interesting to say to him at that moment, but she heard the telltale creaking of folding doors and a soft *splat* as the dirty laundry she'd crammed into the alcove spilled out onto the kitchen floor. Shit.

"Looks like laundry day," he said.

"You might say that." She turned her back on the laundry. It was super-embarrassing that her dirty clothes were all over the kitchen, but there wasn't a lot she could do about it at the moment. Maybe she should stay home tonight and get herself and her life together. "It's so great you're here, but I have a million and one things that need to get done," she said. "Maybe we should—"

"We've both gotta eat," he said.

"I know that, but we...I..."

"It's my day off. You're not ditching me to do laundry, are you?" he asked playfully, his enthusiasm becoming contagious. CB was now licking his face. Why was her cat more affectionate with him than she was with Jillian? "I'd like to think I'm much more fun than the laundry." He bent to put CB back down on the floor and straightened up. "Come on. You're getting out of here for a few hours. Remember when you told me you were going to show me around town a little? It's time for you to pay up."

Before Jillian knew it, she was standing in the corridor outside her front door, purse in hand, and Seth was locking the front door behind them.

"Let's go," he said. He dropped her keys back into her hand, took her elbow in his fingertips, and towed her out to his Escalade. "It's either this, Jill, or I help you with the laundry and the cleaning. You don't want that."

"Why not?"

"I'm not good at it." He unlocked the passenger door for her, ran around the front of the vehicle, and threw himself into the driver's seat. "We'll get something to eat, and then I have a surprise for you."

"Why are you doing this?" she persisted. He just laughed. She rolled her eyes and blew hair off of her chin.

"I heard about this place a few weeks ago. I think you'll like it." He pulled onto the freeway leading to Seattle. "We'll have fun."

"Am I dressed appropriately for wherever we're going?" she asked.

"Absolutely. We'll be there before you know it." He took the exit to Capitol Hill. A few minutes later, he pulled into the parking area below an unfamiliar building. "Okay. Stick with me, and nobody will get hurt," he joked.

They climbed a flight of stairs to the street, moved through an old-fashioned revolving door, and walked into the building.

"Where are we?"

"You'll see."

## *Chapter Eight*

———————————————————————

SETH TOOK JILLIAN'S arm as they crossed the lobby of the building and climbed the steepest staircase she had encountered in quite some time. The decorating scheme of the space was Art Deco, dominated by black, burgundy, and chrome. Walls on both sides of the stairs were covered in antique advertisements, photos of performers, and show posters. At the top of the stairs, they turned a corner. Jillian stood in a dimly lit restaurant with tin-topped tables; an old-fashioned carved, heavy wooden bar; and gleaming hardwood floors, and the whole thing looked out over a ballroom.

"We're at the Millennium Ballroom, snoopy. We're going to have dinner and a private dancing lesson," Seth said.

"Dancing?" Jillian tried to pull away from him; he still held her arm. "I don't know how to dance."

"Of course you don't. You told me you wanted to learn, didn't you? Now, come on. I'm hungry, and our dance lesson doesn't start for a little while." A hostess approached them. "We have a reservation for two under Taylor. May we be seated toward the back of the restaurant? Thanks."

"Why are you doing this? I don't understand." He propelled her forward with his fingertips at the small of her back. "You're going to make me dance in front of a bunch of other people?" The hostess diplomatically ignored Jillian's comments and sat them at a table in the shadows. Menus were put in front of them.

"We all need to start somewhere," he said. Seth gazed at the bar for a moment and focused on the hostess again. "I'd like a Fat Tire, and Jill, you need a drink. What would you like?"

"I'm not sure."

"How about some ice water until my guest decides what she'd like to drink?"

The hostess walked away.

Seth leaned closer and spoke in a low voice. "I know this scares you. It's not the end of the world. We'll have some dinner; we'll try dancing. I think you'll enjoy it."

"Seth, I guess I'm confused. Why are we here?" The water glass and Seth's beer arrived. He held up his glass to her and took a swallow. "Isn't there someone else you'd rather spend your day off with?"

He thought for a moment. "No."

"Don't you want to go out with someone who—well, someone who's available? I know there're so many women who want to date you, and well, you're here with me."

"Really?" Seth reached out to grip the hand Jillian had on her water glass. "I have fun with you. I like your company. We're having dinner; we have a dance lesson, and you're out of the house for a few hours. Are you ashamed to be seen with me?"

"No. No! Of course not."

"Well, then. Why don't you figure out what you'd like to eat for dinner, and we can coax the server over here to order?"

SETH KNEW JILLIAN spent most of her weekends at Treehouse, when she wasn't making sure John and his cronies were comfortable and well fed in the team's luxury suite at Sharks Stadium. He also knew she did errands or household chores on weeknights. She didn't talk much about herself. When he tried to ask her questions about what she liked to do when she wasn't at the office, she started asking him questions. Over the past couple of weeks, though, he'd managed to get Jillian talking about a few of the things in life she'd never tried but wanted to. One of them was learning to dance.

He knew he'd invited her to do something that she found a little scary. He'd already discovered that when he suggested trying something out of her daily routine, she was a bit hesitant. She'd have so much fun, she'd forget about her initial misgivings.

He'd tried to find out more about her boyfriend. Whenever he asked, she'd clam up and change the subject or make jokes. He hadn't seen any photos or male belongings in her place. Either this guy was a first-class absent asshole, or Jillian had her own reasons for making sure he didn't think she was alone.

He felt a strange possessive surge. It might make him a jerk, but Seth had to admit he didn't want to share her attention with anyone else. He hadn't had a female friend for a long time. Jill and Lauren kept him from drowning in the sea of testosterone that was his life.

He glanced over the menu but was distracted by movement out of the corner of his eye. The couple on the dance floor must have been professionals. They moved through a tango as one—fluid, graceful, and very sensual. Jillian couldn't take her eyes off them, and he saw longing in her expression. She leaned forward in her chair.

She was about to learn to dance. Dinner could wait.

He got up from the chair and held out his hand. "May I have this dance?"

A soft flush crept over her face. She nodded at the dance floor.

"We'll learn together," he reassured her.

She was still blushing. She glanced down at her hands clenched in her lap, but she smiled and put her hand in his.

The couple had finished their dance, and the woman called out to them in a Spanish-accented voice. "Our previous appointment canceled. Would you like a lesson?"

Jillian responded before Seth could open his mouth. "Yes. Would you teach me?"

"I would love to," her partner said.

He held out his arms to her, and Jillian walked into them. Seth felt a sharp stab of something in the middle of his chest and ignored it, along with the urge to march over there and grab her away from him. Where the hell did this come from? The woman extended her hand to him, but he paused for a moment so he could hear what the man was saying to Jillian.

"She will be fine," the woman told him.

"I'm not worried about it."

He heard her soft, musical laugh. "Of course you're not. That's why you can't take your eyes off of her. Do you dance?"

"Rarely." He was still straining to hear what the man was telling Jillian. "It might be fun to learn."

"You will be dancing with her before you know it. Come with me."

JILLIAN WAS LISTENING to her partner. "What's your name, señorita?"

"I'm Jillian."

"My name is Carlos." He gave her a dazzlingly white smile. Carlos was probably about six feet tall, with black, slicked-back hair, eyes the color of hot chocolate, and a well-trimmed mustache. Seth was all bulging muscles and height. This guy was in great shape too, but his body was long and lean. "You don't dance?"

"I don't know how." She closed her eyes for a moment. She'd wanted to dance for as long as she could remember, but she felt clumsy. "I want to, though."

"There are many steps to the tango, but right now, we'll dance a little, just so you will see what it's like. I want you to pay attention to the shifts in weight. In other words, you will feel the changes in steps before your feet do. The tango requires all of you—brain, heart, and body. I would like you to follow my lead."

She looked up into his eyes and the warmth of his smile. "What if I can't dance?"

"Everyone can dance. If you can walk, if you can feel the music in your heart, you can dance." He slid his arm around her waist and took her hand in his. The music started, and at first Jillian felt stiff and awkward. She wasn't sure where to move or what to do. Obviously, she didn't know the steps. He murmured into her ear, "Relax. Feel the music. What does it mean to you?"

It wasn't the first time in her life she'd been held in a man's arms, but the intimacy of being so close to a man she didn't know was a bit overwhelming. She closed her eyes to concentrate, feeling the movement of his body and a strong arm around her. To her amazement, she moved. Her body was fluid. What had started out as a walk became dance steps and the sensation of flying across the dance floor.

"I...I'm dancing," she said with a gasp.

"Yes. You are." The song ended; another began. "Let's try again."

Jillian felt the ballroom floor beneath her feet and the feeling of her hand enveloped in his, and she smelled the citrusy cologne Carlos wore. The beat of the music matched Carlos's feet. He whispered the names of the steps in her ear as he danced. He moved her as if she weighed nothing, as if she was as accomplished and graceful as his partner. When she relaxed enough to follow his lead, they moved together without her even trying. The dance was sensual, but even more, being rocked in someone else's arms was soothing. She forgot her nervousness in a rush of joy and confidence.

The music ended, and they came to a stop.

"Okay, Jillian. Let's work on a few of the steps. How's that?"

She opened her eyes. He still held her. "Yes, please. I'd like that."

She glanced around. Seth was several feet away. He caught her eye and grinned at her.

"You will dance with him soon," Carlos said.

"He's probably much better at this than I am." The words came out in a rush. "He's a professional athlete."

"Jillian. *Cara*. You are too hard on yourself. You were dancing. He had a tough time." He let out a sigh. "He'll dance too, but it will be harder for him until he can lead. Let's practice a little more."

Carlos moved Jillian through unfamiliar steps. He spoke into her ear the entire time—lyrical Spanish words she didn't understand.

"Does it bother you if I close my eyes?" she asked him. She couldn't figure out why she felt so shy or why the intimacy of being held in his arms unsettled her a bit. She knew he wouldn't hurt her, and she was safe. She needed to relax.

"No, it doesn't bother me. You can feel the steps as I push and shift my weight. Keep trying. You're doing a great job." She heard footsteps behind them, and Carlos stopped. Seth must have tapped him on the shoulder. Carlos brought her hand to his lips. "I will see you again," Carlos said. "More lessons?"

"Yes, please." She smiled up at him. "Thank you so much."

"You're welcome."

He nodded at Seth, and he and his partner moved into each other's arms again.

"Did you have fun?" Seth asked.

"It was amazing. I danced, Seth. I didn't fall over my feet or step on his toes. Did you see?" She was babbling, and she didn't care. "This is so much fun. I had no idea! I never thought I could do it—"

"Would you like some dinner?"

"Yes. I want to dance some more afterward. Could we dance some more?" She touched his arm. "Will you dance with me?"

He seemed a little surprised. "Sure."

She was so excited that she hadn't even asked him if he'd enjoyed himself. "How did your lesson go? Do you like this? Was it fun for you?"

He sat down at their table and signaled the server. "It was fine. What would you like to eat?" he said.

A group dance lesson was starting on the dance floor. Jillian was immediately fascinated with the movement of the dancers, the colorful swirling of the women's skirts, and the laughter. Seth was still glancing around for the servers. It was probably rude, but the food was the last thing on her mind right now.

Jillian was practically bouncing in her chair from excitement. She saw other people walking out to the dance floor and joining the circle around several dance instructors. In other words, it was okay to join in, and she wanted to.

His voice was low and amused. "I'll bet you want to go out there and see what they're doing."

"I'm dying to," she said. "If you're hungry, though, I can wait."

"You can wait, hm? Are you sure?"

She shook her head, and his laughter rang out. "Come on. Let's get out there."

It felt so natural to slide her hand inside his much bigger one as he led her through the seating area, which was getting more crowded by the minute. He squeezed her hand as he maneuvered around tables and pushed empty chairs out of their way, and her heart rate picked up. She hoped her hand wasn't sweaty. Her entire arm tingled. They were steps from the dance floor when Jillian heard someone call out, "Go Sharks!"

Seconds later, she and Seth were surrounded by people who were waving pens and any piece of paper they could get their hands on and calling out questions.

"Are you Seth Taylor?" a woman in a brightly colored dancing costume asked.

"You're my favorite Shark. Could you sign this 'to my favorite Sharks fan'?" another person said.

"If I knew you hung out here, I'd come here more often. My wife dragged me," a big guy in a Sharks ball cap told him.

"It's really great to see all of you, but my friend would like me to join her for the dance lesson," Seth said.

"She won't mind waiting a few minutes, will she?" the guy in the ball cap said.

"My little brother would just die if I didn't bring him home an autograph," the woman in the dancing costume said.

"It won't take you that long to sign a few autographs," someone else said.

JILLIAN PULLED ON his hand. "Go ahead," she told him. "I'll wait."

"Are you sure?" he said. The excited smile on her face was fading as the crowd grew. In other words, she was doing her best to be patient while he dealt with well-meaning fans who didn't understand that he might want to enjoy his evening out.

"I'll be fine," she said. She squeezed his hand one more time and moved away from the crowd to take a seat at one of the now-empty tables.

## Chapter Nine

AN HOUR LATER, the dancing lesson was over. Couples filled the dance floor. Seth was still dealing with a few fans who had ignored his polite efforts to excuse himself. Jillian had been so excited to pull him out onto that dance floor, but he was willing to bet his car she wasn't getting near it now. She rested her chin on her hand and watched everyone else having a great time. Her bravado was as faded as the patient smile she wore.

He couldn't be pissed at the Sharks fans. They wanted to talk with him for a few minutes and get an autograph. It was part of his job. At the same time, watching her waiting for him struck at something inside. Most women would have stormed off half an hour ago.

He glanced over at Jillian and started to move away from the Sharks fans.

"It was great to meet all of you, but I need to go spend some time with my friend," he said. "She's been waiting."

"Have a drink with us," the guy in the Sharks ball cap urged.

"Maybe another time," Seth said. He reached out for Jillian's hand. "Thanks for your support."

"She can keep waiting," another guy told him. Seth ignored the urge to tell the guy that Jillian was a lot more patient than his wife would have been. *Just keep moving*, he told himself.

"Again, thanks. See you another time," he said. He pulled Jillian up from her chair and set off at a fast pace for the staircase leading to the lobby. He could hear other people calling out his name and "Go Sharks," but he wasn't stopping until they were in his car and heading out of the parking garage.

"Seth," Jillian said. "I can't keep up."

He glanced back at her. She was breathing a bit hard, but he was afraid that if he stopped, they'd get waylaid by even more people who hadn't joined in the first autograph session. He took the risk of something like this happening every time he went out in public, but he never dreamed he'd be besieged by autograph seekers at a ballroom dancing lesson.

"It's a few more feet," he said. "Can you make it?"

She nodded. He shoved the door to the staircase open and reached back to make sure she was through it.

"Let's wait here a sec so you can catch your breath," he said as he felt the door shut behind him.

A few minutes later, they'd negotiated the through the lobby's revolving door, and found his car. He was pulling out of the parking garage. She was resting against the passenger seat and taking deep breaths.

"Are you okay?"

"I'll be fine," she said.

He was hungry, but even more than food, he wanted to spend a little more time with her tonight. He enjoyed her company. She made him laugh. He even liked her crazy little cat, which was a first for him.

If he had to come up with words for his feelings, it was that he wanted to be a better person when he was with her. He gave himself a mental shake. What the hell was going on with him these days?

The bridge to the Eastside was almost empty for once. He pulled into Burgermaster, parked the car, and turned to Jillian. The parking lot was quiet for a change. Typically, every stall was full. The food was brought to customers' cars, so he wouldn't have to have this conversation in front of multiple witnesses.

Jillian gave him a smile that was nothing more than a curve of her lips. "I know you run the risk of being recognized every time you go out in public, but was that unusual? You were telling them politely that you needed to leave, and most of those people ignored it."

"I'm used to it, but I wasn't happy they made you wait." He folded his arms across his chest. "Hungry?"

"Yeah." This time, he saw warmth in her eyes. "Would you be terribly insulted if I told you that I really do prefer cheeseburgers?"

"Well, then, we're at the right place." He shifted in the seat. Kim would have ripped the building apart with her bare hands if he'd made her wait for him and then taken her to a burger place instead of an expensive restaurant.

Jillian wasn't Kim.

She was studying the menu. "Have you had the veggie burger? How is it?"

"You're not a vegetarian—"

"It might be good. I'd like to try one, and I'd like the garden salad. So, go on." She turned to face him and unfastened her seat belt. "What happened?"

He noticed her normally expressive face had settling into a mask of blank composure. He wasn't going to find out how she felt about this, and he wanted to know. She had to be angry with him, and he really didn't blame her for it.

The carhop appeared at his window. He took his time giving their order. Finally, he had no other options, especially since the carhop went back into the restaurant, and they were alone.

He felt the hot, uncomfortable surge of embarrassment wash over him. He knew he should have handled tonight's situation better.

"I apologize. You had to wait a long time, and I should have been more insistent that we had plans." He let out a sigh.

"Then they would have been mad at you for not talking to them," she murmured.

"It's pretty flattering to talk to people who think I'm great or want my autograph. You missed another dance lesson, though." He glanced up through the sunroof and blew out another breath. "Maybe we could try this again sometime."

"Maybe," she said.

Jillian's mask abruptly cracked in half. She looked stunned, but she turned toward the window so he wouldn't see it. She wasn't fast enough. She picked up her purse off the floorboard. "I need to visit the ladies room. I'll be right back." She opened the car door and hopped out. He watched her walk away.

JILLIAN WALKED INTO the ladies room, stuffed one fist into her mouth, and let out a muffled scream. She knew she wasn't supposed to be seeing him. If—well, when—John found out, there would be problems. Going for a walk was one thing. Going on what could be construed as a date was something else entirely, and this wasn't the first time. Seth kept asking her to do things with him, and she wanted to go. The more time she spent with him, the more she enjoyed it.

She knew he used to spend most of his time hanging around with Drew McCoy and Derrick Collins. Maybe he was bored and looking for something to do because his two best buddies now spent most of their time hanging around with their wives.

She was never, ever getting involved with Seth, she told herself. Actually, she already was. Why lie? Whenever he was around, she was breathless. She couldn't think, and her heart beat so fast and so loudly that she wondered if someone else could hear it. Her palms were sweaty. Her mouth was dry. She knew he wasn't interested in her romantically, and she still felt this way. There was no limit to how stupid she was and how badly she was going to get hurt if she kept hanging around with him. He'd laugh if he knew she remembered how his hand felt when he'd impatiently taken hers on a hiking path or in the ballroom tonight, or how he smelled—the freshly showered, woodsy soap scent she couldn't seem to get out of her head. He'd probably come up with some kind of "I'm flattered" crap if he had any idea how she felt.

She'd rather die.

She took care of business, washed her hands, and fluffed her hair with her fingers. She had to go back to the car, or he'd come in here after her.

JILLIAN HOPPED BACK into the passenger seat, dropped her purse on the floorboard, and took the plastic container of garden salad he'd just handed her. "Thanks." She spread a napkin across her lap. So far, she wouldn't meet his eyes, and she wasn't talking.

"You're welcome. I ordered a veggie burger for you to try if you'd like." He grabbed his own container of salad. "I wasn't sure what kind of dressing you liked, so I took a guess."

"Thank you. I should have told you what dressing I wanted before I went to the ladies' room." She poured the small container of vinaigrette dressing over her salad. "This is great, though."

"Hey, do you mind making one more stop on the way home?"

"No, I don't mind," she said. He probably wanted to run into the store or whatever. She turned slightly to look into his eyes. "Thank you for the dancing lesson. I had fun. I'm glad you invited me."

"I had a great time too. I meant it when I said we should try that again."

She nodded as she took a bite of her food. Hopefully, she'd enjoy what he had planned next.

Half an hour later, he pulled up in front of the large gazebo in Kirkland's Marina Park on the shores of Lake Washington. The park was usually crowded with families and joggers; right now, they had the place to themselves. Nobody was on the lakefront after dark on a weeknight. The moon was full and glistened off the water. It wasn't chilly. The only sounds were the slap of waves on the shore and the rustle of leaves as the breeze blew.

"What are we doing here?" Jillian asked.

"You never got that dance," he gruffly said. "Come on."

"Are you serious?"

He turned off the engine. His iPhone was still hooked up to the car's sound system, and he found a song he thought Jillian might like out of some girly stuff one of his former girlfriends had downloaded onto it. He got out of the car, left the door open so they could still hear, and held out one hand.

"I believe this is my dance," he said.

Obviously, they weren't going to tango. Before tonight, he hadn't danced for a long time, but he wanted to dance with Jillian. He reached out and pulled her into his arms.

He saw the color rise in her cheeks again.

He noticed she didn't move away. She didn't resist him at all. Her hands rested on his forearms. He was close enough to see the pulse madly beating at the base of her throat as she looked up at him. The top of her head was barely to his shoulder.

"When was the last time you danced with someone?" he asked.

"Before tonight? Years." She smiled a little. It must have been a good memory.

"Put your hand on my shoulder. Let's see if we remember how." He thought he'd try some kind of old-fashioned waltzing thing, but all he could remember was junior-high-quality slow dancing. She seemed to remember it too.

He felt her hands move over his biceps and gentle on his shoulders. There was less of Jillian than there had been the first time he hugged her. Her clothes were looser too. His arms tightened around her. She let him touch her, but she wasn't plastering herself against him as another woman would have done. He was torn between thinking it might be a good thing that she held herself away from him and wanting to hold her closer.

ONE DANCE WITH him, and then Jillian would pull herself out of his arms and get back into the car. She could dance with him and not get emotional about it. He was just another guy. She was not going to let herself get stupid over someone who was clearly only interested in her as a friend.

His hold on her was gentle. He smelled good. She saw the flash of his smile when she peeked up at him. She'd felt shy with Carlos because she didn't know him, but she didn't have that problem with Seth. She wanted to move closer but knew she shouldn't.

She tried to remind herself that Seth probably had more than a few friends with benefits, even if he was between girlfriends at the time. He was a guy. He probably wasn't celibate, and he and she weren't romantic with each other. There was also the tiny fact that anything that happened between them was not going to end well.

She was in more trouble than she knew how to get out of.

AT FIRST, JILLIAN rested her head against his cheek. A minute or so later, she laid her head on his chest. They swayed together, feet barely moving, and he realized his heart was pounding. He'd never experienced anything as romantic as dancing late at night in a deserted city park to a song playing on his car's sound system. The darkness wrapped them in the softest cocoon. He glanced down at her as he felt her slowly relaxing against him.

*It's not the pale moon that excites me*
*That thrills and delights me*
*Oh, no*
*It's just the nearness of you*

He took a deep breath of the vanilla scent he'd recognize anywhere as hers. His fingers stroked the small of her back, and he heard her sigh. Slow dancing was even better than he remembered. Then again, he wasn't in junior high anymore, and he was holding a woman in his arms, not a teenage girl. There was a lot to be said for delayed gratification. Dancing with Jillian was all about the smallest movements and letting things build. He laid his cheek against hers.

"I shouldn't be doing this," she whispered.

"Why not?" he whispered back.

"It's not a good idea."

"We're just dancing, Jill."

And if things got any hotter between them, they'd be naked. She didn't try to step away from him. If she'd resisted him at all, if she'd shown reluctance or fear or hesitation, he would have let her go and walked away. Her fingers tangled in his hair.

They were just friends. He didn't think he had those kinds of feelings for this woman—the sexual, amorous, bow-chicka-bow-wow feelings—despite the fact his pulse was racing, his fingers itched to touch her, and he knew he should let go of her. It didn't matter that he was still having hotter-than-the-invention-of-fire dreams about Jillian most nights. He wasn't going to consider what kind of tricks his subconscious played on him. Instead, he pulled her a fraction of an inch closer. He slid one hand up her back, feeling her long, silky-soft blonde hair cascading over his fingers, and she trembled. He cupped her cheek in his hand. He couldn't take his eyes off her mouth. Just a couple of inches more, and he'd kiss her. He moved slowly but purposefully.

He watched her eyelids flutter closed, felt her quick intake of breath. He wondered how she tasted. He'd know in a few seconds.

"I want to kiss you," he said in a breath against her mouth.

The silence was broken by the screaming guitars of Guns N' Roses.

That would teach him to use the shuffle function.

## Chapter Ten

A FEW DAYS later, Jillian put her disposable coffee cup down on her desk as she dropped her car keys into her purse and shoved the whole thing into her desk drawer. She'd gotten a three-shot skinny latte at the Starbucks drive-through. If there was ever a day she needed a caffeine IV, it was this one.

She hadn't seen Seth for several days. He'd evidently forgotten about her. She hadn't slept well last night. She kept reliving how it felt to be held in Seth's arms. She'd been so sure he was going to kiss her as they danced beneath the gazebo in the park. He'd said he wanted to, and then he jumped away from her like she was made out of molten lava. There wasn't a lot of conversation on the way home that night either.

If she had any guts at all, she would have told him how she felt the last time she saw him—that she was hurt and confused, and she didn't understand what she'd done wrong to make him react the way he had. Maybe she should have kissed him. Instead, she sat in the passenger seat of his car and stared out the window as he drove.

No matter how hard she'd fallen or how she yearned for him, she was back in the friend zone. Again.

SETH HADN'T SLEPT well for the past several nights either. He'd barely managed to haul his ass out of bed this morning. If he didn't move it, he'd be late for practice, which would be expensive. He didn't need the coach on his back. He pulled on some warm-ups and his cross-trainers, pointed his Escalade toward the Sharks' practice facility, and tried to forget the look on Jillian's face when he didn't kiss her the night they went dancing. He'd watched the emotions flit over her face: Confusion. Sadness. Hurt. She'd backed away from him and wouldn't meet his eyes.

There were so many things he should have said to her at that moment while his fucking iPhone blared Guns N' Roses, and he shuffled his feet like a seventh grader whose voice was just starting to change. He should have told her that he knew they'd talked about being friends, and "friends" meant no physical stuff, but right now, he wasn't into being friends. He wanted more. He wanted to kiss her until they were both breathless. He wanted to get close enough that he wasn't quite sure where he ended and she began. Mostly, he now knew that whole thing about their being "just friends" was crap. He wanted her. Bad.

More than his current physical discomfort, he'd be a real ass if he treated Jillian like a one-night stand. He'd want to kill another guy who did the same thing to her. She wasn't in the market for just one night; he wasn't in the market for happily ever after, at least not right now. He wasn't ready to settle down yet.

He could picture Jillian in a cozy house, reading a story to a couple of blonde cherubs before bedtime while her adoring husband (who remained faceless; he couldn't think of any other guy who actually deserved Jillian) told himself one more time how damn lucky he was. The guy didn't even exist, and Seth hated him already.

She'd told him that John had said he'd fire her if she got romantically involved with anyone from the team. He knew John was probably blowing smoke, but to someone like Jillian, it was sufficiently scary to the point that she wouldn't take that risk.

"It's getting late," he'd said like a dumb-ass the last time he'd seen her. "We'd better leave."

She gave him a quick nod, an "uh-huh," and got into the car.

She'd hardly said a thing on the way home either.

He wished there was a way he could show her that he really wasn't that much of an idiot and get back to where they'd been before. He took the freeway exit to the facility and stepped on his brakes a bit. The cops loved to sit in the brush by the little bend in the road and hand out speeding tickets like breath mints as a result. He drove past a squad car and gave the officer a wave.

It took him a while, but he'd managed to get Jillian to tell him a few things about herself and her life. He was pretty surprised to learn she'd been on her high school's swim team, for instance. She also said she hadn't been swimming in years. An idea dawned as he pulled into the parking space with his jersey number on it and got out of the car. Team sponsors and advertisers gave out free stuff to the team all the time; why shouldn't he share the wealth with her?

He strolled into the Sharks' locker room a few minutes later. Most of his teammates were there to lift before practice started. He headed toward Drew McCoy's locker.

Drew gave him a fist bump. "Nice to see you could make it."

"You too," Seth said. "How's Kendall?" Drew's wife was still working for the Sharks' arch rivals, the San Francisco Miners, but she'd struck a deal with the team's ownership to work remotely four days a week.

"She's kicking ass and taking names." Drew smiled. "Our Tessa is at her nana's. We'll pick her up tomorrow."

"You're a lucky man."

"The luckiest," Drew said. "What's up with you today?"

"Didn't that gym across from Bellevue Square give you some free membership passes or some damn thing when you did those ads for them?"

"Yeah. I'm guessing you want at least one."

"Both, if you're not already using them. What would you like in exchange?"

"By the time I get out of here, it's not like I want to go to the gym again. Kendall has a trainer. We won't use them," Drew said.

"How about a gift certificate to John Howie Steak or a weekend at that hotel by Chateau Ste. Michelle Winery in exchange? Your wife would love the spa."

"Don't worry about it. I'll bring the passes when I come in tomorrow. The gym shouldn't squawk either. More people join if they think we hang out there." Drew's mouth twitched. "Two passes, huh? I know you're not bringing Morrison. Who's your plus-one?"

"She's just a friend," he said.

"Oh, sure. Just a friend." Drew laughed out loud. "That's how Kendall and I started too."

Seth lifted, went to practice, met with his position coach, and grabbed a sheaf of fan mail out of the cubbyhole in the locker room with his last name and jersey number on it. He needed to make a phone call before he left the facility for the day. He sprinted out to his ride and got into the driver's seat.

"Performance Gym."

"Hello. This is Seth Taylor of the Sharks. I'd like to talk with your general manager, please."

The gym already sponsored the Sharks, so it was a quick-and-positive conversation for Seth. The general managers offered two gym memberships to Seth in exchange for his appearance at a one-hour meet-and-greet party with the gym's members, which would be scheduled at Seth's convenience after the season was over. He wouldn't need to make off with the McCoy family's passes, which was good news. Seth also managed to obtain private use of the gym's pool for two hours this evening.

He couldn't stop grinning. Hopefully, Jillian would forgive his being so clueless the other night if she got to revisit another activity she'd enjoyed once upon a time.

Plus, Jillian could swim to her heart's content. He wasn't opposed to splashing around in a pool that was above freezing for a couple of hours. He thanked the gym's GM, ended the call, and pointed his ride toward a local department store. Jillian was going to need something to swim in.

Seth wasn't an expert at swimsuit shopping, but he remembered there was a store at the mall that sold nothing but swimsuits—it would be hard to go wrong. He managed to find a one-piece the saleswoman insisted would fit Jillian perfectly after he gave a demonstration of her shape and size in the air with his hands.

"She's curvy," the saleswoman said.

"Yes. And she's about this tall." He held his hand up to just below one of his shoulders.

The salesperson reached out to grab a bluish-purple one-piece suit off the rack. She started talking about built-in bra cups and its being "tugless." He didn't care about that. Mostly, he hoped Jillian would like it. He also wanted to see her in it. If that made him a dog, so be it.

Seth also bought a pair of board shorts for himself. He could hardly wait to see the look on Jillian's face when she found out what they were doing tonight.

JILLIAN HIT THE button on her desk phone that sent all calls to voice mail overnight and dropped her face into her hands. She didn't mind being busy at the office; she loved her job, and the days flew by as a result. Today, though, was something else entirely. John's business trip had been extended. Early this morning another franchise's owner had decided to fire his son, who was the team's general manager and CEO. The other team owners were notified of an emergency meeting in New York City next Monday morning to deal with the situation. John was cc'ing her on texts and e-mails as quickly as he could type them out. He needed Jillian to alert his pilot to the change in John's schedule. (The pilot was with him. One would think he could call the guy on his cell, ask if he was busy on Monday, and go from there, but he wanted Jillian to do it.) John needed hotel reservations and restaurant reservations, and he wanted a world-famous department store to let his current girlfriend in an hour before opening so she could go shopping with his credit card.

When Jillian wasn't dealing with John's to-do list, she was planning the Sharks' season ticket holders' 5K race. The Sharks' PR department had offered to help, but there were a few things she couldn't delegate. One of them was getting out of the chair at lunchtime and walking another mile. She'd walk another mile before she went to bed tonight too.

If she'd had this kind of day four months ago, she would have ordered a pizza, curled up on the couch in her pajamas with CB, and rewatched *Sleepless in Seattle* for the ten thousandth time. Maybe that was a slight exaggeration, but she owned the DVD, and she watched even a few minutes of it whenever she had a bad day. It always made her smile.

*Sleepless in Seattle* was getting a workout this week too. Between the fact that Seth seemed to have forgotten she existed and her insane workload, she wondered if maybe she should order up a few more rom-coms from Amazon.com.

Jillian's cell phone rang. She pulled open her desk drawer, grabbed it out of her purse, and hit "Talk" when she saw John's personal cell phone number pop up on the screen.

"Hi, John, how are you doing?"

"You turned the phones over," he said.

"It's six fifteen here," she said. She was typically off for the evening at five PM.

He let out a sigh. "You're right. My mistake. Listen. Will you do one more thing for me? Just put it on the list. It doesn't need to happen right now, but I wanted to make sure you knew so you could start the planning."

"Sure, John. What can I do for you?"

"I'm playing poker with a few of the boys. I need a hotel suite in Seattle, food, booze, the works. And a professional poker dealer. If you can't find one here, I'll pay for him to fly in from Vegas for a couple of days."

"Do you want to go to Vegas? I can make the arrangements."

"No, no. Too hot right now." He laughed at his own joke. "This is going to be a really high-stakes game, so I want to make sure everything is perfect."

She could only imagine what he meant by "high stakes." Money was no object for John. He'd expect something extraordinary for his guests too. She'd better put on her thinking cap.

"I'll do my best, John."

"I know you will, Jillian. Have a nice evening. I'll talk with you tomorrow."

He ended the call, and she wrote "poker game" on a sticky note and stuck it to her computer monitor. A few seconds later, she heard the front door of the lobby open and felt a gust of cool air.

"We're closed for the evening," she called out.

"Good," Seth said. He strolled up to her desk. "You're done for the day, right?"

She wanted to jump out of her chair and throw her arms around his neck, but she managed to stay seated. She reached in her desk, grabbed her purse, and dropped it onto the desktop. She pretended like she wasn't thrilled to see him.

"I am," she said.

"I have a surprise for you."

She looked up into his face. "I don't know how I feel about surprises right now."

"You'll love this one." He held out his hand. "Come on. Let's get out of here."

"I've had the worst day ever—"

"I'll help you forget all about it," he said. He was at his most charming—twinkling eyes, dazzling smile—and she was the center of his attention. "Come with me."

Oh, she'd like to, and she felt the heat of a blush climbing up her neck as a result. She put her hand inside of his and grabbed her purse—and they left the building.

SETH PULLED INTO the parking garage below the gym twenty minutes later. Jillian had spent most of the ride trying to guess where they were going.

"What kind of surprise would it be if I told you?" he said.

His feelings for her, and he finally had to admit that he had some, were confused at best. He'd started off wanting to talk with her because she was sassy and funny. Every time he saw her now, though, it was all he could do to keep his hands off her. He wanted to spend every spare minute with her. He felt protective of her. And he did not want any other guy from the team talking to her at all. About anything. He'd seen that asshole Kade flirting with her because Kade knew it got under Seth's skin, for starters.

Seth had a thing for her. He wondered what she would say if he told her how he felt about her. He reached into the backseat of his ride and grabbed the bags from the swimsuit place.

Two minutes later, he was holding her hand again, and they were in an elevator to the gym. She was still trying to guess where they were going.

"There's a styling salon here. Are you taking me to get my hair cut or something?"

"No." He pulled breath into his lungs. "I like your hair the way it is." That was an understatement. He'd like to run his hands through it right now.

She looked a little shocked. "Thank you. That's such a nice thing to say."

He hit the button for the correct floor while she was still regarding the printed list of businesses and restaurants in the building. "O Chocolat?" she said hopefully.

"Not today."

Seconds later, the elevator stopped, the doors slid open, and they walked into the lobby of the gym, which looked like a spa instead of a place people went to sweat.

She shook her head a little. "Where are we?"

"We're going to do something you told me you really love, but you haven't had time to do in a while now." He handed her the bag with her new swimsuit in it. "Go change. We have the entire place to ourselves for a couple of hours." He pointed at the arrow on the wall with a sign overhead that read Ladies Locker Room. "I'll see you out there."

She took the bag from him and peeked inside, and her mouth dropped open. "That's a swimsuit," she said.

"Yes, it is."

"We're going swimming."

"Yes, we are." He couldn't stop grinning. She was going to have such a great time, and he was so stoked he'd come up with something she loved to do.

She swallowed hard, gave him a nod, and turned the corner to the locker room without another word.

JILLIAN SANK DOWN on the bench inside the locker room and pulled the swimsuit out of the plastic bag. He'd chosen a simple tank style in a shade between cobalt and purple. Despite her panic, she had to admit it was pretty. She grabbed the tag and looked at the size. He must have thought he was picking out a suit for his little sister; there was no way in hell this thing was going to fit her.

She dropped the empty bag onto the bench next to her and stifled a groan. She wasn't sure what was worse—the day she'd had at work or the fact she might have to put on a swimsuit in front of another human being. Then again, she could handle the anonymous person she'd never have to see again. Seth was going to see it all, and she wasn't sure she wanted him to at this particular moment.

She glanced around the locker room. Luckily, she'd have no witnesses if she at least tried the damn thing on. If it didn't fit, she wouldn't have to wear it. The gym wasn't going to let her swim in her underwear (or nothing at all, which was even more terrifying). She'd be off the hook. She got up from the bench, grabbed the bag to put her clothes into, and dropped the suit on another bench inside of a curtained alcove.

She couldn't believe he had no idea that most women would rather have a root canal with no anesthetic than be seen anywhere in a bathing suit. Maybe the women he knew thought it was fun and couldn't wait to put on a bikini. She sure didn't know any of those women. Kari was thin, and she wouldn't wear a swimsuit in front of anyone but her husband. Then again, he'd seen her give birth. Maybe Kari forgot to feel shy about her body after that experience.

Seth was so excited, though, about bringing her somewhere he thought she would love. She knew he didn't do it to laugh at her or to tell her all about her figure flaws. He wanted her to have fun. If she could get past the whole "Oh my *God*, I'm in public in a swimsuit, in front of a guy I really like" thing, it melted her heart a little to know he'd gone to so much trouble for this. He thought he was doing something good. So he was a little oblivious. She couldn't be mad at him for it.

Jillian stripped off her clothes, folded them carefully, and tucked her socks inside of the flats she wore to the office. There was a full-length mirror in the dressing area. She'd looked at herself in the mirror over the vanity in her bathroom at home, but it wasn't the same. Her body was changing. She was currently wearing the smallest size of pants she'd owned since she was in college. Maybe it wouldn't be so bad after all. Maybe somebody slipped some type of mind-altering substance into the coffee she'd had earlier this afternoon too.

She grabbed the suit off the bench and stepped into it. "Breathe," she told herself as she stepped into the other leg hole and started pulling the suit up over her thighs. She closed her eyes as she slid her arms through the armholes and yanked it up the rest of the way. She adjusted and wriggled.

The suit fit.

She would probably look like a miniature Buddha to anyone else, but she realized (through the fading haze of panic) she didn't look too bad. She still wasn't sure she wanted to be seen in the suit, but now she had no excuse at all.

"Here goes nothin'," she muttered to herself.

She ripped the store tags off of the swimsuit, grabbed the bag with her clothes and shoes, and walked to the shower area to rinse off.

SETH'S PHONE RANG as he pulled on the new pair of board shorts he'd bought for himself. It was Lauren, so he hit "Talk."

"Where the hell are you? Owen, the chef, wants to know if you want dinner," she said.

"Aww, shit. I forgot to tell him I'm not going to be home for a while. If he wants to cook something, will you ask him to put it in the fridge for me? Of course he's getting paid."

"I'm guessing you have other plans tonight. So, where are you?" Lauren reminded him of…himself. Dammit.

"I'm at the swimming pool at Performance Gym in Bellevue."

"Since when do you swim?"

"I'm taking Jillian swimming tonight."

He heard a sharp intake of breath as she punctuated every word. "You're. Taking. Jillian. Swimming. Are you insane?"

"She loves to swim."

"She's not going to want you to see her in a swimsuit! Seth, I can't believe you thought this would be a good thing to do. Seriously?"

"She seemed like she was excited about it—"

"Riiight," his sister said. "Okay. I have to go. I'll see you later."

He heard the click as she ended the call, and he sat in dumbfounded silence for a minute or so. He'd made a bad situation worse. What was he going to do now?

JILLIAN WRAPPED TWO clean towels around herself as she walked into the pool area. She didn't have a locker, so she left her belongings on one of the benches that ringed the pool. Seth wasn't out here yet. Maybe she could get into the water before he arrived. That left the problem of how she was going to get out of the pool without his seeing her entire body, but she could come up with a strategy later.

She dropped the two dry towels over another bench and slid into the shallow end of the pool. Of course it was a little cold, but she'd feel better in a minute. She could wade out a bit and get used to the temperature of the water. She swished her arms around a little for additional warmth.

She preferred to believe that the cool blue water rendered her somewhat invisible. A girl could dream.

She turned around as she head Seth's voice. He dropped his belongings next to hers on the bench. She heard the slap-slap of his bare feet on the tile surrounding the pool. She couldn't stop staring at him. She prayed she wouldn't start drooling.

He'd rinsed himself off in the shower too. He was tan. Drops of water clung to his dark hair and slid down his chest, trickling over his six-pack and heading lower. The board shorts clung to his hips and thighs. He approached the deep end and jumped in. Of course, he emerged looking even better than he had before he'd gotten into the pool. He slicked his hair back with both hands and pushed the water out of his eyes.

New life rule (at least for Jillian): never go swimming with a man who should have his own calendar. He was flawless, and she wasn't. The self-confidence she'd felt when she realized the swimsuit actually fit was circling the drain. She wrapped her arms around herself.

"I'm not quite sure how to say this, Jill, so I'll just spit it out," he said as he approached her.

"You hate the swimsuit," she said.

He moved a little closer. She told herself to breathe.

"No. You…it looks great on you," he said. He opened his mouth like he wanted to say something more but stopped. They stared at each other for a few seconds. "And my sister told me I'm an idiot." His dark eyes were always intense, but tonight they were riveted on her. Her heart was going thump-thump-thump at his sweet compliment.

"Thank you," Jillian said. He took another step toward her, and she swallowed hard. "What's up with your sister?"

"I know you used to swim. You told me you really missed it. I thought you might like being able to try it again. I was stoked that we'd have the entire place to ourselves," he said. "Lauren said that I should have asked you first, and that most women would rather die than be seen in a swimsuit." He glanced away from her. "Is that true?"

She was shocked to see the normally confident Seth momentarily regressing to a shy high schooler in seconds. He knew he'd screwed up, but her heart melted at his obvious discomfort and remorse. She reached out to catch his hand in hers.

"I…I was a little scared about it…" Well, a lot scared about it, but that would make him feel worse. "It's just us. Not a big deal." She shrugged her shoulders as he met her eyes again.

"Why do you feel that way? Any man would be attracted to you, no matter what you were wearing, Jill."

Jillian saw the shock on his face as he realized what he'd just blurted out, and he glanced down at the water between them again. She told herself to breathe. She wanted to tell him everything in her heart, but right now, maybe keeping things light was the best way to proceed.

She splashed him a little. He let out a laugh.

"Want to swim with me?" she said.

She pulled away from him and threw herself into the water.

## *Chapter Eleven*

NEXT MORNING, JILLIAN could hardly move. She'd enjoyed her time in the pool last night, but every muscle she hadn't used for several years was aching and sore. She shoved the front door to the Sharks' practice facility open with her forearm and flinched.

Maybe stretching a little before the next time she got in the pool might help. Seth gave her the free membership pass to the gym when he brought her back to her car.

"Could I write you a check for this?" she said. "How much was it? And I owe you for the swimsuit you bought me."

He waved his hand at her. "Your money's no good here. It was free. It also covers stuff like the water aerobics classes or whatever. You could go swimming whenever you want to."

She wanted to swim, but she wasn't sure about a pool full of hard-bodies. That might take some getting used to. "Thank you so much."

"Don't thank me. Thank the Sharks' PR department," he teased. He pulled up next to her car. "I'll see you around, Jill."

She didn't quite know what to do, and he didn't seem to know either. She reached out to hug him. She laid her cheek against his scratchier one.

"Thank you for the pass. I had fun tonight."

"Me too."

He waited until she got in and started her car. He followed her out of the Sharks' parking lot and onto the freeway home.

It was her turn to suggest some activity he might enjoy, and maybe that would be a tiny payback for a free gym membership that was probably worth thousands. She wasn't sure she was up to any mountain climbing, but maybe he'd like to come along if she attempted a short, easy hike on one of his days off. Maybe she could look up a few during her lunchtime today.

She walked into the administrative area of the building to start her workday.

Tom Reed, the Sharks' QB, ran up to her. He was already dripping sweat from lifting weights. She wondered if any of these guys ever spent rainy days propped up in bed with a ton of pillows, reading a novel on their Kindles. Probably not.

"Jillian. I need your help," he said.

"Tom, I gave up pro football a year ago. The groin pulls are such a bitch," she said.

He gave her his thousand-watt grin and reached out to grab her forearm. "I gotta talk to you about this." He walked her through the office toward the Sharks' locker room.

"What do you need? Why can't we talk in the lobby?"

"I'll get a fine. Come on." He shoved the locker room door open and tugged Jillian through it.

"I can't go in here—oh my God! Are you serious?"

The guys who were attempting to change after practice continued doing what they were doing: namely, walking around in little or nothing after their showers. She glimpsed the Sharks' star defensive end, Kade Harrison, naked as the day he was born. He was big all over. Her face was already getting red.

Kade didn't seem to be alarmed that a woman was standing two feet from him with her mouth hanging open. He locked eyes with Jillian. "Well, look who's here. How ya doin'?" Kade lifted an eyebrow.

She was incapable of answering him. He let out a snort and walked away. Of course, Jillian tried not to stare at his ass.

"Settle down," Tom told her. "I know it's shocking."

"You'll get a fine for talking to me in the lobby, but you won't get one if I'm in the freaking locker room? Tom, have you lost your mi—"

"Shhh. Listen." He pulled her down on the bench in front of his locker. "My publicist gave away a party for a kids' sports team with me as the host. The publicist is pregnant and on bed rest. My wife is at her mother's with our kids for a couple of weeks. I am not asking her to fly home for this. Can you help?"

"Sure. What do you need me to do?"

Tom looked a little wild-eyed. He was typically unflappable. She knew something beside the fact his wife wasn't in town right now must have really rattled him.

"They drew a name out of online entries," he said in the same tone that someone might use to say, "The accountant moved to Central America with all of your assets," or "It's triplets."

She reached out to pat his forearm and did her best to ignore the half-dressed guys who wandered around the locker room. They were all staring in her direction.

"That's not a problem. We'll get some snacks, a few balloons. I'll get some goody bags together. We can handle this, Tom. What's the issue?"

"They drew a little girl. It's a little girls' soccer team. What am I going to do for two or three hours with twenty little girls?"

Jillian bit her tongue before the biggest smart-ass remark ever fell out of her mouth. To a man who had three sons and spent his days with fifty-two male team members, this was his idea of hell.

"So, when's the party?"

"Saturday. Early afternoon."

She had less than thirty hours to pull off a miracle or at the very least, something that wouldn't get all of them arrested for child endangerment or something.

JILLIAN STOOD IN front of a conference table at the team headquarters, loading goody bags. The food was taken care of. The cafeteria staff took pity on her when she told them

Tom was being descended on by twenty little girls and came up with some extra-special party food. Jillian also spent some time recruiting Tom's teammates to show up.

Kade of the birthday suit found this endlessly amusing. At least he'd put some clothes on before approaching her again.

"So, what's in it for me if I join the party, doll-face?"

Brandon McKenna materialized out of nowhere. Actually, he walked around the corner of the weight room. He'd retired from the league a couple of years ago and gone into the broadcast booth for Pro Sports Network, but he still came in to lift when he was in town.

He gave Kade a hard glare. "How about a black eye? I could make that happen for you," Brandon said.

The two men stood motionless, sizing each other up. Jillian wondered when one of them would start pawing the carpet and snorting like a bull. Kade had taken Brandon's roster spot when Brandon retired from the league, but Kade was everything Brandon wasn't—brash, arrogant, and egotistical. Kade was sufficiently good at his job to ensure the Sharks put up with his less than stellar personality to get the double-digit sacks he brought to the table each season. Brandon, however, did not need to put up with Kade's BS on a daily basis and had shown before he would take action if he had to.

Kade glanced away from Brandon. Jillian pulled air into her lungs with relief.

"That won't be necessary," Kade said. "What time should I be here tomorrow, Jillian?"

"Eleven thirty. Thank you so much. I really appreciate it." She patted him on the arm. He grinned at her and brushed the hair off of her shoulder with one big hand.

Brandon glared at him.

"You have enough guys, right, Jillian?" Brandon asked. "I don't fly out to San Francisco to work the game until later tomorrow afternoon. Want me to stop by for a few minutes?"

Jillian resisted the urge to throw her arms around Brandon. "I would love that. I know the kids will love meeting you."

"You're good for my ego. This is the only part of the job I really miss, so you're doing me a favor," Brandon said. He shot her a quick grin and ambled away, pointedly ignoring Kade, who moved a bit closer.

Jillian took a few steps closer to the front door. Kade followed and rested one arm against the wall over her head.

"So, Jillian, you've seen me naked." Jillian blushed to the roots of her hair. Her face was on fire as he continued. "Usually, that doesn't happen until we've at least had dinner. Let's go get some beer, and I'll let you beat me at pool." He typically looked ferocious, but the smile he was treating Jillian to at the moment made her think of how everything looked when rain clouds parted, displaying brilliant sunshine. "How about it?"

Jillian could not have been more shocked if Brad Pitt had just strolled through the front door of the facility, confessed to leaving Angelina Jolie, and asked her out. She was fairly sure she was the last woman Kade normally would have wanted to spend time with.

"I...oh, Kade, it's really nice of you to think of me, but I'm...I'm not allowed to date the players."

"You spend all that time with Taylor, and the two of you aren't dating?" His lips twitched while his face registered disbelief. "Okay. We'll call it pool, and we'll go in separate cars. I won't tell anyone if I happen to buy you dinner to go with that beer. Come out with me," he said in what he probably thought was his most persuasive tone.

She was obviously dreaming. Even more, what on earth could Kade want to discuss with her? He wasn't romantically interested in her. This couldn't be a work thing. He obviously had something up his sleeve. She wasn't sure what it was, but she had to get out of this as gracefully as possible.

"I'm really flattered, but I'm going to have to say no. Thank you so much, though."

"Don't give me the 'I'm flattered' stuff. Let's go. I promise you'll have fun," Kade said.

"I'm sure I would, but it's really not a good idea. Thanks again."

She slipped out from under his arm and hurried away.

JILLIAN ARRIVED AT the practice facility early the next morning. The cafeteria staff had worked wonders with the food for Tom's party. She looked over heart-shaped tea sandwiches, a fruit tray so gorgeous it should be criminal to eat it, and shark-shaped sugar cookies decorated with pink frosting. She wasn't sure little girls liked raw vegetables, but there was a selection of dips and dressings to go with them. She brought out a box of the goody bags she'd loaded the previous afternoon and set about decorating tables with a profusion of pink favors, a Sharks window cling, and a place card at each setting.

Seth walked through the space, and her heart skipped a beat. She wished she had a little more control over her emotions. She attempted an unconcerned facial expression.

"Hey, event planner."

"So, you've decided to join us, huh? Don't eat that," she said. Her palms were getting sweaty. It might be easier to resist Seth if he wasn't so cute.

He hovered over the food table. "Just one."

"No. Unless you're a five-year-old girl, it's off limits."

He rolled his eyes and heaved a heavy sigh. "I'm the entertainment. Someone should feed me."

"What are you talking about?" Jillian frowned at the contents of one of the goody bags that had been haphazardly stuck into the box. Either she dropped some of the stuff she'd already loaded in it on her way up here, or there was a problem. It was full of gift cards. "What the hell is this?" she muttered to herself.

"Oh. Oh. Give me that." Seth crossed the room, holding out one hand. "I'll take care of that."

"What's with the gift cards?"

He shook his head and wagged one finger. "If I tell you all my secrets—"

"Come on, Seth. Tom's really nervous about this party. What are you up to?"

Seth shoved a raw carrot in his mouth and talked around it. "Oh, Tom knows."

"Why won't you tell me, then? I'd like to know."

Seth swallowed the mouthful and took the bag from Jillian's fingers. "The little girl who won the party—her dad's been out of work for a while. Tom offered to catch them up on their bills, but the guy wouldn't accept the cash. So a few of us got together and bought a couple of gift cards. We'll put it in her stuff and send it home. What's he going to do?"

A "couple of gift cards"? Jillian's mouth dropped open. "How many are in there?"

"More than ten, less than fifty. The coaches chipped in too." Seth gave her a lazy grin. "So are you going to feed me? I understand we're playing soccer later. A man's gotta eat."

"The chef made some food for the adults that should be ready in a few minutes." She flicked through the gift cards. The little girl was going to need a ride home in an armored vehicle if the amounts she was seeing were accurate. It was a very sweet gesture, but she needed to get this equivalent of a bag of cash into a safe place before the party started.

"Want me to get you something to eat too?" Seth called out as he walked into the kitchen.

"That would be great," she said. "Thanks."

JILLIAN TRIED TO pretend like having him around wasn't a big deal and that she was paying attention to the party and the group of girls more than she was tracking Seth as he moved around the room, teasing the little girls and giving his teammates crap. Instead of showing up and standing on the sidelines, Seth was doing his best to interact with the party guests. She was doing her best not to dissolve into a puddle of goo as Seth coaxed and charmed.

He dropped to one knee in front of a shy little girl who was still clinging to her dad's pant leg.

"You'll teach me how to play soccer, won't you? I don't know how."

The girl let out a giggle. "Maybe."

"Maybe? What can I do to change your mind?" He gave her a heart-melting grin. "I know. I'll bet you want another one of those pink shark cookies, don't you?"

The girl nodded.

"Well, then. I'll work on that. In the meantime, would you like to play?"

The girls who'd formed a knot around Tom Reed drifted slowly in Seth's direction as their friend let go of her dad's pant leg and reached out for Seth's hand.

Jillian glanced over after refreshing some of the food platters to see that another girl had whipped the pint-sized plastic-and-rhinestone tiara she'd received in her goody bag off her head and held it out to Seth.

"You want me to wear that?" he said, widening his eyes in mock horror.

"Yes!" six little girls shouted.

"Well, okay. Just this once," he told them. He put the tiara on to a cacophony of giggling. "Do I look silly?"

"*Yes!*"

"I thought I looked nice. You're not making fun of me, are you?"

"Nooooo."

Another little girl had Brandon McKenna by the hand and tugged him over to the group. The grin on Brandon's face told Jillian he loved every second of the attention. While some of the other Sharks were milling around in the kitchen or standing a distance away from the girls, any much-larger male showing interest at all was dragged into the midst of the fashion makeover.

One of the little girls dug around in her pocket for the lip balm Jillian told them was "makeup."

"You need makeup," the little girl informed Seth.

"I see," he said.

The little girls applied as much of the barely pink-tinted stuff as they could to him.

"He looks pretty now," one of them said.

"Let's put some on Brandon," another girl insisted.

"You don't have to do that," Brandon said. "I will wear one of your tiaras, though."

Seth turned to face Brandon. "Aww, come on. It's not so bad," he said. "The stuff tastes like strawberries."

"Strawberries, hm? Maybe I'll give it a try." Brandon gave the little girl who wielded the "makeup" a raised eyebrow. "If I do this, will you teach me to play soccer too?"

"Yes!" the girls screamed.

"Well, then. I'm all yours," he said.

Jillian grabbed her cell phone out of her pocket to snap a picture. She'd have to ask Brandon later if he minded her sending the picture to his wife. She knew Brandon was crazy about his sons, but if there was ever a guy who needed a little girl of his own, it was him.

The Sharks' photographer also circled the scene, snapping away. A few minutes later, the makeup application was complete, and the face painter arrived to add the Sharks' logo to Brandon's and Seth's faces before the little girls clustered around them for even more pictures.

"Hey! What about me?" Tom called out. "I don't have any little girls at home. I want in on the action. Where's my makeup? I need one of those crown things too." He glanced over at Jillian. "Will you take a few pictures of us with my phone?"

Tom sat down on the carpeting of the Sharks' cafeteria as three of the girls smeared what was left of the lip balm on him and attempted to secure the tiara on his head. His hair was so short, the tiara kept falling off, which brought more giggles and redoubled efforts to get the tiara to stay on. Jillian managed to get several pictures and took a couple on her phone too. She'd met Tom's wife; she could only imagine what Megan Reed would have to say about them when she got a look.

A few minutes later, the guys were propelled out to the practice field by the group of girls. The team photographer followed them out the door. If Jillian finished the cleanup, she could go outside for a few minutes to watch too. She turned to grab her sweater off of the back of a chair as she heard Kade's voice.

"It's cold out there. Let's pull up a chair and relax." She felt his fingertips brush the small of her back as he dropped into the chair next to her. She was startled and pulled away from his touch. He didn't seem to notice. "I like kids, but the screaming's giving me a headache.

How about you?" He popped a slice of kiwi fruit into his mouth as he watched her.

"I'm going to clean up a little more and go out to see what they're doing," she said.

She picked up the trash bag she was using and moved a foot or so away from him. She knew there were enough parents and Sharks personnel out there that they really didn't need her help, but she was a little freaked out that Kade seemed to be stepping up his "get to know Jillian" campaign for whatever reason.

He pulled out the chair next to him. "Keep me company, won't you?"

Most other women probably would have jumped for joy to get any attention from him. He wasn't unattractive. He was tall, dark-haired, hazel-eyed and, like every other Shark, in great shape. She'd never been a fan of guys who didn't take no for an answer, though, and she'd already politely told him she wasn't interested.

"I really need to get this stuff cleaned up a little, and then I'll go outside to keep an eye on what's happening," she said.

He gave a low chuckle. "Let the cafeteria staff do the cleanup. Isn't that what they're there for?"

She wanted to snap at him. She took a deep breath and concentrated on using a casual tone. "They've already done a lot of extra work for us today. I don't want them to be left with a huge mess."

"Aww, c'mon. You're not avoiding me, are you?" He smirked at her.

"Of course not," she said.

Yes, she was, and she needed to get herself outside with other people. He was making the hair on the back of her neck stand up. Maybe she was paranoid, but she didn't like his continued pursuit.

He got up from the chair and strolled over to where she was clearing off dirty paper plates and cups. He was much too close, and she surreptitiously glanced around for the exits. If things got weird, the best option she had was to drop the bag and run outside to the field where everyone else was.

"Why don't you let Reed deal with the rest of this, and we'll go have a drink? You have to be parched," he said.

He reached out to brush the hair out of her face. She'd passed annoyance a few minutes ago and went straight into panic. Maybe some women were okay with a guy they really didn't know touching them, but she didn't like it.

"Please don't do that," she said.

She backed away from him, holding the garbage bag up to chest level in an effort to put space between them.

"Do what?" he said.

He took another step toward her. Her mouth went dry with fear, and she could feel herself shaking. Maybe she was overreacting, but she needed to get out of here. She set the plastic bag down next to another table and spun away from him.

"I'm going outside," she said. "I'll finish this later."

As he reached out to grab her arm, she heard the glass door to the practice field open.

SETH HAD GLANCED up from tying a little girl's shoes and, through the panoramic windows that faced out on the practice field, saw Kade Harrison chasing Jillian around the cafeteria. Jillian looked terrified. She kept backing away from him, and he wasn't getting the hint.

He reached out to grab the sleeve of Derrick Collins's sweater.

"I'll be back," Seth said. "Gotta take care of something."

It was more like rescuing Jillian from one of his overly competitive teammates, but he couldn't control the surge of protectiveness and anger when he'd seen the look on her face. She was scared, and that asshole Harrison wasn't leaving her alone.

"Fine," Derrick said. "Leave me here with a bunch of five-year-old girls. I can take it." Two of the little girls were clinging to his pants leg and waving one of the plastic-and-rhinestone tiaras at him.

"Man up and wear a tiara!" Seth shouted to him as he crossed the practice field to the building at a run. If he wasn't so freaked out right now, he'd laugh at the mental picture of the six-foot-five, three-hundred-pound Derrick brought down by a few little girls.

"You just want another pink cookie!" Derrick shouted in response.

Seth hit the door into the facility at full speed. The look of relief on Jillian's face when she saw him made anger spike through him anew. He wanted to rip Harrison's head off.

"Get away from her," he growled.

Seconds later, he'd crossed the room and shoved Harrison away from Jillian. Seth knew Reed would kick his ass if he spoiled the party for his guests, but he saw red.

He wasn't going to dwell on the consequences if he beat the shit out of Harrison, who'd had it coming for a long time. Getting grabby with Jillian was the least of Kade's problems right now.

He felt Jillian's hand on his arm. "Seth, I'm okay. Everything is fine. Stop it, you guys!"

"I'll take care of this. Get behind me," Seth told her, but Derrick's voice rang out behind them.

"What the fuck are you doing? Knock this shit off. We have guests," he informed them. He got between Seth and Kade, grabbed both shirt fronts in his big fists and pushed them away from each other. "You can kill each other during practice. Not now."

The three men stared at each other. Seth felt Jillian's hand still holding onto his arm.

"No means no, asshole," Seth said to Kade, who laughed out loud in response.

"Tomorrow," Derrick snapped.

## Chapter Twelve

JILLIAN HURRIED THROUGH the employees' parking lot at the Sharks' headquarters during a light rain a few days later. The typical Tuesday morning rush featured a new wrinkle: the dress pants she'd put on earlier were now so loose they fell off her. She was going to have to make some time later to go to the mall and buy a pair of pants that actually fit. She'd managed to cinch up the pants by poking an additional hole in one of her belts and pulling her now-baggy sweater down to hide this fact. Hopefully, the pants would stay up throughout the day.

She was still ignoring the scale, but she couldn't ignore the fact that she was shrinking out of her wardrobe. She was going to have to weigh herself. She'd been avoiding it so far, just because she wasn't sure she wanted to see a number. If she saw a number, that meant she'd start obsessing over it. She didn't want to find herself running to a scale every day and worrying if it didn't reflect her increased activity.

Seth strolled into the building minutes later and winked at her.

"Hey, Jill, it's wet out there," he said. "Is John in yet?"

She ignored the urge to tell him he had a keen eye for the obvious. "He's out of town for the next couple of days. Would you like me to tell him you're looking for him when he calls in?"

"I'd love that." He plunked down in the chair next to her desk. "What's up, Buttercup?"

She laughed at the silly nickname. The phones were quiet, Vivian was at a dentist's appointment, and Jillian felt butterflies in her stomach, but she had to tell someone else besides Kari. "I need some new pants. The ones I have don't fit anymore."

"Is that so?" he said, but his eyes twinkled. "I wondered when you'd start to notice. Have you weighed yourself yet?"

She'd talked to him a couple of weeks ago about her hesitation to go anywhere near a scale. The typically teasing Seth greeted this news with silence and hadn't said a word about it since. She wasn't sure if she should be insulted or touched that he didn't push her in an area that was still pretty sensitive.

"No," she said. "I haven't. I'm afraid I'll be running in there every morning and be upset if there's no change—"

"Then concentrate on feeling better. A number doesn't define you."

She bit her tongue before telling him that for women, numbers defined them and always would. Their ages.

Their heights and weights. Their bra sizes. So many numbers. She shook her head.

"What happens if you don't answer the phone for a few minutes?" he said.

"John gets mad at me."

"He's not here today. It'll go to voice mail." He got up from his chair and said, "I was just in the weight room. There's nobody in there. If you want to get on the scale, now's a good time. He patted her on the back. "If not, don't worry about it." He gave her a nod and loped away.

Two minutes later, she was shaking from head to toe as she approached the scale in the weight room. It was a good thing the place was (temporarily) deserted. She knew Seth was right about the fact that a number didn't define who she was inside, but she was afraid of this one.

She took one huge step onto the metal base, squeezed her eyes shut, and took a deep breath. "Oh, God. I can't look," she muttered.

Maybe she should turn around, open her eyes, and run back to her desk before she saw the readout. Or maybe she should gather her courage and be proud of the small changes she'd already made, no matter what the number on the readout said.

She pried one eye open and glanced up as she told herself to breathe.

She'd lost thirty pounds.

LATER THAT DAY, Jillian and Kari braved the rain to visit the local mall. Just like most women, Jillian was excited about getting some new clothes, but she was also worried about how much this trip was going to cost. She had a little extra money right now, but it didn't mean she should go insane with it.

Kari led her through the swinging double glass doors of Nordstrom without a second thought.

"Come on. I can't wait to see you pamper yourself a little, girlfriend. We're going to dress up the new you. And then we're getting a glass of wine to celebrate."

Kari looked like she wanted to do a little dance on the all-weather-carpeted mat right inside the front doors. Jillian was happy about the fact she'd lost weight, but Kari was beside herself with glee.

"I'm just buying a few basics, Kari. I don't want to spend a ton of money—"

"You're buying well-made clothes instead of cheap crap. Everything you get will last instead of falling apart the first time it goes through the washer." Kari led her to the escalator that went to the women's clothing departments. "And we're getting you a new bra. You need something that fits correctly and shows off the girls."

"I was thinking a couple of pairs of pants and a few tops. Nothing crazy," Jillian said.

"Yeah, yeah, yeah," Kari teased. "Let's have some fun."

A tall older woman in an effortlessly stylish outfit approached them as they walked into the Point of View department. "How are you this evening?"

"I'm fine," Jillian said. "I need some tops and pants I can wear to the office. I'd prefer clothes that don't need to be dry-cleaned."

"She needs a pair of jeans too," Kari chimed in. "And some casual clothes." Kari elbowed Jillian a little. "What if Seth asks you out? You'll have nothing to wear!"

"Do you mind?" Jillian said to Kari, but she had to laugh.

"Nothing she owns fits her anymore," Kari said.

The saleswoman grinned at both of them. "Well, let's get her some clothes that fit, shall we?"

After a little questioning about Jillian's favorite colors, how dressy or casual the office was, and how much she'd like to spend, she and Kari were on their way to the dressing room when Jillian spied a bright turquoise asymmetrical one-button fleece wrap cardigan on a mannequin. She typically wore dark colors or anything that didn't draw attention to herself, but she wanted that bright, pretty cardigan.

"I'd like to try that on too, please."

"Yes!" Kari said and fist-pumped the air.

One hour later, the saleswoman had helped Jillian assemble several outfits that mixed and matched. Even better, she'd encouraged Jillian to try on a few things she would have avoided before—vivid colors; soft, clinging fabrics; and a bit sexier than her typical crew-necked long-sleeved sweaters and loosely fitting slacks. The saleswoman also helped Jillian find clothes she loved that wouldn't blow a gaping hole in her savings account. Jillian was even fitted for a pretty new bra. Jillian's new wardrobe was taken out to the check stand by another salesperson while the woman they'd been working with knocked on the dressing room door one more time.

"I know you said you weren't sure about buying a dress, but every woman needs a little black dress," she said. "You can dress it up or down. Plus, this one's on sale."

The dress was knee-length jersey with a scoop neck, long sleeves, and a gently flared skirt.

"Try it on," Kari said.

"I've already spent so much money—"

The saleswoman held it out to Jillian. "I'll leave it with you. If you change your mind and want to try it on, it's here."

"Don't you still have some black heels at home?" Kari said.

The fabric was so soft in Jillian's hands. The shoes she already had would look great with it. She'd have something pretty to wear if she and Seth ever went out on a date that didn't require athletic equipment or sweating.

She pulled the dress off of the hanger. "Okay. I'll try it on," she said.

Two days later, Jillian was wearing one of her new outfits as she arrived at the office—the pretty turquoise cardigan over a coordinating soft knit top and a pair of black dress pants. She'd even treated herself to a cute bangle bracelet. Even more than the new clothes, the happiness she saw when she looked in the mirror thrilled her. Her self-confidence was building.

She was still trying to make a dent in the huge amount of work John had left for her. She'd shown up at the office this morning at seven o'clock; every effort she made on the list was interrupted by a ringing phone or yet more pleas for help from Seth's teammates. She'd helped Tom, so obviously she was available to "help" every other guy on the team. Even more annoying, someone on the team managed to get her cell phone number, and he'd passed it around. The chiming of incoming texts was enough to make her want to bang her head on her desk. These guys didn't need coaches. They needed a den mother—or ten!

I NEED A RESERVATION SEASTAR @ 8 FRI NIGHT. A LITTLE HELP?

WILL YOU GET AND MAIL MY LITTLE SIS A B-DAY GIFT? IT'S TOMORROW. SHE H8S GIFT CARDS.

THE INTERIOR DESIGNER PICKED COLOR FOR LVNG RM THAT'S WACK. HERE'S HER NUMBER.

If Seth was responsible for this, she was going to kill him.

She opened another expense spreadsheet and tried to concentrate on reconciling it with the receipts she'd finally managed to pry away from John before he left again; the chime of yet another text on her phone sounded.

EVAN'S BACHELOR PARTY NEEDS DANCERS. WILL YOU GET SOME FOR US?

"That's it," she said and slapped her phone down on a pile of paperwork in the middle of her desk. One of the more interesting side effects of making a few life-style changes was self-preservation. She wanted the guys on the team to like her, but they didn't get to push her around. She grabbed the receiver on her desk phone, hit the extension for the weight room phone, and waited for someone to pick up.

A slightly out-of-breath voice answered. "Daffy Dan's Pussy Par—"

"This is Jillian, John's assistant," she said. "Who's this?"

"Morrison," he said. He was the second-year offensive line player who spent most of his days tangling with Derrick Collins during practice. "What's up?"

"Who handed out my cell phone number? I don't appreciate it."

All was silent on the other end of the line.

"Clay? Are you still there?"

Jillian heard Clay put his hand over the mouthpiece and muffled voices in the background. She waited for him to respond.

"Uh, Jillian, we're not sure—"

"I'll come in there and find out myself."

She hung up the phone and set her line to voice mail. This shouldn't take longer than five minutes, and she could explain to John if he happened to call while she was away from her desk. She stalked off to the weight room. She knew she shouldn't be mad at them; the team really needed to hire someone whose entire job was to babysit what could sometimes be grown men who still lived like college students. She didn't mind helping them out once in a while, but she drew the line at obtaining "dancers" for a bachelor party.

Jillian pushed through the glass door to the weight room. Twenty-five men had abandoned their lifting to form a knot in the middle of the room. They'd also managed to select a spokesman in the two minutes it took to get from her desk to the weight room door.

Zach Anderson stepped forward and extended his hand to her. "Jillian, we didn't mean to upset you. We apologize." She saw his bashful grin. "We'll quit driving you nuts."

"Yeah," Clay said.

"You do a lot for us, and we appreciate it," Caleb said. Caleb was dating Zach's youngest sister, Whitney. Jillian wasn't surprised he was backing Zach up.

"I still need some help with a paint color. It looks like baby barf all over my living room! I'll pay you," Terrell said. He whipped a money clip out of his workout shorts pocket. After a glare from the twenty-four other guys, he put the cash away.

"T, she's not an interior designer."

"Taylor's going to kick your asses if you keep bugging her," Drew McCoy said.

Jillian held up both hands. "Okay. Here's my new policy. First of all, who decided to give the entire team my cell number?" She glanced around at a lot of foot-shuffling. They wouldn't look at her. "Great. How would you feel if I gave out your cell numbers?"

"Not cool."

"I'd be pissed."

"Don't think about it, girl."

"All right, then." She took a deep breath. Three months ago, she would have been running herself ragged to help them out because she wanted them to accept her. She knew enough about most of the guys on the team to know that if you gave them an inch, they'd take a mile. They didn't respect anyone who didn't stand up to them. She wanted their respect. "I like you all, but I'm not your mama, your sister, your girlfriend, or your wife. This is my workplace." She let that one sink in for a minute or so. She glanced at Grant, the backup QB, who hadn't looked at her since she walked into the weight room. "I respect your time and your privacy. You should respect mine too."

She glanced around to see twenty-four heads nodding in agreement. Grant didn't nod.

"Got it," Derrick Collins said.

"Absolutely," Clay said.

"Thank you, Miss Jillian," Caleb told her.

"I have to get back to work now. I'll talk with all of you later," she said and turned to leave the weight room. She heard the low murmur of male voices as she opened the door to the lobby.

"I guess this means she's not finding us some strippers for E's bachelor party."

A COUPLE OF hours later, Jillian heard Seth's voice behind her.

"Hey. Let's get out of here for the night."

"I still have to do my workout," she said. She'd rather curl up on her apartment couch with a blanket, a good book, and CB, but it would be at least another hour before she could get some time to herself.

"Sometimes it's good to play hooky," Seth told her. "Come on. I want you to see my house."

"There's all this work—"

"It'll wait until tomorrow," he said.

Twenty minutes later, Seth turned onto a tree-lined street with rolling lawns and perfectly maintained landscaping that framed huge homes. She'd heard about this Bellevue neighborhood, but she'd never actually been here before.

Seth pulled into one of the driveways, shut off the ignition, and turned to Jillian.

"Is this your house?" she gasped.

"Of course it is," he said. She stared at him. "It's just a house."

"Yeah, and my entire apartment probably fits in your broom closet."

"Laundry room." He grinned at her. "Let's go inside. You have a cell phone in case we get separated, right?"

"You're funny."

Seth's house was framed by a lush, manicured front lawn. The landscaping was pristine. No weeds dared to grow in this yard. The exterior of the house was painted a shade that probably came straight out of a Starbucks cup—after all, it was the perfect shade of latte, with white trim framing multiple bay windows that sparkled in the sunlight. There was another pair of windows in the apartment over his three-car garage. She noticed blue-green shutters flanking the second-story windows. She realized her mouth was hanging open, and she shut it.

"Just a house," he repeated. He stepped up to the front porch that ran the length of the house and unlocked the front door. Jillian followed him inside.

"Pee-Wee! Hey, brat. I'm home," he called out and tossed his keys in a flat art-glass dish that sat on a wooden table against the wall in the entryway.

Maybe Pee-Wee was a cat or something. Jillian was still staring. The floors were dark wide-plank hardwoods, polished to a high sheen. Unless she was really wrong, a decorator had left his or her stamp on his house, and Seth liked earth tones. There was a formal living room to the left of the front door, but the effect was somewhat spoiled by a sock monkey stuffed animal among the cushions on the old gold-colored, overstuffed couch. He saw her glance at the stuffed monkey. "Too damn stuffy," he explained. "I put a pink flamingo in the yard when I moved in, but I got a fine from the Homeowners Association."

"Where is it now?"

"I left it in the HOA president's front yard with a note." He continued down the hallway. "Come on. I'll give you the big tour." She glanced at a staircase broken by a landing featuring another huge window on her left. "Stairs to the second story. Half-bath is to your right. This is my favorite room. Well, other than my room." The kitchen had glass-front cabinetry that complemented the floors. The walls were a warm light-cocoa color. The countertops were veined copper granite.

Jillian could happily spend the rest of her life in this kitchen. He had two ovens, a center island that featured a wine refrigerator, plenty of room for pots and pans, a top-of-the-line refrigerator, and gas cooktop. A lower counter on the other side had a built-in computer desk. Even more beautiful than the kitchen design was the light that streamed through the house. Maybe you got better light when you spent a lot of money. She had to smile at the sight of one cookbook stored on the shelf over the counter.

"Betty Crocker?"

"My mom tried to teach me how to cook. Now I have a chef," Seth said. "Gotta eat, don't I?"

She shook her head.

Just beyond the kitchen of any woman's dreams, a wooden table and four Bentwood chairs sat on a patterned wool rug. The family room beckoned. Part of Jillian expected an empty beer-can pyramid and a Shark Babes calendar, but his family room had leather couches, a hardwood coffee table, and a huge flat-screen television mounted on the wall neighboring the gas fireplace. She had to smile at the video-game controllers scattered over the tabletop.

"The guys came over to play games last night."

Jillian heard footsteps rapidly approaching and turned to see a tall, slender, beautiful young woman with long, straight dark hair, a mischievous expression on her face, wearing a T-shirt that read "My life is a complicated drinking game."

"Hey, Pee-Wee, where ya been? I was yelling my head off down here."

"I was on the phone. And don't call me Pee-Wee."

"Sure, you were." Seth reached out to ruffle her hair. "Jillian, this is Lauren, my bratty kid sister. Be sure to call her Pee-Wee. She loves it."

Lauren gave her big brother a shove. "Hey, knock it off." She stuck out her hand. "It's nice to meet you."

"It's nice to meet you too," Jillian assured her.

"Lauren lives here when she's not at her sorority house at the U. Then again, I think she's here more than she is there," Seth commented.

"It was living with Mom and Dad or living here. You won, butthead." Lauren seemed to have the same missing filter between her brain and her mouth that her brother did, but she was teasing him. She turned her attention to Jillian once more. "Have you gotten lost yet? This place is gigantic, isn't it?"

"It's only four thousand square feet," Seth said with a groan. "You act like it's Bill Gates's house."

"Seth has a chef," Lauren confided. "He has a house-cleaner. He even has a guy who does the yard, and he wonders why I didn't want to live with my parents when I'm not at school."

"You wanted to stay here because you could wear rude T-shirts Mom hates. Plus, it doesn't matter to me if you drink my beer, as long as you're not driving. You want to hang out with your friends in the spa too."

Evidently, it was one long fight, but Jillian didn't miss the easy affection between them. She felt the familiar stab of pain at the fact she had no siblings to tease and talk with; no parents she loved, who loved her in return. She didn't know what it was like to have shared experiences and memories with anyone but Kari. She was so grateful for Kari, but Kari had a family of her own. Jillian wanted that more than she wanted anything else in life— the opportunity to belong, even to just one person. To be loved and needed as part of her own family.

"Speaking of the beer, you're all out of Hefeweizen."

"Thanks for the update," Seth told Lauren. "I suppose you'd know nothing about that."

"That's right." She beamed at him.

"So, I'm trying to give Jill the tour, and then I might persuade her to have some dinner here. Would you like to join us?"

"Where did you think I was eating?" Lauren said.

"Well, I know that you've decided you're a vegetarian now. We eat meat around here, missy."

"I eat fish," Lauren informed him.

"Oh, okay. What if I want a steak?"

She made a huge face. "Eww!"

"I'll ask Owen to make you one of those vegetable gratin things he made the other day. Will that work?"

"Fine." She reached out and patted Jillian's arm. "It was nice to meet you. I'll see you at dinner."

Lauren scampered away as quickly as she'd arrived, and Seth let out a sigh.

"Someday, she'll find a place of her own, and my life will be complete."

"Are you serious? Wouldn't you be bored?"

"Well, yeah. I'd miss her. Don't tell her." Seth took her elbow in his fingertips. "My chef will be here in an hour. Would you like to have dinner with us? Maybe I should have asked you first, but it seemed like a good idea at the time."

"Sure. It would be fun."

"Great. We probably have some steak, and I'll talk him into that vegetable gratin thing. It's really good." He moved through the kitchen to another staircase. "Want to see more of the house?"

"I'd like that."

They arrived on the second floor. Lauren's room was first, closest to the staircase. Jillian glanced through the open doorway to see her sprawled on her bed with her cell phone clutched to her ear, laughing at something someone was telling her. They walked away.

"She likes to think she's such a rebel," her brother told Jillian. "She thinks she gets away with a lot here. I'm stricter with her than our parents are." He kept walking, past what must have been a guest bedroom, past the office.

"My office. If you want to see it, you can, but it's not all that interesting." Jillian gave him a nod. "Bathroom, linen closet, laundry room. Another bedroom." He opened the door at the far end of the hallway. "Here's where the magic happens." He grinned to soften his narcissistic comment.

"You're ridiculous," she told him, but he laughed.

Seth's room was nothing like she'd expected either. The room was dominated by a light-cherry king-sized sleigh bed. The bedding was a mix of soft olive-green leafy print on white, with plenty of fluffy pillows adding coziness. His iPod was charging on the night table next to the bed, and a mushroom-colored throw was tossed over a chair in the opposite corner. There was a gas fireplace too. The windows were covered with privacy sheers that still let the sun stream in. The ceiling was recessed. Mostly, it looked informal and comfortable, and it was very, very neat.

"Don't you believe in clutter?"

"I haven't lived here long enough to amass a lot. It's all in my office. Go check out the bathroom."

"Why?"

"I thought I was going to have to physically remove Lauren from the jetted tub."

The tub was the least of it; there was another fireplace set into the wall at one end of the bathroom. More light streamed in through a window made up of beveled glass squares, glittering like diamonds, and looking over a greenbelt. The floor was tile; the countertops were quartz, and Jillian marveled at how beautiful it all was. A double shower with multiple shower heads dominated the opposite wall. The toilet had its own little room, with a built-in padded bench next to it.

"There's a refrigerator in your bathroom?"

"It was here when I bought the house." Several bottles of beer and a bottle of champagne waited behind the glass door.

"How do you ever leave this place? I wouldn't."

"Sure, you would. You'd get bored after a while."

"You can't be serious."

Seth sat down on the side of the tub. "The house is just a house. Somewhere to live. I'm not home much." Jillian noticed a somewhat evil twinkle in his eyes. "I'll bet you'd never get out of the tub."

"You have a chef, and there's a refrigerator in here? You're right."

"I could be persuaded to rent the bathroom…"

"I couldn't afford it."

JILLIAN CROSSED THE bathroom and walked back into
Seth's room. He was enjoying her reaction to his house
more than he liked living in it. Yes, it was comfortable.
He was glad he had enough room for Lauren to stay with
him; he didn't worry about what she was doing so much.
He knew his parents worried about her a lot more than
he did.

He was feeling more at home here than he'd ever felt in
his house in San Diego. He tried to tell himself that maybe
it was because Kim didn't live here, but mostly it was the
fact his family was twenty minutes away. He'd meet some
new people that he could socialize with, but his parents
were close enough to see whenever he wanted to.

Jillian wandered over to the easy chair in one corner
of his room and ran her fingers over the cashmere throw
he'd pulled off the bed last night. She moved to the mantel over the bedroom fireplace and studied the framed
photos the decorator had grouped there.

"Seth?"

"Yeah?"

He walked back into his room, and an invisible icy
hand closed around his gut. He swallowed hard. He knew
what she was looking at.

"Who's the guy in the photo with you and Lauren?"

He had two options: Tell her, or distract her. He
knew by now that she was as persistent as he was, and
he would have kept asking until he got an answer. He
thought about Liam every day, but he typically discussed
him with nobody but his family. Publicists in NFL front
offices loved to offer stories to sports media about how

different players overcame adversity to succeed. Seth wasn't about to exploit his family's ongoing pain to give the team or the local papers another feel-good story.

He took a breath. "That's my brother, Liam." He licked his suddenly dry lips and tried to pretend he didn't want to blubber like a baby. Still. "He died five years ago."

Jillian turned to look at him. "Oh, Seth, I'm so sorry for your loss." He saw compassion in her eyes. She was as speechless at this news as everyone else his family knew.

"Thanks."

He sank down on the side of his bed. She picked the frame up off the mantel and came over to sit next to him. The picture was of Seth, Liam, and Lauren on the beach in Maui. He'd just signed his first NFL contract, and he had plenty of money to take everyone on a trip before his first training camp. Lauren's brothers had wrapped their arms around their giggling little sister after an afternoon of snorkeling. Their mom snapped the photo. None of them had the slightest idea that less than a month later, Liam would be dead.

Jillian bit her lip. "I'll understand if you don't want to talk about it."

"You probably want to know what happened."

"Seth, your parents must have been crushed."

"They were," he said.

*I was too*, he wanted to tell her, but the words wouldn't come out. He'd never forget the way his mom's mouth twisted in pain, the wail she let out when the doctor told them Liam was gone. She dropped to her knees, and he knew she didn't know where she was or what she was doing. His dad aged twenty years in thirty seconds. Lauren wanted to cling to Seth. He wanted to be alone. He could scream and cry, and nobody else would tell him that he should "be strong" for his parents or that he'd feel better someday. It never felt better.

"I'd appreciate it if you didn't discuss this with anyone else," he said. "My family—"

"I understand," she said. He was willing to bet the deed to his house she would keep his secrets.

He looked at the pattern in the rug into which he was currently digging his feet. "Liam died of meningitis. It didn't last a day. We didn't know what was wrong with him, and then it was too late."

He saw Jillian move a little closer out of the corner of his eye, and she laid her hand over his. He realized he'd clenched his fist in the comforter on his bed. He told himself to let go, to take a breath. He wasn't going to cry in front of a woman he was still getting to know. They sat there for a few minutes, neither speaking. She brushed his hand again with hers, and he took it. She looked at the photo again.

"What was he like?"

He forced out every word. "He was my best friend." Seth did nothing but breathe for a couple more minutes. Jillian still had his hand. "We both played football, but while I was screwing off and not studying, Liam was getting all A's. He was going to start premed at the U in the fall. He couldn't play football and become a doctor, so he decided he would be a doctor. I know that every time someone dies, we remember the good stuff. In his case, it was all good stuff. I mean, obviously, he was a guy, and guys aren't always on their best behavior. Liam cared so much about other people, though, and they cared about him. If he was sitting here right now…" Seth paused for a moment. The tears rose in his eyes, and he fought them back. He spoke over the lump in his throat. "If he was sitting here right now, he'd be drinking my beer, and he'd give you a hug."

"Me? You're the one who needs a hug," she said.

He'd done stuff in this bed with other women that would make a porn star blush, but when Jillian moved closer and her arms slid around him, the only urge he had was to lay his head on her shoulder. He heard her murmur in his ear, "I'm so sorry that I'll never get to meet him."

"Yeah. Me too." It was all he could get out.

She held him. The knot in his stomach unraveled a little. He felt her arms slowly withdraw, and he sat up again. He had no idea what to say. She was silent, but the silence wasn't uncomfortable. How did she know exactly what to do when the hospital social worker, the counselor the entire family saw after Liam died, and the team psychologist didn't seem to get it?

He heard Lauren shouting from downstairs. "Seth, Owen's here. He wants to know how many people are coming to dinner."

"Let's go." He stood up and reached out for her hand.

Jillian and Seth walked into the kitchen to find Lauren heckling the chef. Owen had a shaved head. He was several inches shorter than Seth. He sported a beer belly, tats, and hoop earrings. He evidently favored brightly printed chef's pants, a spotless white chef's coat, and Chuck Taylor high-tops. He also seemed to love giving Lauren all kinds of grief.

"Listen, little girl. I hate to break it to you, but your brother signs my check. Therefore, I cook what he wants for dinner. Maybe you should try talking with him."

"He told me that he was going to ask you to make the vegetable gratin."

"He told me that he wants steak for dinner, so there."

Seth gave him a nod. "Remind me to give you a bonus. She needs to understand that I'm the boss of her."

"I'll put starch in your boxers, buddy," Lauren retorted.

"Oooh. Color me scared." Seth mussed her hair as he walked past. "Hey, Owen, you have the stuff to make the gratin, don't you?"

"Yeah. I'll start it right now."

Lauren stuck her tongue out at Seth.

"Is there anything I can do to help with dinner?" Jillian asked.

"Things are under control," Seth reassured her. He picked up the platter of perfectly done steaks to put on the kitchen table. "Want to eat with us, Owen?"

"I'd love to, but I have another job tonight. Thanks, man." He fist-bumped Seth. "Tomorrow night?"

"Yeah. How about seven?"

"Perfect." Owen picked up his knife case and let himself out the front door.

Seth, Jillian, and Lauren took seats at the kitchen table and passed the food around. Seth took a sip of his glass of Syrah and glanced over at Lauren.

"Listen, Pee-Wee, Jillian and I were talking earlier."

Lauren took a bite of her food. "This is even better than it was the other night. What's up?"

"I was talking to her about Liam."

Lauren's head snapped up. She looked panicked.

"I want to put something in the backyard for him. We're both here now. He should be here too. Will you help me pick it out?"

Lauren's fork hit the plate with a clatter. She put one hand over her mouth and sat motionless.

"Mom and Dad have a bench. Maybe we should get something like that." He had to see that Lauren's face was papery white. She was shaking. Tears swam in eyes that looked anywhere but at the two of them. "I go out in Mom and Dad's backyard sometimes, sit on the bench, and talk to him. It's weird. It's almost like he can hear me." He reached out for Lauren's hand. "If you don't like that, we can look at some other kind of thing."

Jillian felt like she was watching a car wreck in slow motion—the cars were spinning out of control toward each other, the drivers wrenched the wheel, tried to swerve, prayed, and it did no good. They'd collide no matter what, and all she could do was look on. Seth was probably trying to cope with his own grief the best way he knew how—talking about it—but Lauren was obviously still too raw inside to even consider discussing her feelings in front of anyone who wasn't a family member.

Lauren's voice came from a million miles away, rusty and indistinct. "No."

She jumped up from the table and ran through the kitchen. They heard her footsteps on the stairs.

Seth and Jillian sat for a few minutes. She wasn't sure what to say. He took another sip of wine.

"She really needs you right now," Jillian said before she could bite it back.

His voice was rough with emotion. "I'll go up there in a few minutes. I have to figure out what the hell I'm going to say." He picked up his wineglass again and set it down. "She...my mom told me that sometimes she needs to cry, and I should understand that, but I feel like someone stuck a knife in my gut every time I see tears."

He leaned back in his chair and dropped his hands into his lap. His appetite was evidently gone.

A few hours later, Seth climbed the stairs to Lauren's room. He'd almost figured out what to say to her.

The door stood open. Moonlight bathed his sister's sleeping form. She still had her cell phone in her hand. He moved silently across the bedroom rug, extracted it, and put it on the night table. He picked up the lavender blanket off the chair and spread it over her. She rubbed her nose with one hand, but she slept on. The big talk he wanted to have was going to have to wait until tomorrow.

He lowered himself into a chair by her bed, stretched out his legs, and closed his eyes. He'd dropped Jillian off at her car a couple of hours ago. He hadn't wanted her to leave, but she had things to do.

HER KEY RING had jingled as she pulled it out of her purse. Her face had been in shadow, even if the moonlight painted her hair a silvery blonde.

He'd stuck his hands in the front pockets of his jeans. "Listen. I didn't mean to get you in the middle of some big family argument. I should have waited and talked to Lauren about my idea later and let her have a chance to think about it." He had shrugged his shoulders. "I really screwed up."

She reached out to pat his arm. "You're too hard on yourself. Plus, she was probably reacting more to discussing Liam in front of someone she just met than to your idea. I'll bet if you go back to your house and talk to her, she'll have had some time to think, and she'll react differently." Jillian took a breath. "I know you tease each other, but she loves you so much. She misses Liam as much as you do."

He'd handed Jillian a chance on a silver platter to make him feel like crap over the fact he didn't get how upset Lauren was about any mention of Liam until it was too late. She hadn't done it. Instead, she'd looked up at him with gentle, concerned eyes and told him she knew he could fix it. She always believed the best about him, even when he gave her evidence that he wasn't always perfect. He had felt at ease with her, which was—in his experience with women—a completely new sensation.

He'd given her a nod. "Thanks. I'll give it another try later," he said.

He had taken a step toward her, but pulled her car door open and got inside.

"I'll see you tomorrow," she said. "Thank you for dinner." She'd turned the key in the ignition, backed out of the space and drove away. He'd gotten back in the Escalade.

HE HAD DRIVEN around for a while before he went back home. He thought about calling one of the guys to meet him somewhere for a beer, but he wouldn't be great company. He was still mystified by what he was going to say to Lauren. Finally, he drove to his house, put the car in the garage, and came up here to have the talk he'd been dreading.

His thoughts were interrupted by his sister's sleepy voice.

"Seth? Why are you here?"

"I wanted to talk with you about what happened at dinner."

Lauren reached out to turn on the bedside lamp. "So you thought you'd sit there and wait for me to wake up?"

"Pretty much." He leaned forward, resting his forearms on his thighs. "Listen. I owe you an apology. I should have picked a better time to talk with you about a little memorial for Liam. I didn't mean to make you cry, and I'm sorry."

She was rubbing her eyes like the little girl she used to be. He almost smiled at the raccoon-like smeared mascara around her eyes.

"I'm sorry I freaked out in front of Jillian." Lauren pulled the blanket up around her shoulders. "I wrecked the dinner, and she probably thinks I'm a baby."

"No. She doesn't. She likes you. She talked to me a little about what happened."

"What did she say?"

"She said that it upset you, and maybe the conversation should happen when she's not around." He thought for a moment. "Hey. I know I give you a lot of crap, but I'm wondering about something. What do you think of Jillian?"

His sister propped herself up on one elbow and gazed into his eyes. "Why are you asking me?"

"I just wondered—"

"BS," his sister informed him. "Do you want the truth?"

"What do you mean? Of course I do."

"Well, I'd like to stay here," she joked, "but believe it or not, I want you to be happy." She gave him the little-girl grin he still saw once in a while. "If you haven't already figured out that she's the greatest, you're an idiot. You don't talk to anyone else about Liam. She makes you laugh. She's pretty, and she's really nice too. I like her a lot. Mom and Dad will love her." She gave him a little nod.

He realized with a shock that maybe she was right. He wasn't going to admit it, though.

"You've got it all wrong, Pee-Wee. We're just friends."

"Sure, you are," his sister said. She grinned at his discomfort. "Uh-huh. That's why you're in here asking me what I think of her."

"Plus, she's not like anyone else I've ever dated." His argument sounded weak to his own ears.

"That's why I like her," his sister informed him. "You should marry someone like her. She'd make you happy." Seth stared at her in shock. "Do you think I want to wait forever to be an aunt?"

He grabbed both arms of the chair and hoisted himself out of it. "Got it. It's time for me to say good night."

"You don't want me to tell you the truth about anything else?"

He leaned over Lauren and kissed the top of her head. "See you tomorrow, Pee-Wee. Good night." He shut off her bedside lamp and turned to go.

His sister's voice halted him in his tracks. "Let's get a bench for Liam. I'll help you pick it out, okay?"

## Chapter Thirteen

ONE WEEK AFTER Jillian came to his house for dinner, Seth walked into Strikes Bowl on a Wednesday evening and glanced around. Most of his teammates were here already, with assorted wives, girlfriends, and a few significant others. It was the yearly fund-raiser for Zach Anderson's foundation, which sponsored college scholarships for underprivileged kids.

Seth avoided most of these things. He usually ended up getting stuck in a corner somewhere with an overzealous male fan, who wanted to recount every minute of last season, or an overzealous female fan, who wanted him to sign body parts that would get him a fine from the commissioner's office. Zach asked him if he'd attend a few days ago. He really didn't have a good excuse, so he was here. Last year, he had Kim to run interference for him. This year, he didn't have a date.

Seeing this, one of the Shark Babes attached herself to his arm. God, he hated strong perfume on any woman.

"Hey, Seth. Can I count on you for the Special Olympics fund-raiser next month? Those kids would all love to meet you." If the look in her eyes was any indication, she'd like to meet him too, preferably later tonight in her bed.

Seth tried to pull away, but she wasn't budging. She was now rubbing one breast against his forearm. She had to know that any man under ninety was going to react, and sure enough, he did.

"When and where is it?"

"It's at Sharks Stadium, silly. Tom's our featured speaker. We're trying to get as many of the guys there as possible to sign autographs. Plus, people will give more money if they can meet the players."

"Let me talk to my agent. He arranges all that stuff."

"Sure." She didn't move. "So, you probably know about the after-party."

Oh, he knew about the after-party. He couldn't figure out how she knew. The guys guarded that information pretty carefully. Plus, cheerleaders weren't allowed to date players, but it seemed like they always did. Well, other players. He wasn't going to find a reason to piss off the coach.

"Yeah. Thanks for the info." He finally managed to extract his arm. "You're Jennifer, right?"

She laughed like this was the funniest thing she'd ever heard.

"No. I'm Ashlee. You're Seth."

"Yes. I am."

He moved away from her. He wouldn't be attending the after-party unless he wanted to spend an entire evening avoiding yet another situation he shouldn't end up in.

The bowling alley was crowded. Even with thirty lanes available, fifty or so current and former Sharks, their guests, and the coaching staff, not to mention cheerleaders, front-office folks, and fans who'd paid to get in, blocked every possible exit. He needed a beer. He headed toward the bar, only to notice a familiar blonde woman a distance away, chatting and laughing with a couple of former Sharks.

Jillian was here, which was the best news he'd had all day. This would fix everything. He'd have someone to talk with; he could introduce her around. She'd want to go to the after-party just to see what was going on. She hadn't told him she was coming tonight. Then again, she didn't spend a lot of time socializing, as far as he could tell. He was still trying to get through the crowd to her.

Damian Drake, the shutdown cornerback who had retired from the Sharks one season after his buddy Brandon McKenna hung up his own cleats, handed Jillian the Full Sail Ale IPA he'd just bought her.

"Girl, stay away from that nasty lite beer," Damian insisted. "There's better beer. Tell her, McKenna."

"You're doing a fine job, Drake," Brandon said. He nodded at the IPA Jillian held. "I see the ladies got the drinks I sent over."

Brandon's wife, Emily, sat at a table a short distance away with Damian's date and Matt Stephens's newly pregnant wife, Amy. He'd ordered a round of club soda with a lime twist for the three women, and the bartender had managed to scare up a plateful of fresh saltine crackers for Amy, who was battling twenty-four-hour-a-day morning sickness.

"Jillian, stick with us. We'll have you drinking the good stuff in no time flat," Brandon told her.

Jillian grinned at both of them. Brandon was frequently in and out of team headquarters due to his job with Pro Sports Network. He'd always been friendly with her, and she enjoyed talking with him as well. Obviously, he was handsome and charming, but even more, he made an effort to get to know her.

"So, your wife's sitting in the pregnant section. Is there something you'd like to tell me?" Damian slapped Brandon on the back.

"There's not, but I wouldn't object if there was." Brandon winked in his wife's general direction. "I keep telling Emily that I want a little girl with red hair just like hers. She's afraid the boys will use her for tackling practice, but they're not touching my little princess. I'll make sure of it."

Jillian had to smile at the mental picture of a tiny red-headed girl, curled up in her big blond daddy's arms.

Damian rolled his eyes.

"Listen, man. She might show the two of them how things are. She'd have your genetic material, wouldn't she?" Damian said.

"That's right. I'll have to remember that." Brandon turned to face Jillian. "So, where's your date? I'd like to meet your young man."

Amy Stephens approached the group. "Oh, no, you don't," she said. Amy gave her brother-in-law a gentle punch in the arm. "Jillian, do not let him near anyone you're dating. He'll check his credit score and threaten bodily harm if the guy does not treat you like a lady at all times."

"Hey. It worked with you, didn't it?" Brandon reminded Amy.

"Yeah, it did after you scared the pee out of everyone else but Matt."

Brandon laughed and leaned down to kiss Amy's cheek.

"How are you feelin', squirt?"

"Awful." Amy smiled, though. "All I want is another healthy baby."

SETH FINALLY MANAGED to reach the small knot of chatting, laughing people. Jillian evidently felt comfortable enough with the group she was talking with to tease them a bit.

"So, Brandon, when are you and your wife going to ask me to babysit?" she said.

Brandon saw Seth approach over Jillian's head, nodded to him, and said, "You know, we'd like that. Our usual babysitters are all out of town or out of commission over the next week or so, and I'd like to take my wife out to dinner. Let's put something together."

Jillian beamed. "That would be great. I love kids, and I'd love to spend time with your little boys."

"Hey, Jill. It's nice to see you here." Seth reached out to cup Jillian's elbow in one hand.

"Seth! I didn't know you'd be here!" He realized with a shock that she was genuinely happy to see him. Amy had vanished into the crowd while they were talking, most likely on her way to the ladies' room.

Damian gave Seth an elaborate handshake.

"I'm a fan. Minnesota's QB won't forget your name for a while, will he?" Damian said.

"I'm sure it has nothing to do with the fact I carved it into his ass as he crawled off the turf," Seth assured him.

Brandon caught Seth's eye and raised one eyebrow.

"Sorry, Jill," Seth said.

"For what?"

"Ladies are present," Brandon explained. "Listen, Jillian. John won't mind if I stop by next week and firm up that babysitting thing, will he?"

"No. I don't think so," she said. Brandon reached out to give her a side hug.

"If you'll excuse me, I need to spend some time with Mrs. McKenna. You're bowling with us, aren't you, Jillian?"

"Sure. Of course." She beamed up at him.

Seth wondered what he could do to get Jillian to smile at him that way. Did she have a crush on McKenna? Shit. Then again, half the wives and girlfriends of guys on the team had a crush on McKenna. What was it about him, anyway? Seth was just as handsome. He had a little money too. All women liked that stuff.

"I'll meet you all over there," Jillian said. "Will it be all right if Seth joins us?"

Brandon's eyes narrowed slightly as he glanced over at Seth. They were friendly when talking as part of

Brandon's job or in the weight room, but Seth got the general impression that Brandon wasn't crazy about his spending any time at all with Jillian, for some unknown reason. "Oh yeah. We'll fit him in." He shook Seth's hand once more and walked away.

Damian was already sitting in the lane's seating area with his date. Seth listened to the noises of those practicing before the bowling tournament started, people chatting, and a little music.

"I wasn't sure if you were bowling with someone else, and I didn't want you to feel left out," she said to Seth. She looked a little worried.

A pity date. This was getting better by the minute. He'd fended off six women on his way across the bowling alley, but the one he'd headed for believed he needed social help.

"Jill, it's fine. I'll get some shoes. Would you like something else to drink?"

"Yes, please." She wrinkled her nose as she looked at the beer that was still three-fourths full. "This isn't my favorite," she confided.

"Let me help," Seth said. He took the beer out of her hand and polished it off with a few swallows. "What can I get you instead?"

"I'd like a…" She thought for a moment. "I'd like one of those hard-lemonade things."

"Coming right up. Why don't you find the lane we're bowling in, and I'll see you in a few minutes."

He sauntered off. There wasn't a line for the shoes, which were the most butt-ugly things he'd ever seen. He'd been in several of these bowling events now. Maybe he'd remember to buy some shoes of his own at some point. Damian was at the bar, getting more club soda.

"Hey. Where's Jillian?" Damian said.

"She went to warm up."

Seth placed his order and turned to watch the activity in the lanes as he waited.

Damian took a swig of the beer that still sat in front of him. "My date wants to fix her up with some guy at her office."

"Is that so?"

"Oh yeah. She met Jillian at the fund-raising event last month, and she's been talking about it for days. She thinks they'd like each other. The guy seems okay, and we really like Jillian."

"Does the guy know she's dating someone else?" Seth knew Jillian's alleged "dating" was fiction, but it might be fun to tease her a little with it.

Damian's mouth dropped open. "What the hell? She never told us. Where is he tonight?"

"Hell if I know."

Seth took a swallow of the beer the bartender had just delivered. He picked up Jillian's drink as well and made his way across the bowling alley.

THE TOURNAMENT STARTED. The athletes turned out to be fairly good bowlers. The females in their party gave it their best efforts, but it was quickly apparent there hadn't been a lot of practicing. Amy wasn't bowling. Her sister, Emily, was helping Brandon keep score. Then again,

Brandon must have had amazing powers of concentration. His wife was sitting in his lap, whispering in his ear, and generally draping herself all over him.

"Emily just got back from performances in Italy this afternoon. She was gone for a month," Amy told Jillian.

"And they're here?"

Amy took a tiny nibble on another saltine.

"The boys are at Grandma and Grandpa Hamilton's, and they're staying in a hotel half a block away. They'll probably stay another hour or so, and then they won't surface for a couple of days."

Jillian let out a laugh. Maybe someday she'd know what it was like to be in love, but she wondered if she'd ever find what Brandon and Emily obviously had.

Matt Stephens sat down next to his wife and pulled her close.

"Fifi. Sweetheart. Let me take you home. You're not feeling that well, are you?" He laid one big hand on Amy's belly.

"I want to visit with everyone. Maybe in a little while," she said.

He whispered something in Amy's ear; Amy blushed and batted playfully at his hand. "I am already pregnant, thanks to you, mister."

Matt Stephens was a former Shark who'd left Pro Sports Network to open a microcredit firm that lent to women-owned small businesses. The business was thriving. When he wasn't involved with that, he showed up at events like tonight's to sign autographs and bring additional attention to the charity in question.

"Hey!" Brandon McKenna was supposed to be taking his turn bowling, but he turned to face Matt. "That's my sister you're feeling up, Stephens."

"She's married. Mind your own business," Matt said, but he got up from his seat to hug his brother-in-law.

Seth dropped onto the bench next to Jillian.

"What's going on?" he asked her, nodding at Matt and Brandon.

"A family thing." Jillian felt the familiar stab of pain in her chest. "You're bowling, right?"

"Oh yeah. I might break a hundred," he joked. "Are you bowling?"

"As little as possible. I suck at it." She took a sip of the drink Seth handed to her.

"You're probably better at it than you think," Seth observed. Jillian was pleased by his confidence in her, but she knew that would change when he actually saw her in action.

"Well, aren't you sweet?" Amy called out to him.

Seth gave Amy a nod and a smile. Jillian noticed Brandon's eyes on Seth as he walked back to the scoring table. He didn't look happy. She wondered why.

Seth got up to take his turn for practice and called over his shoulder, "Watch this, Jill."

He lined up on the floor in front of the lane and swung the ball with grace; it rolled smoothly along. Strike. Jillian applauded, and Seth made an exaggerated bow.

"Let's see that again!" Damian shouted.

"Of course." Seth lined up once more and swung the ball as gracefully as he had the first time, but for some reason, the ball had a mind of its own. One lone pin stood.

"Shi—crap."

"You got most of them," Jillian reassured him.

"Most of them isn't good enough, Jill." He dropped onto the bench again. "Are you hungry?"

"No, thank you."

"I'm going to go get another beer."

He loped off. Brandon glanced around to see where Seth went, folded his lips, and returned his attention to his wife. Damian plunked himself down in the seat Seth had just vacated.

"So, Jillian. What's this I hear about you having a special friend? You never told us you had a boyfriend."

Several heads swiveled around.

"Huh?"

"We haven't met him yet."

"Why didn't he come with you?"

Amy, ever the diplomat, blurted out, "Where is he?"

Jillian stifled a sigh. She should never have made up a story; now she was caught. She thought for a moment. "He had something else he had to do this evening." She shrugged her shoulders and tried to look casual.

"How long have you been together?"

Jillian shrugged her shoulders again. She was busted, and there was no way out. "A few months."

"Has he met Seth?" Brandon asked.

"No. Not yet."

Emily looked up from nuzzling her husband's ear. "How did you meet him, Jillian?"

"Oh, we met on Facebook."

"You're kidding."

"No." She let out a shaky laugh. "Kinda weird, huh?"

Matt and Brandon exchanged a glance, and Damian spoke.

"Well, that's too bad. My friend Kiara, here, knows a guy at her office we wanted to introduce you to." He slid his arm around his date's shoulders and gave her a squeeze. "He'll be disappointed." Damian gave Jillian a wink.

Jillian waved one hand. "That's so nice of you both to think of me, but things are fine. He's kind of shy. Maybe he'll show up at something soon and you can all meet him."

Matt and Brandon were still exchanging looks. Jillian wished she knew what the two of them were thinking, but maybe she didn't want to know. Brandon helped his wife to her feet, said something into her ear, and squeezed Jillian's shoulder with one big hand as he passed by.

"Excuse me for a moment," he said.

There was a short break before the next game started. Matt and Damian drifted off toward the bar. Jillian saw Brandon walk over to them, and Matt snagged Seth's arm to pull him into their group too. The discussion was animated, but Jillian couldn't hear any of it.

Amy moved over closer to Jillian, and Emily sat down on her other side. They both seemed to have as little interest in bowling as Jillian did.

"This is all Brandon's going to talk about when we get out of here," Emily said. "He'll make sure the guy you're dating is on the up-and-up." She grinned at Jillian. "He lives for this stuff."

"He's such a meddler," Amy said, but she smiled as she spoke. "I can't imagine what's going to happen if Emily ever has a little girl."

Emily let out a groan, and all three women laughed. Emily did her best impression of Brandon's deep, Southern-accented voice. "She's not dating until she's thirty-five."

"That's going to happen," Amy said.

Dread curled sticky, uncomfortable fingers around Jillian as she chatted with Amy and Emily. Oh, God. She hadn't thought of this. What would she do? She didn't want to admit that she'd made up the whole thing, but she really didn't want to tell them there was no boyfriend. She'd really stuck her foot in it this time. Maybe it was better that they think she was some kind of a lonely loser than find out that she'd deceived all of them.

"So, Jill—you don't mind if I call you Jill, right?" Amy said.

"Of course not. Seth calls me that all the time."

"You two are just friends?" Amy said.

"He really is a nice guy, even if sometimes it doesn't seem that way," Jillian joked. She caught movement out of the corner of her eye. Brandon and Matt appeared to be grilling Seth somewhat. Damian was looking on.

The three women fell silent for a few minutes.

"Jill, I gotta ask you a question," Amy finally blurted out.

"Sure."

"What's with all the kids' clothing we've seen in the back of your car? Do you have a family or something?"

## Chapter Fourteen

JILLIAN BIT HER lip while Amy continued.

"I don't mean to be so snoopy, but Matt and I passed your car in the lot the last time he came in to have lunch with John, and we noticed what looked like a hundred sets of winter hats and gloves in the backseat."

"My sister's an amateur detective when she's not running her flower shop," Emily said. Amy made a face at her, and Emily laughed harder.

"Oh, come on. You want to know too," Amy said.

Jillian wouldn't be able to lie about this. She swallowed hard. "I volunteer with a local organization that helps foster children."

"So they were donations."

"Yeah. I saw a great sale, and I scooped up as much as I could afford."

Jillian wrapped her arms around her midsection. Even more than envying Emily's marriage, Emily and Amy made her wish she had a sister. What would it be like to spend time with someone who'd known you since you were a baby, someone who might fight with you once in a while but, on the whole, loved you? Their laughter and teasing were fun to watch, but it made Jillian's heart ache.

"Have you volunteered for a long time? What organization is it, if you don't mind my asking?" Emily took a sip of her club soda.

"I volunteer at Treehouse. Treehouse provides things and experiences that foster children need in order to have a better childhood. They also help the older kids with college applications or finding a job." Jillian took a sip of her drink. "I've been doing this for a long time now."

Emily draped one arm around the back of the bench.

"I've heard great things about Treehouse. They help a lot of kids, and they do it on a modest budget. What made you decide to pick this particular organization?" Emily said.

Jillian hugged herself a little more. "I was a foster child. Treehouse wasn't in the business when I was younger." She tried to smile. To anyone else, it probably looked like a grimace. "Maybe I can help someone else."

Emily's hand cupped Jillian's shoulder. She squeezed. Amy was silent. Finally, Emily spoke. "You didn't live with your parents."

"No. My mom was killed in a car wreck when I was three," Jillian said. "I never met my dad."

"I'm so sorry about that," Emily said.

Amy nodded. Jillian saw tears swimming in Amy's eyes.

Jillian moved restlessly in the chair. She dropped her hands into her lap and fidgeted. Amy laid her hand over Jillian's and hung on.

"I usually don't tell people my situation. They don't know what to say," Jillian said.

"Kind of like us," Amy muttered.

Emily gave Jillian's shoulder another little pat. "Well, you're in the right place."

"What do you mean?"

"The guys here could fund that charity's programs for a year with their walking-around money. Tonight. They'd never even miss it." A fierce light shone in Emily's eyes. "I can help too. What do they need?"

"I don't understand."

"Will you tell me how to get involved?" Emily asked. "I realize this is pretty spur of the moment—"

"You think?" Amy interrupted.

Jillian had to smile, just a little. The two of them were so funny together. She imagined that sometimes they disagreed, but the love that bound Emily and Amy felt like she could reach out and touch it.

"Well, I'm still a fairly new mom. I can't imagine my babies all alone. I just can't." Tears glistened in Emily's eyes. "Plus, I want to do this, but I also wonder if I'd go to the headquarters and want to adopt every kid I met there."

"Like Brandon would be against that," Amy told her. "He'd buy you a bigger house. Hey, Jillian, I don't know if you've spent enough time talking with him to figure this one out, but he has a gooey marshmallow center. He's a total pushover." Amy let out a bark of laughter. "Ask him if you can borrow his black American Express card. He'd let you too."

Emily let out a decidedly unladylike snort. "Oh yeah, and your husband is no different. Jillian, I'm telling you—I don't know how your guy is, but one whimper from Amy, and Matt's cleaning out Tiffany's if it'll make her smile." Emily reached over and grabbed Amy's wrist. "Do not tell me he bought you another ring. I *love* that! Baguettes and rounds? Gorgeous."

"We're pregnant. He wanted to celebrate," Amy muttered.

"Oh my God. There isn't any room left on your finger now. What's he going to do when the baby makes an appearance?" Emily rolled her eyes. Jillian couldn't stop the laughter that bubbled out of her. "Listen, Jillian, Brandon's coming back here any minute, but could we exchange cell numbers? I want to talk to you about this some more." Emily whipped an iPhone out of her handbag.

Jillian didn't have the sheer number of accessories her two new friends did, but she managed to exchange cell phone numbers with both Amy and Emily. Emily threw the phone back in her bag and got up from the bench.

"Hey. I'm really glad we had this chat, but I gotta go. Give me a hug. My husband needs to be dragged off to a hotel room." Emily threw her arms around Jillian. "We are so having lunch."

Emily hugged her sister too, and raced away minutes later.

"Is she always like that?" Jillian said.

"She's jet-lagged, but she'll be calling you. I have questions too, if you don't mind." Amy glanced around. "Where are the guys? The second game should have started by now."

"They're probably talking with some fans or something."

"Probably." Amy pulled a chair around to face herself and put her feet up on it. "So, Jillian, how do you like working with this bunch? I know some of them are harder to deal with than others. Plus, how did you get to know Seth?"

Jillian thought for a few moments. "Yeah, some of these guys are more challenging than others. Most of them, though, are nice. Just hanging around Seth was really surprising to me. People approach him everywhere. It doesn't matter what he's doing. He said he was in the men's room the other day, and some guy asked him for an autograph."

"That's happened to Matt before." Amy grinned. "The last time we went to the OB/GYN's office, the radiologist asked him if she could get his autograph for her brother while she was smearing that cold goo on my belly."

"Does it bug you?"

"Matt's pretty used to it. I don't like it when it's obvious someone wants to talk to me because they want to meet him."

Jillian wondered how Seth's girlfriends coped with this. She didn't talk about where she worked when she was outside of the office, because people tended to ask for tickets or if they could meet a team member. The team gave her two tickets for each home game. She was always up in the suite with John and the other VIPs, so she donated them. If she ever found a real-life boyfriend, he'd probably want to go. She heard footsteps behind her, and Seth sat down on the hard plastic seat next to her.

"Hey. You miss me?"

Amy smothered a laugh behind her hand. Jillian glanced over at him.

"Where're the guys?" Jillian said.

"Well, McKenna took off out of here with his wife. Amy, Matt was signing autographs with Damian. I don't know if they're going to bowl the next game." He slung his arm around Jillian's shoulders. "Want to go to a party with me later?"

"I have to go to work tomorrow—"

"Just for a while. We'll have fun."

Amy watched them with a speculative look on her face. Jillian never did answer the question about how she'd met Seth, and Jillian knew there had to be questions about what they were doing together. She also wondered if Seth wanted her to go just so he could drink and she could drive him around.

Matt materialized a few seconds later. "There's my beautiful girl. Fifi, let's go home."

Jillian couldn't help herself. "Why does he call you 'Fifi'?"

"It's my alter ego," Amy told her. She slowly rose from the chair. Matt slid one arm around her waist.

"Well, Jillian, Amy's parents were…inventive. Yeah. That's what she told me the night we met." He brought

Amy's hand to his lips and kissed the back of it. "Little did I know."

Jillian got to her feet and hugged Amy good-bye.

"I'll call you," Amy said into her ear. "Let's have lunch, okay? We'll bring Emily along."

"I'd like that," Jillian said.

"Great." Amy nodded at Seth. "Don't let him keep you out too late."

Jillian got a hug from Matt; he shook hands with Seth, and he and Amy walked away.

"So," Seth told her. "Let's get out of here. I have things to show you."

SETH WALKED JILLIAN through a courtyard to an elevator bank in the same building the bowling alley was in. She was a little overwhelmed by the numbers of people she saw moving through the corridors of the bowling alley, movie theaters, and multiple restaurants in Lincoln Square. She felt Seth's fingertips brush the small of her back.

"I won't lose you," he teased. "We're going to hang out with a bunch of the guys and their guests. We'll have some drinks, we might play some pool, and you can relax a little."

"Me? Excuse me. I can't believe—"

Jillian was interrupted by the rapid tat-tat-tat of someone in high heels behind them.

"Aren't you Seth Taylor?" a feminine voice cooed.

Seth took Jillian's elbow. He had a choice: turn around and talk to a woman who was now trying to catch up with them, or pretend he didn't hear her. Even better, he heard another pair of high heels on the highly polished floor. He pasted a smile on his lips he didn't feel and turned to face them.

The two women who came to a complete halt well into his personal space obviously didn't see Jillian—or they disregarded her. It was all there—the artfully rumpled, highlighted blonde hair, far too much makeup, breasts that were definitely aftermarket and shown off to their best advantage, tight jeans, and stiletto heels. A few months ago, he probably would have had a drink with them, at least. The difference between them and Jillian was pronounced. Where they were done up—hair, makeup, and clothes strategically seductive—Jillian wore jeans and had her long blonde hair pulled back in a ponytail, with a natural pink flush on her cheeks. He was fairly sure the women in question felt positive he would choose them over her. It would have been amusing if he didn't know it probably wasn't going to end well.

"So, Seth, where you off to?" the taller one asked. She gave him a sultry glance. In other words, all this could be his.

He could see Jillian smiling at them out of the corner of his eye. He wasn't sure if she knew this already, but they were trapped. The elevator bank was behind them. The escalator wasn't going to work. Any Shark who went out into the public area of Bellevue's Lincoln Square right now was going to get mobbed. There were thousands of people in the area's restaurants and movie theaters tonight.

"Ladies, we're off to a team meeting. It's nice to meet you, though." He stuck out his hand. The woman who'd tried to catch up with him brushed it aside.

"A handshake? How about a hug? I'm a big fan." Her friend moved forward too. He wasn't getting out of this. The elevator doors behind them opened, and Jillian tugged on his sleeve.

"Excuse us," she said to the two women. "Are you ready?" she asked Seth.

The women followed them into the elevator, as he could have predicted.

JILLIAN LEANED AGAINST the elevator wall. The two women who joined them inside were doing whatever they could to get Seth's attention, up to and including one of them rubbing her breasts on his forearm and asking if she could buy him a drink. The scent of their perfume was almost overwhelming. She wondered what it would be like to have that kind of bulletproof self-confidence.

"I appreciate the offer, but no, thank you," he told them.

Jillian wondered what would have happened if he had had this encounter while she wasn't around. They were also stuck in the world's slowest elevator. How long did it take to go up three floors anyway? She remained amazed at how much hair-tossing, hip-thrusting, and breast jiggling had already happened. Maybe she should have cut them some slack. After all, if she saw Seth walking around in public, she'd want to talk with him too, but this was getting a little ridiculous.

"Well, how about you buy us a drink?"

The elevator stopped on their floor. It took a moment for the doors to slide open, but he was ready. He gripped Jillian's hand and bolted out of the car, pulling Jillian after him. "We're already late. Nice to meet you," he called over his shoulder.

"Wait! Wait!" one said. Jillian was fairly surprised that anyone could run in stilettos on a highly polished floor, but these two obviously had practice. "How about an autograph? My nephew just loves you."

"Yeah. My little brother is a huge Sharks fan too."

Seth was still moving. "If you'll write to Sharks head-quarters, I'll make sure they both get an autographed photo. Tell them I said hey."

He was heading toward the front door of an upscale pool room, which Jillian had read about but had never seen. It seemed she was about to.

The guy at the door nodded at him and waved Seth inside.

"They're in the back room."

"Thanks, man."

Jillian could hear people calling out to Seth, see the heads of people in the lounge area swiveling to see him, but he didn't stop. He hauled her down another dimly lit corridor. Another doorman sat at the entrance.

"Tyrone."

"Hey, Taylor."

"This is Jillian. She needs a bracelet."

"Of course." Tyrone wrapped a neon-blue Sharks insignia plastic bracelet around her wrist and fastened it with a snap at one side. "There you go, Jillian."

Seth fist-bumped with Tyrone. "T., you're going to be here, right?"

"Yeah. You got followed, didn't you?"

"I might have."

"I'll take care of it. Have a good evening."

He opened the door for them. Seth ushered her into another huge room, but this one wasn't as crowded. Current and former Sharks, the team's cheerleaders, and their guests milled around talking, laughing, and settling in to have a few drinks.

Two hours later, Jillian escorted a somewhat buzzed Seth to his Escalade and drove him home. Luckily, she only had to drive a couple miles in a vehicle much larger (and much more expensive) than the one she was used to.

"I shouldna had those last two beers," he said. He threw his forearm over his eyes.

She hid her smile. "You were all having fun."

"Gonna have a headache tomorrow."

"You'll need some aspirin and some water before you go to sleep," she said. She pulled into his driveway, praying she wouldn't hit the side of the garage as she drove inside it. "I'll walk you upstairs."

"You take my car home," he said.

She didn't want to drive a vehicle that cost more than her business-major college education, but she couldn't leave his ride at the parking garage while she went to get her car. The whole thing was ridiculous.

He wrapped his arm around her shoulders as she slid her arm around his waist. "Take it easy," she said as they walked up the stairs. He wasn't stumbling around, but she wanted to make sure he'd get into his room safely. She was torn between laughing a bit at his antics and scolding him for getting drunk when he had practice in the morning.

He flopped onto his bed. She pulled off his shoes as she spoke. "I'll get your aspirin and water here in a minute."

"Thankssss, Jill."

At least he remembered who she was.

She rummaged around his medicine cabinet until she found some ibuprofen and got him a glass of water to wash them down with. She pulled the blankets over him, made sure the bathroom light was on so he wouldn't wake up and be disoriented, and brushed the hair off of his forehead.

"Go to sleep," she murmured.

"Where are you going?"

"Home. I'll pick you up in the morning."

He reached out to grasp one of her wrists. "Stay with me."

"What? No. I can't do that."

"Yes, you can. Stay here. Get some sleep." He moved to the other side of the bed and folded the blankets down in open invitation. "Come on, Jill."

"I shouldn't be doing this."

Spending time with Seth was one thing, but getting physically involved with him was something else. She remembered John's threat to fire her if she got romantic with Seth, and she remembered Vivian's reinforcement of this fact too. She'd told John nothing was going on between them. She couldn't say that anymore, not by any stretch of the imagination.

"Please?"

Against every bit of wisdom she possessed, she kicked off her shoes and stripped off her jacket. She dropped it on the floor by the closet.

"You need one of my T-shirts. They're in the dresser, third drawer down."

"I should leave my clothes on."

If she left her clothes on, nothing was going to happen. Sure it wasn't. She'd cling to half an inch on her side of the mattress all night and wouldn't touch him. She would have rolled her eyes at her own justifications if he wasn't looking directly at her.

"You won't sleep well."

He'd sleep like a baby. He always slept more deeply when he wasn't alone. Plus, he didn't want her to leave.

"I . . ." She didn't finish. He could practically see the wheels turning in her head. Should she, or shouldn't she?

"Don't be a chicken. Plus, no sheets on the guest bed." She hadn't seen much of the guest bedroom when she'd visited before. The bed in there was always made. And he was a liar.

"Fine." She got in the bed and flipped on her side away from him. He could fix that. He pulled the blankets up to her shoulders and slid one arm around her midsection.

"Stop it," she protested, but there was no heat in her voice. She didn't shrink from his touch.

"Shhh," he soothed.

"Why are we doing this?"

He pretended he didn't hear her question. "I'm too drunk to drive you home, and you're too sleepy to drive yourself. Close your eyes." He buried his nose in her hair. "Good night."

SHE'D BEEN PLAYED.

Seth shouldn't have been behind the wheel of his car, but she'd bet her own car he wasn't drunk. He was lonely. He didn't want to sleep alone. He'd had plenty of opportunities to find someone else to warm his bed tonight, and he'd taken advantage of none of them, as far as she could tell. Jillian wasn't sure why he'd chosen her, but she had to admit that nobody forced her into his bed: She'd climbed in herself. His hand was flat against her belly, and he pulled her against him. She felt his body relax against hers. His warm breath tickled the nape of her neck. The clean, freshly showered scent of his hair and skin surrounded her.

She could wait a few minutes until he fell asleep and then go home, but she knew she wouldn't. She let out a long sigh. She'd also told Emily and Amy, two women she hardly knew, all about her personal history. She hadn't told Seth yet. Why was she still holding back? He wasn't going to use the information to hurt her.

This was a hot mess.

"Whatsss wrong?" she heard him murmur. He kept trying to pretend he was drunk. It was a good thing he played football for a living because he was a terrible actor.

"Nothing." She covered his hand on her belly with her own. He laced his fingers through hers. "Go to sleep, you big baby."

"You must miss sleeping with the guy you're dating."

The silence in the room grew as she hesitated. She wanted to tell him everything, but she couldn't. Plus, what would he do when he found out that she was as lonely as he was? It would be one long misunderstanding. She'd lose his friendship, and right now, she wasn't ready to do that.

"Yeah, I do." She let out a breath. "He's insatiable, you know."

Seth let out a snort of laughter.

She closed her eyes. He was so warm. The feeling of his body against hers was comforting. At the same time, every hormone in her body was wide awake and screaming for relief. She knew something was happening with him. She could feel him, hard against her. She resisted the urge to roll over and do something about it. She was in bed with a man most women would do almost anything to be with, and nothing was going to happen tonight.

This was a thousand-thread-count, hotel-mattress version of hell.

SETH AWOKE SOMETIME in the wee hours. All he heard in his room was the sound of Jillian's breathing. She was asleep in his arms, her head pillowed on his shoulder, one small hand flat in the middle of his chest. The bathroom light illuminated the room enough for him to watch her sleep.

It wasn't the first time he'd invited a female friend into his bed, but he really needed to stop doing this. He'd want to kill any other guy who did the same thing to her. After all, Jillian deserved better. She made him laugh and made him think. He enjoyed spending time with her, even when she insisted on telling him things he wasn't sure he wanted to hear. The party in his shorts had started when he saw her in the crowd at the bowling alley, and things had just gotten worse. It was the external indication of how he felt when he saw her. Happiness. Relief. Couldn't wait to talk with her. To say he was miserable right now was an understatement, but he reluctantly conceded he had nobody to blame but himself.

She stirred a little and rubbed her nose on the side of his neck. If he was hard before, he could now pound nails with it. They were supposed to be just friends. He wouldn't have shared half the things he did with her if they were more than that. It would be too risky. He didn't want to fuck this up—whatever they had. What was it about her? She was everything he'd never wanted. She didn't have a perfect figure. She was attractive, but he'd always been partial to dark-haired women. Jillian wore little makeup, didn't get a mani and pedi once a week, and wasn't interested in fashion. When she smiled at him, though, he forgot it all.

*One kiss*, he thought. *Just one kiss*. He could do it. He'd kiss her. Then he'd go back to sleep. He was kidding himself, but he had to touch her.

He smoothed the hair out of her eyes, and he saw one side of her mouth move into a faint smile. His fingertips trailed down the soft skin of her jaw. She arched into his hand like that damn cat of hers did, even in her sleep. He dragged his thumb over her lower lip. Her scent, the way she cuddled up to him—he wanted her to stay forever.

He wasn't big on poetry. He thought it was pretty much a pain in the ass when he was in school. He wished he'd paid better attention. He didn't have the words to describe how it felt to touch her, and he wished he did.

He was out of his mind. *Leave her alone*, his newly discovered conscience shrieked. Get out of the bed. Go into the other room. The only way this was going to end was with them both naked, and it was wrong. Before, he didn't care who got hurt, but now he did. He couldn't hurt her. He couldn't.

There was enough light in his room to see Jillian open her eyes. Her voice was sleepily husky and the sexiest thing he'd ever heard. "Seth?"

He tipped her chin up and sealed his mouth over hers in one quick motion. She tasted sweet and clean, like water. Her lips fluttered beneath his. She was kissing him back! His heart banged around in his chest. The blood roared in his ears. Mostly, he wanted more. He'd kissed so many women before, but none like this. He wanted to plunder, but even more, he wanted to savor. Everything and everyone before was a warm-up.

He heard a groan and realized it came from him. He slid his tongue into her mouth, exploring and tasting, and he just about exploded when he felt her shy forays into his mouth with her tongue. Their tongues did a complicated dance, and her moan was muffled as she kissed him. She slid her fingers into his hair. He pushed her T-shirt up and moved his hand up until he palmed her breast. She was still wearing a bra. He'd be taking care of that shortly. He rolled onto her, pinning her beneath him but supporting his weight on one forearm as he fisted his hand in her hair. She cradled him between her thighs. He felt her arms clasping him, her hands roaming over his back, and heard her unsteady breathing as he came up for air.

"Jill," he managed to rasp, "I want you." He pulled the hem of her T-shirt up and tried to take it off over her head.

It was like someone had thrown a bucket of cold water on her. One moment, she was kissing him as if he held all the oxygen left in the world and she would die without more; the next, she pulled her mouth off his, cried out *no*, and pushed against his chest with both hands. She threw herself off his bed, grabbed her shoes, and hopped around the room until she managed to cram them onto her feet.

"I have to go."

"Now? Don't leave. Come back here." He held the blankets up so she could slide back in.

She attempted sarcasm. "It's too late on a school night. Gotta go."

She grabbed her jacket and ran out of his room. He was off the bed in a flash and chasing her down the hallway.

"Wait! Wait. Where are you going?" He reached the front door before she did and leaned one hand against it.

Her eyes were wild. Her clothes were pretty messed up. He couldn't take his eyes off her mouth, though. The reflection of the porch light shining through the glass panels in his front door revealed swollen lips stained cherry-red by all that kissing. Anyone who saw her would know exactly what she'd been doing.

"I need to leave. Please let me leave."

"I will, but just one thing." He cupped her cheek once more and slowly rubbed his thumb against it. Standing close to her was like a drug he could never kick. She stood stiffly, but he kept at it until he heard her breathing return to normal, and he saw her relax. "Jill," he said softly, "why, baby?"

She bowed her head. "I...I can't," she choked out. "I shouldn't have kissed you. I shouldn't have been here in the first place. I have to go."

He heard the jingle of his car keys in her hand, and he stepped away from the door. She wrenched it open and closed it behind her, and he hurried to hit the garage door opener in the mud room. Seconds later, he heard the Escalade start.

That went well.

# Chapter Fifteen

JILLIAN PULLED INTO the driveway at Seth's at seven thirty the next morning. If he'd take her over to get her car, he could go back to bed, and she'd go to the office. Well, she'd go to the office directly after she got rid of the piece of toast and coffee she managed to force down. She couldn't decide which was stronger right now—the urge to cry or the urge to throw up. She was shaking like a leaf. Her stomach was churning. She hadn't slept at all last night, and the reason why was probably still tucked up in bed, asleep.

She walked up the path to his front door on rubbery legs. She could leave the keys on the little table inside his front door and walk to the parking garage. It was only about half a mile away. That would work. Just as she tried to fit the key in the lock, the front door swung open to reveal a fully dressed Seth. He had on worn jeans, an Under Armour "Protect This House" T-shirt, cross-trainers, and a scowl.

"I…oh, here." She held out his car keys. "Thanks for letting me borrow your car. I'll walk over there to get my car out of the garage."

"No. I'll drive you." He pulled the front door closed and locked it behind him. He headed off to his car. She kept walking. "I don't know if you heard me," he called out. "I'm driving."

"I'm walking." She hoped she could get away from him before she did something incredibly embarrassing, like lose complete control of her bodily functions. He backed out of his driveway, pulled alongside her, and rolled down the passenger window.

"Please get in the car."

"No. I'm not in the mood to carpool this morning."

Obviously she was acting childish, but one more glance at that hard mouth reminded her how soft it had been when he kissed her.

"Jill, you'll be late for work. Just get in."

They were attracting attention. Seth's vehicle was sufficiently large to offer no clear view around them. Three cars lined up behind him in quick succession. Nobody was honking yet, but that was a matter of time. Jillian tried to pick up the pace. Unfortunately, Seth could drive faster than she could walk.

"Just go away," she called out.

"No. I won't. I want to talk to you, and you're running away from me." The driver directly behind Seth's vehicle gave his horn a quick tap. Seth ignored this. He slowed even more.

"I'm not running away from you. I have to go get my car. I have to work for a living, unlike other people who exercise all day."

"That's it," he told her. The guy behind him laid on the horn. Seth pulled over to the curb, jumped out of his running vehicle, and ran back to the guy who'd honked at him. "Have you ever had an argument with a woman before?" he shouted. Jillian couldn't hear what the guy said to him in response, but Seth continued. "Great. Let me get you guys out of here, then." She glanced back. Seth was now directing traffic around his car. He cleared off everyone who waited behind him, and she heard the pounding of his shoes against the sidewalk as he ran. He stopped in front of her. "Please get in the car so I can take you to the parking garage."

Her eyes traveled up from the pavement, over the chest she'd snuggled against last night, the arms that had closed around her, the shoulder she'd laid her head on, the espresso-brown waves sun-streaked with caramel that slipped through her fingers like liquid satin. The eyes she saw in her dreams. Oh, God, his mouth. She swallowed hard. Cold sweat trickled down her spine. He reached out one hand to her. "Jill."

She didn't take his hand, but she crossed to the passenger side of his car, opened the door, and got in. He threw himself into the driver's seat.

It took ten minutes to get to the parking garage from his neighborhood. He had ten minutes to try to explain himself. It was obvious that Jillian hadn't slept last night.

She was near tears, and she probably had an upset stomach too. Whenever she was upset, the first thing she did was start clutching her stomach.

He was still wondering why she'd launched herself out of his bed. She had kissed him back. She had touched him too. There was something else going on here, but she wasn't talking. She scrunched herself into the passenger seat and looked away from him.

He braked at the stoplight in front of the parking garage. Thank God. Sixty more seconds while they waited for the light to change.

"Jill, let's talk a little about what happened last night." She didn't speak. "I woke up and you were close and I got carried away." He took a deep breath. "I'm sorry."

She turned to look at him. He watched the color drain from her face.

"You kissed me, and you're sorry?" The glimmer of tears rose in her eyes. "You're sorry. Oh, God. Just let me out." She tried to open the door, which he quickly relocked. He wasn't letting her step into traffic! She flopped back against the seat, closed her eyes, and hugged herself even harder.

"That's not what I meant." Of course, the light changed at that moment, and he needed to concentrate. The stricken look on her face—this couldn't possibly get any worse. He made a left-hand turn into the garage, pulled the ticket out of the machine, and threw it on the dashboard. She hadn't said a word, but she brushed at her cheeks with an impatient hand. "I enjoyed kissing you. I wanted to kiss you again. I…well, it upset you, and that's what I meant." He pulled to a stop behind her car. She grabbed her purse, threw the door open, jumped out, and ran to the driver's side door.

She jabbed her key in the lock while he got out of the car again. She glanced up, and his heart just about stopped. She looked at him as if he were a stranger—and an unwelcome one.

"If you wanted to kiss someone, there were plenty of volunteers last night. Why didn't you pick one of them? They were all over the place," she cried out. "They…you don't care for me. You acted like you were going to kiss me weeks ago, and then you didn't. You're not interested because I'm not what you're looking for! You're not into me. I'm someone convenient that you run to when you're bored or you're lonely. Why did you kiss me when you didn't mean it?"

He couldn't have been more surprised if Dallas's offensive line had suddenly materialized in the parking garage and clotheslined him with extreme prejudice. He could see her trembling, her sweet pink mouth a spot of color in an otherwise chalk-white face. She finally managed to get the car door to unlock and threw her purse onto the passenger seat. "I have to go." She jammed the key into the ignition and slammed the car door at the same time.

He'd boxed her in. He could sit and wait; she'd have to talk to him eventually. Instead, he jogged back to his car, got in the driver's seat, and drove away.

JILLIAN PULLED HER cell phone out of her purse and dialed John's direct line. She heard the smile in his voice as he answered. "Jillian. Are you going to tell me you're late for the first time in three months?"

"I don't feel well," she said. That was an understatement. She wanted to throw up. "Is there any way I can stay home today?"

"Of course you can. I'm sorry to hear you're not feeling good. Did the guys keep you out too late last night?"

"No. I...maybe I have some food poisoning. I feel really awful." It wasn't exactly a lie. If her stomach was churning before, now it was so painful that all she wanted to do was go to bed and never get out again. "I'm going to go back home and get some rest."

"Well, I hope you'll be feeling better soon. If you're up to it later, could we talk a little about the rest of the week? I'll be at meetings in Las Vegas, and there're a few things we should go over."

"Of course, John. Would you like me to call you at noon or so?"

"Perfect. Jill, take care of yourself."

"Thank you so much."

She ended the call and drove out of the garage. Her apartment was fifteen minutes away. All she wanted was her bed.

## *Chapter Sixteen*

JILLIAN WALKED THROUGH the front door of her apartment twenty minutes later, dumped her purse on the little built-in desk in her kitchen, and kicked off her shoes. At least the drive home wasn't bad. Her stomach was still churning and painful from her encounter with Seth. Maybe she should try eating something to make herself feel better.

The only thing that usually helped when she was this upset was chocolate. Of course she'd tossed it all. She didn't think she needed the candy bars anymore. Well, she needed one now. Or fifty of them. Whatever worked.

She had a bad feeling that she could eat her way through the entire contents of the candy aisle at the grocery store, and all she'd be when it was over was ill. She'd told herself a thousand times already that Seth was going to break her heart, and sure enough, he had. He was sorry he'd kissed her. Sorry! The tears rose in her eyes again. She stifled a sob. Why did she think she could interest a man so many other women wanted? Why didn't she set her sights on meeting someone attainable, someone who cared for her in return?

She realized that they'd said they were "friends," and she should have been content with that definition, but she wasn't. She should have had the courage to tell him that. She'd run out of his bedroom last night like it was on fire. And it was stupid to get emotionally or physically involved with someone who insisted he was just a friend. She was as much to blame for this mess as she currently thought Seth was, but right now, she didn't feel like being rational, calm, and mature. She wanted to stuff her face with chocolate, watch TV, and blame everything on him.

CB wound around Jillian's ankles and tried to grab her toes as she stormed into her bedroom.

"No, kitty. Stop it."

She heard CB's *prrt* as the kitten tried to grab the sleeve of the brand-new sweater she pulled off. She needed to go to her happy place for a few hours, which meant she was going back to bed in her softest flannel nightgown and huge socks, propping herself up in a cocoon of pillows, and watching anything on her laptop that might make her feel better. CB could play with Jillian's toes to her heart's content when they were covered with several blankets and a comforter.

She grabbed her laptop and phone as she scrambled into bed. CB scampered over her legs to cuddle against her. She pulled the pillows on her bed into a formation that she could sit up against while she stroked her kitten's fur.

"He kissed me, kitty. He finally kissed me, and then he said he didn't mean it."

She couldn't help it. The hot tears overflowed. She knew the best thing she could do was get good and pissed off. She deserved better. She could tell Seth to go perform an anatomically impossible act on himself (like she'd ever said that to another person before in her life) and concentrate on other things that made her happy instead. All she had to do was find a few.

Actually, that wasn't accurate. She had interests and goals for the future before she met Seth. Maybe she needed to stick to her guns, ignore the hell out of him, and concentrate on her own life again. She was making progress on the "Couch to 5K" instructions she'd downloaded a couple of weeks ago. She was walking twice a day and thrilled to notice more changes as a result. She had plenty to do at the office in the next few weeks before the Sharks' season-ticket holders' 5K too. She could sign up for more volunteer hours at Treehouse when she wasn't babysitting John and his buddies in the Sharks' suite. She could get a makeover. She'd also love to spend more time hanging out with Kari.

She glanced over at the clock on her nightstand. Kari would be trying to get the baby down for his nap right now. This would give Jillian some time to quit crying and pull herself together. She could call Kari and ask if she wanted to get a coffee or something when the baby woke up.

CB scrambled up Jillian's front to lick her cheek with her scratchy little tongue. It hurt, but Jillian gave the kitty a kiss on her pink nose. "Thanks, kitty." CB purred a bit more and gave her a head-butt. "Maybe we should watch a movie or something. Want to watch *Must Love Dogs* with me? We can cuddle." CB seemed to think this was a fine idea. She curled up against Jillian.

She and her kitty had a date. To hell with Seth.

FOR THE SECOND time in less than a week, Seth had said something idiotic to a woman and was again in the position of figuring out how in the hell he was going to fix it. He wasn't even counting the incident with Lauren at the dinner table the other night over the bench for Liam. She was his sister. She expected him to say some dumb-ass thing that she'd freak out over on the regular.

After spending another night tossing and turning, it was evident he needed to get his shit together. What was wrong with him? He knew that he wanted a lot more than being friends with Jillian, but he wasn't sure about her feelings. She didn't seem to get at all that he'd kissed her because he wanted to, and he'd wanted to for a long time now. Then again, he wanted to save face if his advances weren't what she wanted, and he'd told her he was "sorry" for kissing her, which was probably the worst thing he could have said to her.

She was shy around men. He'd earned her trust and her friendship a little at a time, and he wondered what he was going to have to do to get it back again. He should have been honest. He had nobody to blame for all of this but himself.

He couldn't believe he was actually afraid to declare how he felt, once and for all, and find out if she felt that way about him too. He'd never worried about whether or not any woman wanted him—he'd make his move, she'd indicate interest in return, and that was that. He was having a tough time reading Jillian. She didn't shrink from him when he tried to hold her hand, and she didn't tell him she was too busy to spend time with him. She wouldn't have freaked out so much if she didn't care at all. If she wasn't interested, she would have made an effort to meet someone else or taken up Kade Harrison on it when he'd asked her out. Then again, Jillian had no problem making it clear to Harrison that she really wasn't interested.

If there was anything he could attribute to his momentary lapse of balls, it was the fact he could walk away from the women he'd been involved with previously. No harm, no foul. The relationship would run its course, both parties would meet someone new, and he didn't have to deal with his broken heart. It wasn't enough that he wanted Jillian physically. He'd fallen hard for her sweet, sassy personality, her sense of humor, and her gentle, compassionate heart. She was his friend first. Physical involvement was the next logical step, but he wondered what would happen if and when they decided they didn't want to be lovers anymore.

He didn't want anyone to have the power to hurt him that way. He didn't want to be vulnerable, wear his heart on his sleeve, or any of that crap. He didn't want to surrender his heart to her, but he knew she wouldn't accept anything less.

She would give her heart to him. What if he broke it?

He could muse on the problem all day, but it might help if he focused on what was happening at the moment: He was getting his ass kicked by his teammates at practice. The coach was all over him like white on rice too.

"Taylor, where the hell are you today?" he shouted after Seth missed tackling one of the running backs.

"Sorry," Seth said.

"Do it right next time," the coach called out to him.

The center snapped the ball, Tom Reed dropped back to pass, and Seth busted through the offensive line with a perfectly executed spin move to give Reed a hard shove before he could get the ball off.

"That's what I'm talkin' about," Derrick Collins shouted.

"Much better," the coach told him.

"Thanks."

Reed raised an eyebrow. "Do that on Sunday."

"Fuck, yeah," Seth said.

He managed to focus for the twenty minutes or so left in practice, and he trotted off to the locker room to shower and dress before another of the interminable meetings he had with his coaches during the season. Today's excitement consisted of watching film of Sunday's opponent. He'd have to get some black coffee and something to munch on so he wouldn't fall asleep.

He grabbed the notebook and a pencil he kept in his locker for the film watching. It always helped to chart the offensive plays of opponents on paper; he and his teammates looked for tendencies and obvious "tells," like the dumb-ass QB from Dallas who glanced at the receiver he was about to pass to. Every. Damn. Time. It would be nice to get paid seventy million bucks over five years for fucking up, but no amount of money could compensate Seth for being the butt of league-wide jokes like that guy was.

He found the film room, grabbed the coffee and a bag of sunflower seeds, and sat down. Jillian probably felt better by now, but he wanted to check in with her. Most of his teammates were still in the locker room so he had a couple of minutes. He grabbed his phone out of his pocket, clicked the notifications to "Vibrate," and tapped out a text to her.

HOPE YOU'RE FEELING BETTER. DO YOU NEED ANYTHING?

He hit "Send" and settled back in his chair. Maybe he should call her later. Just to see how she was feeling, of course.

JILLIAN MEANT TO watch a movie, but the soothing alpha waves of a contented, sleeping kitty made her fall asleep too. She awoke to midafternoon sunlight and a chime from her phone. It might be Kari. She scrabbled around in the blankets for it while CB yawned, stretched, and burrowed in again.

Seth had sent her a text. She stared at it for a few minutes. He wanted to know if there was anything she needed. She needed a lot of things, none of which were available in a store. She closed her eyes and let out a groan. CB poked her head out of the blankets and gave her a quizzical look.

"It's okay, kitty. I'm fine."

Her phone rang seconds later. She clicked "Talk" when she noted it was Kari's number.

"How's your day?" her friend said. "Did you have fun last night?"

"Kari, it's awful. I'm at home right now."

"Did you take the day off?"

"No. I had an argument with Seth this morning and called in sick."

"Are you really sick?"

"My heart's broken. It's not contagious."

"Marcus is taking a nap, and his daddy is home today. I'll be over as soon as I can put my shoes on," Kari said. "See you in a few minutes."

Jillian scrambled out of bed, still clutching her phone. She knew she needed to answer Seth's text, or he'd show up at her front door.

I'M FINE. THANKS FOR ASKING, she texted him. "Butthead," she said aloud.

SETH FROWNED AT his phone screen. One of the things he'd learned from multiple women over the years was that the word "fine" meant the woman in question was anything but. The defensive coordinator was giving everyone a fifteen-minute break to hit the toilet and stretch their legs before more film study. He got up from his chair and wandered into the corridor.

Drew McCoy was leaning against the wall and scrolling through the messages on his phone. "What's up, Taylor?"

"Not a lot."

Drew glanced over at him. "John's assistant, Jillian, is out sick today. Her e-mail is set to a vacation message. Wasn't she at the after-party last night?"

"Yeah. I don't know what's wrong." Seth pretended great interest in his phone's screen.

"Wasn't she with you?"

Seth gave him a quick head shake and shrugged one shoulder. "She drove me home."

Drew narrowed his eyes a bit. "'Drove you home'? That's interesting."

"I was shit-faced."

"No, you weren't. You had a grand total of two beers. What the hell is going on between you and Jillian anyway?"

"Were you keeping track of my alcohol consumption last night? That's fuckin' weird, McCoy."

"No, it's not. My wife pointed out to me that she'd seen you drink two beers in almost three hours, but you had to be led out by Jillian." Drew locked his eyes on Seth's. "Maybe I should get Collins over here and ask you some more questions."

"Why is any of this your business?"

Drew McCoy straightened to his full height and slid his phone back into his pocket. "Are you screwing around with her, or do you care about her?"

"We're friends. That's it."

Drew shook his head. "Then you're a fool." He walked away from Seth and headed into the film room again.

Seth made a pit stop and went back to the film room. There was one more phone call he should probably make before they all started up again, but he needed a little privacy to do so. He really didn't need to discuss this kind of shit in front of twenty-three teammates.

The twenty-three teammates were facing the doorway when he walked through it.

"McCoy says you're not dating Jillian."

"She's a nice lady," one of the rookies chimed in. "I'd sure like to take her out."

"High school girls are more your speed, rook. Shut up and let us handle this," Derrick Collins snapped.

The four members of the Sharks' feared secondary moved closer to Seth.

"You spend all your free time with her these days, according to McCoy and Collins," Terrell said. "Shit or get off the pot, man. It's not fair to her."

"What the hell?" Seth said. "Why is this any of your business at all?"

Kade Harrison's voice rang out from the front of the room. "I'm asking her out again the next time I see her. She'll go with me, dickhead."

"No, she won't," Seth said as he lunged at Kade. Four guys held him back as he tried to get anywhere near Kade.

"Aww, fuck," Derrick said as he tried to sit Seth down in a chair. "Calm down, Taylor. And hey, Harrison, you're a real asshole. You know that?"

Kade Harrison raised his eyebrows and grinned at the men still struggling to keep Seth away from him. "That's right. But I have the balls to go after what I want."

"You don't want her," Jasha snapped. "You flirt with her because it pisses Taylor off."

"She'll want me, though. Funny how that works," Kade taunted.

The noise level in the room went up exponentially as every other guy there told Harrison exactly what they thought of him. The defensive coordinator came through the doorway at a run. "Harrison. Taylor. Out in the hallway. *Now.*"

Twenty minutes later, Kade Harrison had been sent home for the day. He was probably getting benched on Sunday too. Seth was watching film again. He glanced down at the clock on his phone. A couple more hours of this, and he could go home for the evening.

Everything would look better after he got some sleep.

## Chapter Seventeen

AFTER AN AFTERNOON full of girl power and wine with her best friend yesterday—she was sure the neighbors enjoyed their dancing around her living room to "Shake It Off" and various other "he sucks" anthems—Jillian awoke the next morning to a wildly pouncing kitten and a stress headache. She knew she had to get her ass out of bed and get to the office. She had so much work to do today that Seth would be the last thing on her mind. She flopped back into the pillows with another groan.

"You don't have to take that from him," Kari had told her yesterday. "If he can't see all the wonderful things about you that I see, he's not worth your tears. There are other guys too. Go in there with your head held high and pretend he doesn't exist."

"That's easier said than done," Jillian said.

He'd said they were friends. Even if she was currently pissed off at him, she didn't know how to deal with the friend part. She couldn't stand to believe that maybe that had been a lie too. She couldn't imagine her life without him at all, at least right now.

Jillian walked into the Sharks' training facility on shaky legs an hour and a half after forcing herself out of bed. The guys weren't scheduled to practice until this afternoon. The building was quiet as a result. She sank into her desk chair.

If she'd felt sick to her stomach over the argument she'd had with Seth yesterday, it was even worse today, and she'd pulled over twice on the way to the office to race for a ladies room. It was time to confess: She needed to tell John the truth. She and Seth were involved with each other, she'd broken his rule, and she'd better accept the consequences. She'd brought one of her cloth grocery bags to pack the few personal effects in her desk before she asked for a few minutes of his time.

Sharks security would search the bag before she was allowed to slink away with her tail between her legs. They'd enjoy cataloging the Sharks coffee mug; a little framed photo of Kari's baby, Marcus; a small box of tampons; and a container of breath mints, she was sure.

John didn't tolerate employees who lied to him. Anyone stupid enough to do so was fired on the spot. He'd warned her several times not to get romantically involved with the players. It was time for her to come clean, and she was pretty sure she wasn't leaving his office with a job. She logged on to her desktop and read some e-mail while she waited for John to arrive. Well, she tried to read some e-mail. She kept reading the same sentence over and over. She couldn't concentrate.

John breezed through the double doors into the building ten minutes later, and Jillian got up from her chair to walk into his office. She'd seen pictures of newborn colts trying to stand up and walk. She had a lot in common with one of them right now. Hopefully, she wouldn't collapse into a heap or barf on John's office floor.

"Jillian, how are you feeling today?"

"I'm okay," she said. She really wasn't, but she needed to talk to him.

"I have some things I'd like you to do this morning," he said.

"I need to talk to you first," she blurted out.

He glanced up from the tablet he was working on. "You're pretty pale. Maybe you should sit down," he said.

She shook her head. "I don't know how to tell you this, so maybe I should just say it." God, she wished she was anywhere else in the world right now.

He sat back in his chair and stared at her for a minute. "Are you giving me your two weeks' notice?"

"No," she said.

"You're moving to Australia?"

"No."

"Maternity leave?" He smiled at her.

She shook her head. She appreciated his lightheartedness, but right now, it was all she could do to not cry—on top of the wanting to vomit and praying she could make it to a bathroom in time.

"Sit down," he said. "Whatever it is, we can fix it."

"That's the problem," she said. "I don't think this can be fixed."

"What happened?"

"Remember when you told me you'd fire me if I got romantically involved with one of the players?"

"Yes, I do," he said. He leaned forward in his chair, rested his elbows on the desk, and steepled his fingers.

She sank into the chair in front of his desk before her legs decided they couldn't hold her up any more. "I have been seeing Seth Taylor. I didn't mean to get involved with him. We were just friends. But we've been spending more and more time together, and he kissed me, and I..." She heaved a long sigh. "We're involved. And I'll have my resignation on your desk as quickly as I can write it." She got to her feet; she was still shaking like a leaf in a strong wind. She reached out her hand to him. "Thank you for the opportunity. I'm sorry that it didn't work out."

He didn't shake her hand.

"I think we'd better talk about this. Do you understand why I made that rule?" He nodded at the chair in front of his desk again, and Jillian sat down once more.

"Your assistant getting involved with a player interferes with her job," Jillian answered.

"I've lost three assistants in the past three years. Two of them left after dating players and the relationships ended badly. The other assistant got married and got pregnant shortly after the wedding." He shook his head. "I'm tired of training and retraining new assistants. I had hoped you might be different."

His displeasure made her feel even worse.

"I'm sorry I disappointed you."

"Jillian, your private life is your own, but I have to tell you right now: I thought you were smarter than this. The vast majority of these guys aren't in it for the long haul. They want someone temporary. They tire of whoever it is they're with, and they find someone new. I don't think that Seth is unique." He let out a sigh. "Do you realize, for instance, that the divorce rate among NFL players is higher than the national average?"

"He hasn't asked me to marry him." She bowed her head. She couldn't stand the disappointed look on John's face. It would have been easier if he'd told her to pack her things and get out.

"Doesn't matter. You're an attractive young woman, Jillian, and you have a lot to offer any man, but you want a future and a family. I don't think he can give that to you. Please choose someone else." He folded his arms across his chest. "Find a software engineer. A doctor. An attorney. A man who wants a family. Not Seth."

Jillian got to her feet. "I've packed my things, so I can be out of here in ten minutes or so. Again, thank you for the opportunity." She gave him a stiff nod, turned, and put her hand on the doorknob.

"I'm not firing you, Jillian."

"Excuse me?" She turned around to stare at him.

"I can't afford the time it will take to interview for your replacement right now. You can stay, but I am letting you know that if your relationship interferes with your work, I will not only fire you, but you will not get a reference." He folded his arms across his chest. "If you want to see him, go ahead, but I'm not happy about it."

She gave him another nod.

"Vivian has the notes from the 5K planning meeting yesterday. I'd like to see what progress you've made on the projects I gave you." He reached out to grab the receiver of his desk phone. "I'd also like you to start the arrangements for the poker game I talked to you about last week."

Jillian opened his office door and walked numbly back to her desk.

*Chapter Eighteen*

JILLIAN MANAGED TO get through the next several hours at the office by delving into her full in-box. She didn't want to think about John's words; they hurt too much. She had told him the truth. She'd expected to be upbraided as a result, especially since John had warned her repeatedly that there would be consequences to her actions.

She'd lived in a house with foster parents, but she'd never really had a dad. John had taken a somewhat fatherly interest in her since she'd been working for the Sharks. She'd worked hard to win his approval. He'd responded by advising her on things like the safest funds to invest her 401(k), or passing on the name of the mechanic who worked on his cars when she needed work done on her Honda Civic.

She understood that John was angry with her. She deserved his anger, but it felt like he'd pulled the rug out from under her this morning. She was embarrassed and humiliated. She tried not to dwell on it as she threw herself into the multiple projects that needed to be completed before she could go home for the weekend.

John had registered his disapproval with her, but he'd made it personal even though he'd told her a thousand times before, "It's not personal; it's business." Jillian loved her job, but she didn't want another encounter with her boss like this morning's. She understood that she could have avoided the whole thing by staying away from Seth in the first place. She'd offered to resign. John didn't accept her resignation. She wondered how she could redeem herself in his eyes besides working hard and rebuilding his trust in her, one day at a time.

SETH WALKED THROUGH the administrative area of the Sharks' offices on his way to the locker room. He glanced over at Jillian's desk. He wanted to talk with her, but now wasn't the best time. They needed privacy. He needed to tell her how he felt.

Jillian looked pale and upset. She held her desk phone receiver to her ear as she scribbled notes on a pad; she didn't glance up as he walked by as she usually did. He shoved the door to the locker room open with one hand and grabbed for his phone with the other.

JOHN LEFT THE office at four o'clock that afternoon to meet up with some colleagues for a drink. He gave Jillian a nod and said, "I'm out for the rest of the day. I'll see you on Sunday at the stadium."

"I'll be there," she said. "Have a nice evening."

"You too." He didn't smile.

She blinked back more tears as he walked away. She could go home in an hour. She was planning on going for a walk after work, but she really needed some chocolate. Maybe she should buy a candy bar on the way home. She was musing on which type of candy bar she wanted most when Amy Hamilton Stephens walked in with a gorgeous bouquet of Casablanca lilies, peach roses, and snapdragons.

"Hey, Jillian." Amy crossed to her desk and held out the bouquet of flowers. "These are for you."

"Excuse me?"

"Happy Friday," Amy said and dropped into the chair next to Jillian's desk. "I told my delivery guy I'd bring these on my way home."

"It's nice to see you, Amy." She stared at the gorgeous flowers. "Who sent these?"

"Can't tell you. Customer/florist confidentiality, you know." Amy gave her a grin.

Jillian grabbed the small white envelope out of the arrangement, tore it open, and read, *Buttercup, let's stay out late on a school night.*

"Well?" Amy said.

She jammed the card back into the envelope, stuck it into her pants pocket, and glanced over at Amy. "Did Matt ever do anything that really hurt your feelings when you first met?"

"Of course he did. He's not perfect. I'm not, either. I accepted his apology, and he's accepted more than one of mine too." She put her elbow on Jillian's desk and rested her chin in one hand. "I'm pretty sure the anonymous flower-sender wants to tell you exactly what a dumb-ass he is, how sorry he is, and how much he wishes you'd forgive him."

"I'll consider it. Maybe." Jillian sniffed her bouquet. "He does have nice taste in flowers."

Amy gave her an impish grin. "Hey, Emily's home next week for a few days. We still want to have lunch with you. We can meet you here, if that works."

"I would love that. Why don't you both pick a day that works best for you, and let me know? There's a really great lunch place about a mile away."

"I'll ask my sis and get back to you."

Amy's phone chimed. She grabbed it out of her pocket, looked at the screen, and raised an eyebrow.

"Is something wrong?" Jillian said.

"My husband just texted me that our kids are staying with his mom tonight and he's got plans for us. He also sent a selfie. I gotta go."

"A selfie?"

"Oh, hell yes," Amy said. She jumped out of the chair and hugged Jillian good-bye. It was somewhat amazing to see how fast a pregnant woman could move. "I'll see you next week."

Jillian laughed as Amy ran through the lobby to the parking lot. She heard Amy's car roaring away moments later. Maybe someday she'd have a husband she'd drop everything to spend time with too.

An hour or so later, Jillian picked up her bouquet, grabbed her purse, and headed out for the evening.

Even more than a candy bar, she wanted a quiet evening at home. Maybe she'd read or play with CB. She really needed to rest and recharge, and she was still thinking about John's comments to her earlier.

Maybe she should talk the whole thing over with Kari tomorrow. It was always good to get another perspective. She'd have plenty of time to think about the day while she drove home; traffic in the Seattle area any time after three PM on a Friday was a nightmare. She could figure out a solution while she sat in stopped traffic on 405, breathing auto exhaust and watching people in other cars pretend they weren't using their smartphones while driving. She could always pull off at the next exit and get some coffee or something.

Mostly, she wanted to get home, put the flowers Seth had sent her on her kitchen counter to enjoy, and not think about anything else work-related for the rest of the evening.

After employing a patchwork of freeway/surface streets/lesser-known shortcuts, Jillian pulled up in front of her apartment an hour later. CB pounced as Jillian let herself into the apartment.

"Okay, kitty, okay. Let me get your dinner," Jillian said.

CB greeted this with a *prrt* and wound around her ankles. She fed the kitty, changed into sweats and a T-shirt, and threw her dirty clothes into the washing machine before grabbing out a clean load from the dryer. She pulled up a channel called *Healing Music* on Pandora as she considered what was in the freezer for dinner.

Maybe she should put her clothes back on and get something that looked a little more appetizing for dinner. It would be good for her to get out a little and quit dwelling on her problems. She had just gotten up off the couch to walk into her room when she heard a knock at the front door.

"Who is it?" she called out.

She hadn't flipped the lock when she came home, and Seth strolled through the front door of her apartment like he owned the place. Her stomach dropped away as she stared at him.

"It's me," he said. His eyes strayed to the gorgeous bouquet he'd sent.

"What are you doing here?" she said.

"I was in the neighborhood." He crossed to the living room couch, sat down, and rested one of his ankles on his knee as he shoved a pile of clean laundry away with one hand. "You must have gotten over what you had yesterday, Buttercup. I saw you at the office earlier."

"That's a ridiculous nickname. Why do you call me that?"

Of course he wouldn't call her "honey," "baby," "sweetheart," or any other typical endearment. It wasn't his style. His lips curved into a smile as he glanced up at her. He was drumming his fingertips against the back of the couch. His expression was casual, but his eyes never left hers.

She grabbed the stack of her freshly folded underwear off of the coffee table. She wondered if she could stash the underwear in a kitchen drawer without his noticing.

She felt a little weird that he'd now seen the silky, pretty things she'd treated herself to.

"I think it fits you." He glanced over at her laptop. "What are you listening to?"

"Music without a beat," she said. She should thank him for the flowers. He was probably thirsty after sitting on the freeway too. "Would you like something to drink? I have filtered water, milk, juice, beer—"

He cut her off. "I see the casual mystery guy isn't around."

"No, he's not." She took a deep breath. "Why would you care?"

Seth got to his feet, crossed the room, and stopped inches from her. "I care a lot."

She opened her mouth, reconsidered what she was about to say, and shut her mouth again. She should say that she was sorry for overreacting. She should tell him she was going to save the little florist card he'd sent for the rest of her life. She should do a lot of things, but right now, all she could do was stare at him.

He sent one hand through his hair. He seemed to make a decision as he stared at her. He reached out for her hand. The stack of underwear she held fell to the carpet.

"I came over here because I have something to tell you. I…I didn't tell you the truth the other day, and I'm sorry. I wanted to kiss you. I've wanted to kiss you for a long time now, and I was too chicken to say so." He reached out to cup her cheek in his hand. "I can't stop thinking about you. I've tried. I dream about you at night. I want to be wherever you are, all the time. You said you wanted to be friends, but I don't want to be just friends anymore. I want you. I hope you want me too."

She was breathless. Her heart was pounding. She couldn't have formed words if her life depended on it. He moved a bit closer to her. She didn't move away. She breathed in the woodsy scent of the soap he liked and felt the heat of his body against hers and the big, roughened hand that was gentle on her cheek.

"I know there's no other guy in your life. If there was, he would have arrived on the scene a long time ago." He stroked her hair. "If you're with someone else, if we're 'just friends,' I can't do this," he said. He pulled her against him with a quick movement tipped her chin up, and his mouth came down on hers. She reached out to grab a handful of the soft cotton of his shirt. She hung on, and he held her.

He lifted his head enough to murmur, "I can't do this, either." His tongue slid over her lower lip, and she tasted the water he must have been drinking before he walked into her apartment. Their mouths clung and shaped to each other. Her arms snaked around his neck. She slid her fingertips under the neck of his T-shirt to feel the smoothness of his skin. He pushed her T-shirt up, and one hand moved to cup her bare breast. She let out a moan as he tickled her nipple with his thumb.

"Imagine what else I can't do." The warmth of his breath brushed her ear. She felt the scratchiness of his cheek against her own. He nibbled on her earlobe. "I want it all, Jill. And I want you."

"I want you too." Her voice shook. She leaned her forehead against his shoulder.

He continued a gentle back-and-forth motion with his thumb on her nipple, which pebbled under his touch. Her knees were getting weak. She listened to his heartbeat as her knees turned to jelly and she leaned against his chest, feeling the warmth of his skin through his T-shirt, feeling the muscles in his shoulders bunch and flex as he held her a little tighter. He was hard against her belly. She moved closer.

Jillian thought she was safe from all the feelings she had for him, as long as Seth thought she wasn't available. She could spend time with him, talk with him, and laugh. There was no pressure. She could be herself, and he could be himself. There was no fear of rejection or the awkwardness of an unwanted confession. Of course, it was all going to be different now, and how would that be for both of them? She couldn't think about it right now, especially since he'd just streaked the tip of his tongue around the shell of her ear.

His voice was a dark, sensual rumble, and his mouth traced her collarbone. "Are you still mad at me?"

She shook her head. "Are you still mad at me?" she said.

"No." He grinned at her. "What should we do now?"

"We could kiss some more," she suggested. She felt his chest move with silent laughter.

"Oh, we could. Or I could pull your clothes off and do every last thing to you I've dreamed about doing since we met." He let that sink in for a few seconds. "The blinds are still open, aren't they?" His voice dropped. "I'm sure your neighbors will enjoy it."

"You really dreamed about me?"

"Almost every night." He pulled in a breath. "I can't wait to see if reality is better than my dreams."

She stood on her tiptoes and leaned her forehead against his. "Come to bed with me," she whispered.

He bent to scoop her up in his arms. A few long strides later, he deposited her on her bed and followed her down. She reached out for him. She buried her nose in his neck and took a deep breath. She couldn't believe this was happening, but she was going to enjoy every second.

"Jill."

"Hm?"

She was in the midst of an exploration of an evidently sensitive patch of skin on the underside of his jaw with her tongue. She felt him shudder. She shoved the T-shirt he wore up so she could run her fingers over his smooth chest, and he captured her mouth with his own. Her hands moved over him, and he stripped off the T-shirt she wore. He dropped it over the side of the bed.

"Now we're talkin'," he muttered. He sucked Jillian's nipple into his mouth, and she arched to meet him. He was pulling at her sweat pants with one hand and stripped them off. She tried to wriggle out of her underwear, but he put one big hand in the middle of her belly. "That's my job."

He pulled them off with his teeth. Slowly. By the time he tossed the black silk panties over the edge of her bed, she was shaking, her breath coming in short, hard pants, and she melted into the bedding. The only thing she was wearing right now was navy blue toenail polish. Seth got to his feet.

"Where are you going?" She was not going to beg. Well, maybe she might. Where the hell was he going?

"I'll be right with you."

He pulled off the T-shirt she'd bunched around his neck with one quick motion and shoved both jeans and boxer briefs to the floor with another. He straightened up, and Jillian lost whatever moisture was left in her mouth. Oh, God. He was beautiful. He was tan. He was muscular. She had seen him in a swimsuit, but it was no comparison to right now. He had hair in all the nicest places—the silky, dark hair that covered his arms and legs, and the vertical line of hair that typically vanished under the waistband of his jeans. She couldn't stop looking at his six-pack. Well, she couldn't stop looking at it until her eyes drifted further down, and she got a good look at a long, thick, aroused penis.

He was flawless, and she was lying here (on display, due to the bathroom light) with every lump, bump, and inches of loose skin on display. Reality had just intruded. No matter how badly she wanted him, she wasn't going to let him see her naked. She reached over the side of the bed and pulled the blankets over herself.

Much stronger hands pried them out of hers, and he landed next to her on the bed. His voice was gentle. "You don't need those, Jill."

"I...oh, maybe we shouldn't be doing this."

She tried to yank the blankets out of his hands again. She couldn't. She rolled off the side of the bed and got to her feet. She was digging around for the robe she knew lay at the foot of her bed. In the meantime, the gorgeous, naked, amazingly aroused Seth pulled the blankets off the bed and threw them to the floor.

"There. That takes care of that."

She grabbed for herself. He was around the bed in a flash.

"Don't look," she begged. "You...you're perfect. I'm...I'm not. I...we...this shouldn't be happening. I don't know what I'm doing. I—"

"Shhh," he comforted her. He wrapped his arms around her again and laid his cheek against hers. "It's okay. So, you're a little nervous. I'm nervous too." He stroked her hair. "Just relax. Everything's going to be fine."

"You are not nervous. Seriously? How can you say that?"

"Oh, yes, I am." His breath brushed her ear. "What if I disappoint you?" His lips grazed her temple. "Let's face it. I have to play in front of seventy thousand people all the time, but they don't see me naked. That's a little intimidating." He rubbed her lower back with one big hand. "See? Just relax," he encouraged. "If you really want to, though, we'll stop."

"I..."

She fell silent. She knew he was teasing her, but she couldn't resist his tender touches and the way he held her. He was still rubbing her back, still stroking her hair, still murmuring into her ear.

"May I kiss you?"

How could she refuse, when he asked so nicely? She lifted her face, and he did the rest. His mouth moved over hers, slowly and gently. She slid her tongue against his, loving the way he tasted. She moaned a little. She heard him once more. "May I kiss you again?"

"Yes."

A few minutes later, she'd melted all over him. He lay her down again, and she whispered to him, "Will you kiss me some more?"

"Of course." He stroked her face. "If you want to stop, just tell me."

She closed her eyes. She took a breath. She looked up at him once more, into his warm brown eyes and his encouraging smile. "I don't want to stop."

## Chapter Nineteen

SETH WANTED TO kiss and lick every inch of her body. He wanted to bury himself inside her, make her scream, hear her beg him for more. He wanted to do every last thing with her that he'd seen in the countless erotic dreams he'd had about her. He knew that the sexy, confident Jillian was still there. She was hiding a little, and the best thing he could do for both of them was to take it slow. His dick, however, hadn't gotten that memo.

She still felt shy about her body. He couldn't figure out why. She was beautiful. Maybe he should show her and tell her why he felt the way he did about her.

He touched her, leisurely and languidly. He moved over her while he paid attention to parts of her body he knew would drive her out of her mind—he kissed her long, slender neck, tickled the skin behind her knees, sucked her breasts, drew a slow finger up the inside of her thigh. Close, but not quite. She squirmed under his hand. She let out a moan.

The whole time he touched her, he talked to her.

"Do you know what I'm going to do to you, Jill?"

"What?" she groaned. She was running her hands over his back, trying to urge him closer. *Not so fast*, he thought.

"I'm going to keep at this until you come, just touching and kissing. It'll happen. Then, I'll find a condom—"

"I have some," she breathlessly interrupted.

"I thought you might. Then, we're going to put one on, and I'm going to slide inside. I'll go slow. This will take hours." He heard a quick gasp. "Guess what'll happen then? You're going to come again. I'm going to come. We'll have a great time. After that, I'll have to start all over again." He let her think about that one for a minute. Her breathing accelerated. "You know what the best part of being a pro athlete is?"

Her voice sounded a little strangled. "What's that?"

"Endurance."

As he promised her, he took things slowly. She tried to rush him a few times. He grinned at her, shook his head, and told her, "Well, now I'll have to start over, won't I?"

"But...but...you can't. Oh, God!"

"Listen. Only one of us can be in charge right now, and that's me. You'll get your chance later. Maybe."

All he heard was another moan. God, he was having fun.

Jillian was funny. Slowly but surely, she forgot whatever she'd been nervous about. After all, he paid attention to the parts she probably thought were ugly: The newly loose skin on her belly and thighs; the breasts she thought were too big but he believed were a feast made especially for him. Finally, he gave her what they both wanted. He moved his fingers slowly through the wetness between her legs, tickling and lingering over the little nub of flesh that made her buck and moan. She moved against his hand, eyes tightly closed.

"Look at me," he whispered to her. "Open your eyes." She did. Seconds later, she arched, she let out a shriek, and he felt her entire body convulse around his hand.

Jillian was quiet for a few moments, and then she rolled over him to reach inside the bedside table. She pulled out a box of condoms. She ripped the cardboard in her hurry to get one out and threw everything but one foil-covered packet onto the floor. He had to laugh at the sweetly determined look on her face. She was naked, she was adorable, and she was all his.

She tore the foil packet open, pulled out a disc of latex, and proceeded to roll it over him. Well, there was some teasing, and by the time the job was done, all he wanted to do was flip her on her back, move between her legs, and dive inside. She had other plans. She pushed on his chest until he was flat on his back, straddled him, and gave him the same temptress smile he'd seen so many nights in his dreams.

"My turn," she said.

JILLIAN AWOKE SHORTLY after dawn. She heard birds singing, but there was no traffic noise outside. Seth was fast asleep next to her. He must have picked the blankets up off the floor sometime during the night and spread them over the bed.

They'd worn each other out. He wasn't kidding about that endurance stuff. Once she got over her shyness of his seeing her naked, she was an enthusiastic participant, and he taught her a few things she'd never tried before. Just thinking about a couple of them made desire, heavy and hot, pool in her abdomen. She felt the heat of a blush rising in her cheeks too.

One of his arms was still around her waist. She'd cuddled up to his warmth all night. She carefully dislodged his arm and rolled out of bed.

Jillian took care of the morning business, slid into a cotton nightshirt hanging on the back of the bathroom door, and fed CB before going back to bed. The kitten was highly disgusted that she'd been kept out of the bedroom by a shut door most of the night. Hopefully, she'd let Seth sleep for a little while longer before he had to go to the practice facility.

Seth opened one eye as she got back into bed. "Still tired."

"I know. I had to get up for a few minutes."

"A little more sleep," he said.

He spooned around her. Before she knew what was happening, the nightshirt was being pulled up over her head and off. He tossed it on the floor. "What are you doing?"

"Don't wear that thing again," he muttered into her ear. "I'll keep you warm." He wrapped one arm around her waist again and cupped her breast in his hand.

## Chapter Twenty

SETH LEFT JILLIAN'S apartment on the run a few hours later. They'd both overslept. There was no time to talk about what happened the night before or what it meant for them. He was due at the practice facility for a walk-through and a flight to San Francisco for tomorrow's game. She was due at Treehouse for a volunteer shift.

"At least my bag's in the trunk of the Escalade," he'd said. He reached out to pull her close. "Why don't we meet up tomorrow night when I get back?"

"I'd love that," she said. "Have a good flight and a great game."

"I will," he said. His mouth touched hers, sweet and tender. He was running late, but he kissed her like he had all the time in the world. He came back for more as she wrapped her arms around his neck. "I'll text you when I get to San Francisco. I'm going to miss you."

"I'll miss you too. Hurry back," she'd said.

She watched his Escalade vanish around the corner of the apartment house parking lot. Her phone rang a minute or so later. Maybe he'd forgotten something. She grabbed it off of the kitchen counter and hit "Talk."

"Hey, Jillian, it's Chip from Treehouse," the caller said. "You haven't left your place yet, have you?"

"Nope. I...I had a guest. I'll be there as soon as I can."

"Listen. Your volunteer group canceled again."

"I'm sorry," she said. "Isn't this the second time now?"

"I know there are lots of kids doing the mandatory testing this week at school." He let out a breath. "Things around here aren't too bad today. Why don't you take the afternoon off? We'll see you next Saturday."

"Are you sure?"

"Yeah. We love having you here, but it's always good to get a little break," he said. "Go do something nice for yourself."

She hung up after the usual "have a great day" stuff that characterized every phone call made between two people in the Seattle area, and she sank onto her couch. She couldn't remember the last time she'd had a day to herself. Maybe she should take advantage of it. The possibilities were endless: She could get a pedicure. She had a gift certificate for a massage. She could go swimming. Maybe she should skip all of it, curl up on the couch, and read to her heart's content. It all sounded terrific, but first of all, maybe she should get dressed.

CB was dive-bombing something in the rumpled sheets of her bed as she walked into her room. Her room (and the sheets) still smelled like Seth and the musky, clean-sweat smell of sex.

"What are you doing?" she asked CB, who redoubled her efforts to shred whatever it was she'd managed to get her paws on. Jillian's hand closed over the underwear Seth had taken off her last night with his teeth. She pulled it away from the kitten, which seemed to think this was an exciting new game. "Those are *my* underwear, you naughty kitten."

Jillian tossed herself down next to the kitten in the crumpled bedclothes. CB purred and rubbed against her. She let out a sigh. "Yeah, I can still smell him too."

She should be ecstatic. She and Seth had spent the night together, they'd both enjoyed it, and their relationship had officially moved from "just friends" to what she hoped would be a lot more. Kari would probably tell her she was nuts to worry and to just enjoy herself, but she couldn't stop thinking about what John had said to her about pro football players and the fact many had achieved every other success in life but a happy home and a family.

Seth had told her before he'd spent almost two years with Kim because he was used to the way things were. Even if he hadn't been happy with the relationship, it was too easy to continue in it instead of finding someone that he'd be happier with. She knew she wasn't remotely like his ex by any stretch of the imagination, but the insecurities she still dealt with reared their heads in an ugly fashion. Would he get tired of her too, when the newness of whatever their relationship was wore off? Would he continue on because he didn't want the tears and upheaval of a breakup, while letting her believe everything was fine between them?

Instead of basking in the afterglow, her thoughts snowballed into something massive and crushing.

They'd started off so slowly, but their friendship blossomed into something more when they shared their secrets with each other. She'd finally summoned the courage to tell him about the fact she'd grown up in a foster home a few days after she talked about her past with Emily McKenna and Amy Stephens. Her heart soared when he listened carefully and asked thoughtful questions. She wasn't looking for pity. She hoped for understanding, and maybe a little patience. Her life was full of things she'd had to rise above and overcome, and he encouraged her.

As Amy Stephens had said to Jillian, Seth wasn't perfect, either, and she knew she wasn't. Her insecurities were so hard to overcome. She worked at self-confidence one day at a time. She still felt shy about her body, even if Seth had told her that every inch of her was beautiful, alluring, and sexy to him as he covered her with kisses.

He'd always dated tall, willowy brunettes, according to the pictures she'd seen of his exes online. She was a short, curvy blonde. Would he get tired of her and decide he wanted someone else instead?

She covered her face with her hands and let out a groan. "Stop it," she said to herself. "You're worrying for nothing." The kitten rubbed against her. "Maybe I should call Kari. She'll kick me in the butt and set me straight."

She didn't want to admit it to herself, but maybe she was a lot more old-fashioned than she'd thought. She and

Seth hadn't agreed to be exclusive. They'd never used the "L" word. She knew she loved him. Her heart would break into a million pieces if he didn't love her in return. It wasn't necessary to love another person to have sheet-scorching sex, however. And again, she was reminded of John's comments.

She wanted a husband and a family. She wanted someone who loved her the way she was too. What did Seth want? And did she have the courage to ask him about it?

Truthfully, now that she'd gotten what she wanted, she was scared. Maybe the best thing to do was to protect her heart, slow things down a little, and make double-sure she'd chosen well.

THE NEXT DAY, the Sharks won. Seth always enjoyed a decisive win, but beating their arch-rivals, the Miners, was even sweeter. He piled into the locker room with his hugging, fist-pumping, and cheering teammates for their post-game celebration. The guys formed a large circle. Their coach stepped into the center.

"Men. Great job today." He waited for the shouts, back-slapping, and cheering to die down somewhat. "The path to the playoffs is clear. Nobody's getting in our way but us." He held up a game-used football. "And today's game ball goes to the defense. We haven't held an opponent scoreless in five seasons. Even better, you also held them to less than a hundred yards of offense. Your teamwork and dedication showed. And I appreciate it."

There was more chanting and cheering.

"So, let's go home. Next week we'll play in front of our fans. And next week, we're going to win again. Because that's what we do."

Seth showered, dressed, negotiated the post-game press scrum outside of the locker room door, and headed toward the waiting team bus. He wanted the comforts of home. Right now, he wanted Jillian even more.

He'd called her a couple of times today. She didn't answer her phone, but he got a succinct CONGRATU-LATIONS! GREAT GAME! text in response. The Sharks would be at the airport in an hour, and he'd be at her apartment two hours later. He parked his ass in a bus seat and pulled on his headphones while he waited for his teammates.

He must have fallen asleep for a few minutes. He opened his eyes to a commotion. Zach Anderson was shaking his shoulder.

"Hey, sleepyhead, wake up. We're going back to the hotel overnight."

"What? Why?"

"The team plane needs repairs, and they need a part flown in to fix it. We're leaving for Seattle in the morning. They *think*. I'd better call Cameron so she doesn't worry." He whipped the cell out of his jacket pocket and turned away from Seth.

Seth grabbed for his own phone to text Jillian. WE'RE STAYING OVERNIGHT HERE. I'LL CALL YOU IN THE MORNING.

He tried to call Jillian several times over the next day and a half. It turned out the part needed by the mechanics working on the team's plane must have been brought in by donkey cart from New Jersey or something. The team was still stranded in San Francisco late on Monday night. Even worse than being stuck, she wasn't calling him back. He knew she was okay; he'd called her desk phone at the office and she answered.

"Seth, I'm so sorry, but I can't talk with you right now," she'd said. He thought he heard strain in her voice. "The phones are crazy, and Vivian's out today."

"Got it," he said. "If our plane isn't ready by late this afternoon, some of the guys are flying commercial to get home."

"It sounds pretty frustrating," she said. "John's line is ringing again. I have to go."

She clicked over to the other call before he could tell her he'd come over to her apartment to talk when he got back. He was climbing the walls in a hotel room, but even more, it was pretty obvious that something was seriously wrong between him and Jillian. She wasn't talking to him, and he couldn't figure out the problem from 750 air miles away.

They'd spent an amazing night together. He wanted her and nobody else. Why was she pulling away from him now?

JILLIAN'S PHONE RANG at eleven fifteen that night. She glanced over at the nightstand. It was Seth. She hit "Talk" and said, "Hello?"

"Listen, Buttercup, we're on our way home. Do you want me to stop by your place when we get there?" He sounded so happy, and it made her heart hurt.

"I have to go to work tomorrow morning. That might not be a great idea."

"Then let's get together tomorrow night for dinner. We should talk about a few things."

"Sure," she said. "I should be able to leave a little after six."

"Got it," he said. "It'll be fun."

"Have a safe trip home."

"Sweet dreams," he said.

"Good night," she whispered and ended the call.

SETH ARRIVED AT the practice facility on Wednesday before six AM for his work week. He hadn't had much sleep last night, but it couldn't be helped. November in Seattle was a challenge. It was still dark. The sunrise wouldn't happen for another two hours. Wispy gray clouds scudded over a midnight-blue sky. The chilly wind off Lake Washington went straight to his bones as he got out of his Escalade. And he couldn't stop thinking about Jillian, who was probably still asleep in a nest of soft, warm blankets at her apartment.

He grabbed the electronic key out of his wallet and swiped it in the card reader that admitted him to the Sharks' locker room. He was here at oh-dark-thirty because he needed to get some lifting and running in before the appointment he'd made with John via text yesterday. It was in his best interest to remain calm and factual during the conversation. Mostly, he'd spent the past two days forcing down his confusion and anger.

Seth finished his lifting and got in a run before he strolled into John's office at a little after seven AM. The meeting he'd asked for two days ago via text wasn't actually until eight AM, but he wanted to say what he had to say and get out before Jillian arrived for work.

Maybe he was taking all of this a little too seriously, but Jillian was pulling away from him. He'd called. She'd barely talked with him. On the flight back he'd finally remembered she'd said something when he was half asleep early Saturday morning about John. About how he wasn't thrilled that Seth and Jillian were romantically involved. Seth couldn't figure out what else was going on with her. He had a few ideas, though. He knew that John's opinion mattered a lot to her, and he'd learned over the past few months that she really needed security. She worried about losing her job or any other situation that could leave her alone and scrambling for the things other people took for granted, like paying the rent or supportive family members.

It pissed him off that John had evidently decided Seth's personal life was his business.

John didn't bother glancing up from his tablet.

"I thought we agreed on eight," he said.

John hadn't had a lot of sleep in the past forty-eight hours. Seth would bet a large amount on the fact that the guys who kept the Sharks' plane in tip-top shape were about to suffer significant consequences, due to the team's being stranded in California until Monday night.

"I have to get checked out by the trainers at eight," Seth said. "I'm here now."

"What do you need, Taylor?"

Seth lowered himself into a chair in front of John's desk and reached back to shove the office door closed. He heard the latch click as it engaged.

"Maybe we should start this conversation by your explaining exactly why you told Jillian she shouldn't be with me."

"I don't know what you're talking about." John must have decided it was a good time to acknowledge there was someone in his office. He stared into Seth's face. "I didn't say that."

"Then what did you say to her? She seemed pretty convinced you told her not to see me. And I don't appreciate it."

"This must be like that old kids' game from the playground—Telephone, wasn't it? One kid whispers something to the kid next to him, it goes around the circle, and by the time it gets back to the original source, it's not the same message." John let out a long breath. "I know that Jillian wants a husband and a family. Maybe not at the moment, but she'd like one in the future. I talked to her a little about the fact that most pro athletes aren't interested in permanent relationships. The divorce rate among NFL players is higher than the national average, for instance. She should know before she gets involved with you that she may never have the things she wants most in life."

Seth's mouth dropped open. "You have no idea what my plans are for her."

"She's a good person. She deserves a man who's in 100 percent, not someone who's going to bolt when he finds someone younger and more beautiful." John narrowed his eyes a bit. "If I had a daughter of my own, I'd want her to be a lot like Jillian. I suppose I'm a little protective of her as a result."

Seth stared at John. What the hell was *this*? And why would John think he'd dump Jillian for anyone else? It was ridiculous.

"She's afraid she's going to lose her job if we're together."

"I told her it didn't matter to me if she got involved with you. I am telling you, though—she wants to get married and have a family. If you don't want those things, get out now before you really hurt her and you have a lot more to worry about from me." John shoved his glasses up on his nose. "Is there another topic you'd like to discuss?"

"I don't like finding out that my boss has such a low opinion of me as a person."

John folded his lips. "Then maybe you shouldn't borrow trouble, Taylor. If she really wanted you, nothing I said to her would make any difference, would it?"

Now it was Seth's turn to stare at John in disbelief. He'd not only insulted Seth, but he'd doubled down on it. He and John weren't best buddies, but Seth had always thought their interactions were cordial and mutually respectful. Evidently, he'd had it all wrong.

Seth stood up from the chair and gave John a nod.

"Thanks for your time, John."

John responded with a grunt.

Seth needed to get to the bottom of all of this, but it was going to have to wait. In the meantime, he was now wondering if he was the one who had been played. Had she decided she wanted to step back, and she was using her job as an excuse? Why would she do that? All she had to do was tell him she'd changed her mind and it wasn't working, which had to be a lie.

Everything seemed to be fine (and hotter than fire between them) last Friday. By Sunday, it was a completely different story, and today, he was left wondering what the hell was going on. It hurt more than anything. The only way to find out what happened was to talk with Jillian.

JILLIAN GLANCED AT the clock later that day. A quarter to six. She already had a lump in her stomach, and she wasn't sure that having this conversation with Seth in a public place was the best decision.

John had been like a bear with a sticker in his paw all day long, but his previous nastiness toward her had mellowed somewhat.

"Hey, Jillian," he called out from his office. "Will you come in here for a minute?"

"Sure," she said. She got up from her desk and walked into his office.

"Shut the door," he said.

She swallowed hard and nudged the door shut with one hand.

He gestured toward the chairs in front of his desk. "Sit down," he said.

"Are you firing me?" she said.

"No. Of course not." He leaned back in his chair. "I have a couple of things to talk with you about, and I'd prefer that they remain between us for the moment."

"Okay." She wasn't sure what to think. John looked exhausted. Nobody must have slept while the team was in San Francisco.

"First of all, I had a meeting with Seth Taylor this morning. I want to reinforce to you again that I told you the things I did last week because I want you to make an informed choice, not because I'm trying to control your love life." He let out a breath. "I think a lot of you, Jillian, as a person and as an employee. You have done a great job for me and for the organization. I know I don't tell you that enough."

"Thank you," she said. He still wasn't smiling, but she felt relief surge through her.

"Having said all of this, I have some information that I am entrusting to you. The paperwork will come across your desk, and you will be cc'd on e-mails over the next few days, so I didn't want this to come as a shock. This information must remain secret until I discuss it with the media at a press conference next week. Also, there will be a change in your status in about a month."

She stared at him in surprise. "I don't know what you are talking about."

He leaned forward in his desk chair. "Remember the poker game I asked you to arrange?"

"Yes."

"We actually ended up playing in Vegas the night before last, which is part of the story. The part that affects you, however, is the following. I am not the controlling owner of the Sharks anymore."

"*What?*" she blurted out. "Did you sell the team?"

"Not exactly." He let out a long breath. "I'm getting older, and I have had health problems. I have been thinking about what to do with the team for a while now. My family members are older too. They're not willing to take on the demands of team ownership. So, let's just say someone else is taking over as a result of the poker game. The team will be under new ownership as soon as we dot the i's and cross the t's. Lawyers are involved," he joked.

"You won't be here every day anymore?"

"No. And that's what I need to discuss with you."

She wrapped her arms around herself. "Does this mean I need to look for another job?"

"Of course not," he said. "Here's what I have for you. You have three choices. It's up to you which one you take."

John explained that she could remain his executive assistant. She wouldn't be working for the Sharks anymore; she'd be working for him at his offices at Carillon Point in Kirkland. The second choice would be working for the new owner of the Sharks.

"He's someone you've met, and I know he would be happy to have an executive assistant who's familiar with what needs to happen around here on a daily basis," John said.

Jillian nodded. She was a little dazed.

"The last choice is one I think you might dump both of us for," he said. "The team is creating a new executive-level job. You'd be responsible for planning and executing the Sharks' charity events year-round. You're perfect for it. You would be working with your own assistant and the PR department, and there's a significant raise involved. If you want this, you'll start the job after my press conference, and the new owner will have to find his own assistant." John grinned at her. "Of course, we're offering full benefits, paid 401(k), four weeks of vacation a year to start, and two free suite tickets for every game." He grabbed a piece of scratch paper off of his desk, wrote something on it, folded it in half, and passed it across his desk to her. "Here's the starting salary. Of course, this is open for negotiation, and there would be a salary bump after ninety days."

Jillian took the piece of paper off his desk, unfolded it, and read the number he'd written. She thought she was seeing things. It was double her current salary and more than she dreamed she'd make a year in her life.

"This is a lot of money."

"Then take it," John said. "You'll be able to buy a house. You'll make enough on your own to be independent."

"I don't know what to say."

"So think about it overnight," he said. "We can talk more in the morning. I want you to remember, though: You'll need to keep everything I've told you secret for at least another two weeks. Got it?"

SETH WATCHED JILLIAN walk out of John's office a few minutes later. She was pale. She also looked as exhausted as he felt. Maybe they should agree to have their conversation another time so everyone could get a good night's sleep first. Then again, he wasn't sure he would sleep until he found out what in the hell was wrong between them.

She opened her desk drawer, shoved a piece of paper into her handbag, and reached to hit the button on her desk phone that sent all calls to voice mail overnight. The slowness of her movements and the fact she still hadn't glanced up at him told him that her mind wasn't anywhere near her job right now. She put both hands down on her desk and hung her head for a few moments.

"Jill?" he said.

She jerked upward like a marionette whose handler was pulling the strings. "Oh. Oh. You're there," she said.

"Yes. I am. Why don't we go and get some dinner?"

"Sure," she said. She gave him a stiff little nod, and he saw the wall go right back up between them.

After a short skirmish over who was driving, Jillian insisted on taking separate cars. He revised his opinion from "something's wrong" to "something is horribly wrong" before she followed him out of the Sharks' parking lot. He'd already asked Owen to make dinner for them at his place; it might be good to have the conversation he'd planned without every other person in a restaurant listening in. Baked ziti; a garden salad; and flatbread brushed with olive oil, sprinkled with herbs, and baked in the oven waited for them, as well as a bottle of wine.

He pulled into his garage. He motioned for Jillian to pull her car in next to his, but she shook her head and parked in his driveway. Dread washed over him like the tide. Unless he was mistaken, he was about to get dumped.

She got out of her car and walked toward him. He drank her in with his eyes. He'd waited days to hold her in his arms again. She stopped a foot or so away as the garage door closed behind them. The normally smiling and effervescent Jillian was anything but, and the lump in his stomach grew.

"Hello," he said.

"Hi there," she said. She looked wary. He couldn't imagine where the sweet Jillian that would run into his arms and hug him with all of her strength had gone.

"May I kiss you?" he said.

She swallowed hard. He held out his arms, and she walked into them. He felt her arms slide around his waist as he tipped her chin up. He rested his cheek against her much softer one.

"Jill, what's wrong? Are you mad at me?"

She was trembling. He heard the telltale catches in her breathing that preceded tears. He felt like someone had swung a wrecking ball into his gut. First the shock, and then the pain.

"Please tell me what I did wrong," he whispered. "I'll do anything to fix it."

"You can't fix it," she said. "We don't want the same things."

"What are you talking about?"

"You never wanted someone like me. You'll get bored, you'll want someone else, and it will break my heart," she said.

He closed his eyes. "I don't want anyone else."

"But you will," she said. "You don't want someone permanent. You want someone you'll be with for a while, and when it doesn't work, you'll move on. You've done it before." Her voice wasn't accusatory or strident. It was sad. "I want someone permanent. I want to fall in love. I want a home and a family. And I'm not sure you're going to want any of those things at any time soon. You might not want them at all. I can't pressure you into it, either. It has to be your choice, or it doesn't work. We're just two people who want different things."

If she'd been nasty or cutting, he would have retaliated. He would survive it, get pissed off, and tell himself it was her goddamn problem. It wasn't her problem. It was his. And he wasn't sure how he was ever going to get over the idea that to love was to expose himself to loss. Again. He'd opened his heart to Jillian, but she saw something everyone else he'd dated and his own family didn't see: He hadn't given his whole self to her. He held back, and he always had. He didn't want to think of what would happen if he was all in and she walked away. It wasn't survivable.

"Jill, I don't want to lose you." He cupped her face in his hands. Her features blurred as tears rose in his eyes.

"I don't want to lose you, either," she said. "But maybe we need to think for a while."

"So we're taking a break."

She nodded.

He rested his forehead against hers.

"A little time-out," she whispered.

"A few days to think," he said. God, he wanted to scream with agony, and he couldn't believe they were having this conversation at all. Having it in a cold, barely finished garage seemed even worse.

"Yes."

His mouth brushed hers, and he tilted his head to kiss her again. He explored her mouth with his tongue. He couldn't bear to think this might be the last time he tasted the sweetness of her mouth, breathed in her soft vanilla scent, or felt the warmth of her body against his, so he wouldn't. Her arms were still loosely clasped around his waist. She didn't squeeze him tight or cuddle into him at all.

"Are you in as much pain as I am right now?" he whispered.

"Yes," she said.

"Then why are we doing this?"

She pulled away from him, reached out to touch the garage door opener, and walked out to her car. She got in and drove away without another word.

## Chapter Twenty-One

SETH WALKED INTO his house a few minutes later on legs that felt like they were made of lead. He'd been through breakups before—even if she'd softened the blow by calling it "taking a break." It hurt for a few days, and then he moved on. He knew this wasn't going to stop hurting any time soon. He wanted to be mad at Jillian; he couldn't. She was right.

He'd pursued her, but he wasn't looking for always. And he should have been, especially with her. He'd been with women who fit the mold of what a pro athlete should be dating—beautiful, accomplished, and desired by many other men. He wasn't happy when he was with them, though. It was expected. They weren't soul mates. They didn't wrap him in their arms and listen while he described the most painful experience of his life. They didn't know him better than he knew himself and care for him anyway.

The lights were on in his kitchen.

"Hey, Owen," he called out.

"I'm here, bro," Owen said. "How are ya?"

Guys shook hands with each other all day long and never divulged what was really going on with them. It was part of being a man, to not show emotion or to exhibit anything but self-confidence bordering on cockiness in every situation. Tonight, he needed a beer. Maybe he'd go sit on the new bench he'd had installed in his backyard for Liam and try to figure out what he should do next.

His little brother would have told him to pull his head out of his ass. He would have told him that he knew the first time he'd met Jillian that there was something about her, something he needed, and he couldn't seem to stay away from her. Liam would have told Seth he was damn lucky to meet a woman who wanted to be his friend as well as his lover, and if she cared for him enough to want to spend her life with him, maybe he should consider himself lucky she'd consider marrying him in the first place. That is, if she did consider it.

"I've been better," he said.

"I heard a car drive away," Owen said. "I thought you left."

"No. Jillian left," he said. He reached out for the refrigerator handle, pulled it open, and grabbed a beer off of the shelf. "Want one?"

"Yeah," Owen said. "The ziti's in the oven, by the way."

It smelled incredible, but right now, Seth wasn't especially hungry.

Seth handed Owen a beer and nodded toward his kitchen table. "Want to sit down?"

"I think I will," Owen said.

The two men drank their beers in silence for a few minutes. Owen leaned forward in his chair and set the bottle down on the table. "Want to talk about it?" he said.

"I know I should say no," Seth said. "I really fucked up."

"We all do sometimes."

"I keep doing it. I don't seem to learn from it."

Owen finished off his bottle, swallowed, and said, "Want one more?"

"Shit, yeah."

"I have trouble learning from my mistakes too, especially with women." Owen let out a long breath. "I think you'll figure it out."

Seth let out a snort.

"Here's something to think about, before we're both drunk off our asses," Owen said. "How badly do you want her back?"

JILLIAN PULLED OFF the freeway a mile or so from her apartment and hit Kari's number on her phone. A cold, torrential rain was falling. It matched her mood.

"Hey, girlfriend," Kari said. "Where are you?"

"Almost to your house," Jillian said.

"You've been crying. What's wrong?"

"I think I just broke up with Seth."

"What? Get over here. And drive carefully. I'll see you in a few minutes. Don't stop at the store. I have plenty of wine and junk food."

"Thank God," Jillian said.

Kari met her at the door with a glass of wine and a hug.

"What happened? Well, let's sit down first. Patrick's in New York for a couple of days. I miss him already." Her friend sighed.

"I'm sorry I keep coming over here and falling apart. You have a life too. Maybe you need a listening ear once in a while," Jillian said.

Kari turned to stare at her. "Get real. You listen to me all the time. Who else could I share the joys of teething with, huh?"

"Sometimes I feel like I dump on you too much." Jillian sipped from her glass of pinot gris. It smelled like heaven in a glass.

"You are so full of crap. Plus, I'd tell you if you were driving me nuts. We've known each other for twenty-five years. It hasn't happened yet." Kari took a sip of her wine. "So, what happened with Seth?"

"We're taking a break. It's all my fault. I fell in love with him, I slept with him, and I shouldn't have taken it all so seriously. If I could just relax and take things as they are, but nooooo. I want a guy who wants a commitment, and I don't think he does. What if he never does?"

"Did you try asking him what he thinks?"

"He doesn't commit to anyone. He stays in the relationship until he's miserable, and they break up. He told me this."

"And this means he's going to dump you too?"

"Don't you think that would happen?"

"No, I don't. You guys were friends for a long time before you got physical. And he was the one who told you he wanted you. Get out of your head for a minute and relax. Plus, maybe you should try asking him what he wants the next time you see each other. He might surprise you. You have to ask, though. You can't read his mind."

Jillian rolled her eyes and took another sip of wine.

"You know I'm right," Kari said.

"Probably," Jillian said.

## *Chapter Twenty-Two*

---

Two weeks later, the line for check-in at the Sharks' season-ticket holders' 5K already stretched down the block at seven AM. Even though runners had been encouraged to pick up their bibs and race T-shirts at a local sporting goods store prior to the 5K, it looked like a lot of people had chosen to wait until the last minute. Jillian glanced up at the leaden skies and hoped the weather guy from the local TV station had told them the truth—it would be chilly, but it wasn't going to rain.

She'd been up since four. She hadn't slept well due to nerves. Even if she was nervous about the details of today's event, however, she loved her new job. She'd started the job after John's surprise press conference a week ago announcing he'd stepped down as majority owner of the Sharks.

Things were going really well for her. Except one: she was still reliving what happened with Seth two weeks ago and wondering if she expected too much from him. If she was really his friend, shouldn't she focus on that first? Maybe they should try talking about their differences. Plus, she missed him more than she ever dreamed. She longed to hear his voice or see his smile. He hadn't ventured into her side of the facility for thirteen long days now. It seemed like thirteen months.

She heard a somewhat breathless voice next to her. "Hey, Jillian. Great turnout."

She glanced over to see Emily McKenna and Amy Stephens in race T-shirts, warm-ups, and hoodies. Amy's T-shirt highlighted her pregnancy.

"What are you two doing here?"

"We're walking the route, and you're walking with us," Emily said. She reached out to hug Jillian. "You've done such a great job with this." Her voice dropped. "Operation Shark is in full swing at the facility too. They'll be here just after nine."

The players were in town this week, and they didn't have their game walk-through until later this afternoon. Jillian was surprised when she was approached a few days ago by a group of current and ex-Sharks who told her they'd like to be involved. She'd had to scramble to get more XXXL run T-shirts and a few more racing bibs, but it was worth it. They were planning on surprising the participants by running the race with them.

"Amy, are you sure your doctor says this is okay?"

Amy Stephens laughed. "Oh, hell yeah. The doc said to take it easy, but he's fine with it. Emily's doctor told her she'd better not wear her Louboutins."

"They're not making a cross-trainer yet." Emily rolled her eyes. "Maybe by my next pregnancy."

"You too? Oh, Emily, I am so happy for you and Brandon!"

"Thank you. This is what happens when we lock ourselves in a hotel room for three days."

"Oh, like you *hated* that," Amy chimed in.

Emily let out a dramatic sigh but grinned at both of them. "Someone has to do it. Plus, he's asking for a little girl. I'd better get with the program," she confided and nudged her sister with one elbow. "Hey. Maybe we should text Holly Collins and see where she is. She wants to walk with us too. She also said that Cameron Anderson is doing interviews today on the route."

Cameron Anderson was Zach's wife. She was also a football analyst for FOX Sports, and was always gathering content for her show, *NFL Confidential*.

Jillian grabbed her phone, looked up Cameron's contact information, and sent a quick text. YOU KNOW THE GUYS ARE SHOWING UP AT THE RACE, RIGHT?

Her phone chirped seconds later with a response from Cameron. I'M TALKING WITH THEM RIGHT NOW. SEE YOU SOON.

"Holly said Derrick was going to drop her off on the way to the facility." Amy pulled her phone out of her pocket.

"I'm not getting in that huge crowd of people at the starting line," Emily said to Jillian. "Let's meet up there about nine thirty. It shouldn't take us that long to walk three miles, should it?"

"Maybe we should stop for ice cream at the end," Amy said.

"That's a great idea. I need to go check on how things are going, okay? I'll see you at nine thirty," Jillian said.

Jillian hugged both of them and hurried to the check-in area, which was manned with even more volunteers wearing Sharks T-shirts and running gear. She'd driven the route at six AM to verify that water and Gatorade stations were set up, the volunteers were arriving as planned, and the timing equipment at the finish line was working perfectly as well. At least they wouldn't have to worry about runners overheating on the midforties, overcast day.

Families and friends of the runners were already sitting in lawn chairs on either side of the street where the race was being held. Local police were keeping the race course secure.

There were a million details, but so far, everything looked great. She breathed a sigh of relief. It wasn't brain surgery, but the sense of accomplishment and pride she got from planning a fun event for so many people was always a rush. She wished she wasn't so tired, but she could sleep later. She'd jumped so many times already this morning, thinking that she'd seen Seth in the crowd or heard his voice. Her longing for him almost drowned out her excitement over the fact that she was actually going to walk a 5K.

The long walks, swimming, and lifting had paid off. She had more strength and endurance and she'd lost almost forty pounds, but even better, she had self-confidence. Kari would always be her best friend, but

Jillian made more friends as she ventured out of the self-imposed isolation bubble in which shyness and insecurity had held her for so long.

The starting area was a mob scene of runners by eight forty-five. Thousands of people chanted "Go, Sharks" as the starting gun went off fifteen minutes later, and the race was on. Emily McKenna, Amy Stephens, and Holly Collins crossed the race route to join Jillian on the sidewalk.

"Hey, Jillian," Holly said. "How are you doing?" She reached out to give Jillian a hug. "This is such a great event, and you're doing a wonderful job."

"Thank you. I'm really enjoying it."

Holly leaned closer and said into Jillian's ear, "Derrick and Drew played games over at Seth's house last night." She patted Jillian on the back. "He misses you."

"I miss him too."

"You two need to talk," she said.

"I know."

Holly gave her a nod. "And Derrick told him to pull his head out of his ass." All four women laughed aloud.

Seconds later, two decorated tour buses drove into the race area, escorted by police cars. Current and previous Sharks players exited and formed a knot in the middle of the street while the spectators lining both sides of the route cheered.

"Men. Let's stretch out a little," Tom Reed called out. The guys formed horizontal lines across the street, did some stretching, and got back into a circle, sticking their hands into the center. "Let's have a good time today, and we'll meet back here at noon to get on the buses for the facility. Ready?"

The men chanted in response. "One-two-three. Go, Sharks," and took off at a fast jog.

Jillian craned her neck and tried to see if Seth was among the guys who'd just stretched out a little, but they were already halfway up the street. She knew he wouldn't miss something like this. Maybe she could find him at the end of the race. That might work. She longed for a glimpse of him. A couple of minutes of conversation would be even better.

"It's our turn, ladies," Emily said. "Come on." She reached out her hand for Jillian's. Amy took her other hand. Jillian held out her hand for Holly's.

"We'll take it easy, Jillian. You can do this," Holly said. "Don't be afraid to grab some water or slow down a little if you need to."

"I'll be fine," Jillian said. "I'm more worried about the pregnant ladies."

"Three miles? As if," Amy said. "I log three miles chasing our son, Jonathan, around the house every morning."

"The boys keep me running too," Emily said. "Piece of cake."

"You're having ice cream with us at the finish line, right, Holly?" Amy called out.

"Absolutely."

The course was flat. The three other women set a slow-but-steady pace, and Jillian was having such a great time joking with them and glancing around at the cheering crowds that she couldn't believe it when she saw the "Finish" banner five hundred feet or so in front of her.

"We're crossing this together," she said to her three new friends. She couldn't believe the sheer amount of noise, the "Team Jillian" T-shirts she saw on multiple people in the crowd, or the handmade signs she saw on both sides of the street:

> *Congratulations, Jillian*
> *You did it!*
> *Jillian wins!*

"They've been waiting for you," Emily said and gave her a gentle nudge. "Go ahead. This is your big moment."

"I want you there too," Jillian said.

"We'll be there," Amy assured her. "I want to see this."

Jillian walked across the finish line to wild cheering, people taking pictures with their phones, and hugs from her coworkers and some of the players who'd waited around for her to finish. She'd remember this moment for the rest of her life. The only way it could have been better would be if Seth was there, but right now, she was going to enjoy achieving her goal.

"So," Holly said. "I can see Derrick and our car. How about riding with us to the ice cream place? We'll bring you back here to get your cars when we're done."

"I'd love to," Emily said.

"I'm in," Amy said.

Jillian scanned the crowd for Seth. She didn't see him, and a pang of disappointment shot through her. Maybe he'd already left; maybe he was still hurt and angry and intentionally didn't show up. Maybe she should have told him how much it would mean to her if he was there.

Emily, Amy, and Holly were having a whispered conference, and Amy spoke up. "We'll meet you at Derrick's car."

"I can go now," Jillian said.

Emily grinned at her. "I think there's someone who wants to talk to you first."

Seconds later, a tall, muscular, dark-haired man wearing a "Team Jillian" T-shirt darted through the crowd, picked Jillian up in his arms, and twirled her around.

"I found you," Seth said. "I'm so proud of you. I knew you could do it." He set her back down on her feet and kissed her forehead. "Did you have fun?"

"So much fun," she said into his ear. "I miss you."

"I miss you too, Buttercup."

They gazed into each other's eyes for a minute or so. There was so much to say. They were surrounded by hundreds of people, but she couldn't stop staring at him. He reached out to stroke her cheek.

"I can't believe you waited for me to finish."

"You've waited for me before. I was happy to do it," he said. She saw his lips curve into a smile. "I'd wait forever for you," he said.

He pressed another kiss into her hair and vanished as quickly as he'd arrived.

## Chapter Twenty-Three

ONE WEEK AFTER he'd watched Jillian's triumphant finish at the 5K, Seth stared out the weight room windows at the Sharks' practice field as his stomach churned with nerves. He jammed his hands into his warmup pockets before anybody else noticed they shook too.

He had never been so scared in his life. At least Jillian was with him now—they were taking it slow, but things were headed in a positive direction, and he was thankful.

He'd faced the biggest and baddest in the NFL, but he'd never experienced anything like this. Twenty-five kids, between ages five and fifteen, waited on the practice field for Seth on an overcast afternoon. It was chilly in the open air, but the covered practice area was the temperature of a meat locker, as usual. Everyone would warm up when they started moving around.

They'd arrived by school bus ten minutes ago, brought by arrangement with multiple organizations that served underprivileged kids and their families. He still couldn't believe how many people and how much paperwork was involved to play with some kids for an hour and a half. The parents who could attend (and who were still in the picture) watched from a VIP area that overlooked the practice field. When he asked for permission to organize the event, the team lent their support by providing lunch and a goody bag for each kid involved.

Jillian was overseeing his event as part of her new job. She reached out to squeeze his hand.

"They're going to have fun. Go play with them," she said. She gave him an encouraging smile and nodded toward the field.

"Are you sure?"

"I'm positive." Her voice dropped, but he could still hear her when she said, "And I am so proud of you."

"That's one of the nicest compliments I've ever had."

"It's the truth," she said. He forgot his nervousness over entertaining a bunch of kids as she beamed up at him.

He had some vague idea of starting an exercise program for the kids who needed it the most—the kids whose parents couldn't afford dance lessons or sports fees. The clinical research he'd read showed that when children played outside for an hour a day, there was less chance of developing obesity or type II diabetes, and children built healthier habits for the future.

If he'd heard Jillian once, he'd heard her say a thousand times, "Kids who don't have a lot don't need your pity. They need your help. If you can show them how to do it themselves, their lives will change."

Yeah. Well, what was going to happen when they all found out he was clueless? He felt cold sweat trickling down his spine. He hadn't even been this freaked out on draft day when he'd waited to hear whether he was going to be number one or number two.

He took a deep, calming breath and strolled out onto the practice field.

"Hey, guys," he called out. Twenty-five heads swiveled in his direction. "It's time to play!"

Some of the kids clapped. The older ones tried to look bored, but they didn't take their eyes off him. An idea took shape, to his relief. They might laugh at him, but they'd have fun. He jogged up to the smallest girl in the group, a blonde, blue-eyed imp who melted his heart.

"You're it," he told her.

Of course, she couldn't keep up with the other kids. He reached out, scooped her up in his arms, and shouted, "Now I'm it, and you'd better run!" He heard his new little friend's giggles. "What's your name?" he asked as he chased the other kids.

"Hannah." She patted his face with a small hand. "Your face is scratchy," she said.

"Is that so?"

"Yeah." She giggled again.

He slowed to a jog. After all, if he ran, the game would be over in no time flat. The "it" in tag switched several times. Then he called out, "Huddle up." He put Hannah back down. She grabbed on to his pants leg and refused to move. It was fairly obvious that some of the girls didn't know what a huddle was, so he motioned with both arms.

"C'mon over here." With a little coaxing, the kids formed a circle around him. Some dropped onto the grass, obviously already exhausted. Others were practically vibrating with excitement.

"Okay. I'm old now, so you're going to have to help me think of some stuff." Some of the kids laughed. Others looked confused. Didn't kids play the same games he'd played as a kid anymore? "Would you like to play another game?"

He heard a chorus of yeahs.

Kickball might work, but dodge ball was out. He wanted to play with them, not maim them. Red Rover? Maybe not. There were too many littler kids.

Hannah came to his rescue. She tugged on his pant leg again. "Duck, Duck, Goose!" she cried out.

It was perfect. The kids who were already winded could still play, and after that, he'd think of something else that required them to chase him.

"Let's sit in a circle, and we'll figure out who's it."

When they'd gathered and the game was about to start, he heard some familiar voices behind him.

"Hey, dawg." Deion sat down across from him. "I love Duck, Duck, Goose."

Zach Anderson shoehorned himself into the circle between two preteen boys, who were open-mouthed and staring at the pro athletes in their midst.

"I want to play too. Can I play?" Two little girls wriggled aside so Tom Reed could sit down.

"Duck, Duck, Goose, huh, Taylor? You're going down." Matt Stephens had changed out of the suit and tie he wore to the office as the newly named majority owner of the Sharks, as he was currently sporting a Sharks logo T-shirt and warm-ups. Seth had heard that Matt won the team on a poker hand. He also considered how much alcohol he'd have to buy Matt before Matt would share the story.

"Okay, everyone. Let me introduce you, okay? This is Deion. He's a safety. That's Tom. He's our quarterback. Zach is an offensive tackle, and Matt owns the Sharks." The kids waved, called out hi, and generally acted like kids did when they had no idea who any of these guys were. Well, most of the kids. The bigger boys were obviously thrilled to have the pros in their midst but were still attempting to act like they saw this every day. Hannah tugged at Matt's sleeve.

"Do you like kids?"

Matt grinned at her. Hannah had rendered another male helpless to resist her.

"Yes. I have a daughter named Samantha and a boy named Jon."

"Where are they? Don't they want to play with us?"

"Well, sweetheart, Samantha's a big girl. She's at school today. Jon is still a baby. I'll bet they will want to play with you someday."

This seemed to satisfy her. She leaned against his thigh.

"So, are we going to do something here?" Deion smirked at Seth.

"For that, buddy, you're it."

Deion pulled himself to his feet. He started off slowly. "Duck, duck, duck…" he chanted, touching the shoulder of each child as he passed. He moved around the circle three times, stutter-stepping and making the kids laugh. Finally, he chose one of the older kids. "Goose!"

The girl scrambled to her feet and started to chase. She'd never catch him, but Deion pretended to trip over a shoelace and landed in a heap outside the circle. She tagged him.

"Well, crap. I guess that means I'm still it." He pulled himself off the grass, brushed himself off, and held out his hand. "Let me assist you, my lady. Would you like to sit down again?"

This was rewarded with blushes and giggles. He was moving around the circle again, and this time, he picked Seth. Their resulting trip around the circle was going to result in a fifteen-yard penalty for unnecessary roughness. Matt shielded little Hannah from the inevitable pile-up, and Deion grinned at Seth from the space where he'd hurled himself into the circle.

"So, dawg, you're it. Go pick someone."

Seth made four circuits of the circle before picking a gangly young man.

The game went on for a few more minutes. Seth was just musing to himself what they should do next when Matt spoke up. "Hey, kids, there's a surprise for you on the other side of the building. Why don't you follow us?" It was a surprise to Seth too, but he played along.

Matt led the group to the sports court at the end of the path that looked out over Lake Washington. Even football players sometimes needed a break, and this basketball court had been the scene of some truly fearsome five-on-fives during free time at training camp. Right now, though, new sports equipment was stacked on one entire side of the enclosed court.

"Gather round," Matt called out. The kids couldn't stop looking at brand-new jump ropes, soccer balls, basketballs, and boxes and boxes and boxes of new shoes. "Here's the deal. There's enough here for each of you to take something home to play with. You have to promise me one thing, though—you'll actually get out and play. You'll invite your friends. The next time we see you, you'd better be whipping the big football players at Duck, Duck, Goose."

The kids were a bit speechless. It was overwhelming. Matt nudged Seth. "It's your party, buddy. They want to play."

"Where'd you get all this stuff?" Seth muttered to him.

"Jillian made some calls."

They still were taking things slowly, but she was helping him behind the scenes. A friend as well as a lover. Happiness bloomed inside of him.

"We'll have to get their parents down here to help with the shoes, but look at my little princess over there," Matt said and nodded toward Hannah, who held a pink jump rope. She was also trying to put on a pair of running shoes covered with pink stars and hearts. "I'd better go help her."

It was hard to believe that Matt, widely known before his retirement from the NFL as a fearsome hitter who had no patience with those who couldn't take what he was dishing out, was now a doting husband and father. It seemed that Seth wasn't the only one who had changes to make. He spoke up so the kids could hear him. They were a little tentative. Actually, they were looking at the stuff like they couldn't believe it was happening.

"So who wants to play some basketball with me?" Seth grabbed a new basketball off the stack, ripped the cardboard off it, and dribbled a little. One of the girls started toward him. She was tall and lanky, with long dark hair and a shy smile. "Okay. I have one teammate. Who else wants to play?" Other kids edged over. "Come on. We'll have fun."

A few minutes later, he discovered that the tall young lady could body check. He was flat on his ass on the basketball court, laughing.

## Chapter Twenty-Four

Two days before Thanksgiving, Jillian's new office looked like a home-improvement warehouse. Boxes and boxes of holiday lights and decorations took up every bit of available space. A folded Santa costume waited on one of her desk chairs for the director of facilities; he had been Santa Claus for the past ten years at the staff's get-together, which was happening next week. Employees were encouraged to decorate their work spaces for that extra bit of holiday cheer. Most of the staff and all of the players weren't able to go home for Christmas because football season didn't end until after New Year's. Everyone pitched in to make the office festive during a time when many people missed their family and friends.

Zach Anderson and Tom Reed walked into Jillian's office as she stacked a few of the boxes someone had left on the credenza behind her desk. She'd have most of this stuff out of her office by the end of the day. Right now, she'd like to be able to cross the room without falling over something.

"Good morning, Jillian," Tom said.

"Well, good morning, guys. What can I do for you?"

Zach gave her a nod. "Have you finalized the arrangements with the Christmas Ships people for December 14? Is there anything else we need to do to make this happen?"

The players planned their own holiday party each year. Typically, the offense and defense had separate parties; this year, they wanted to celebrate together with guests. They'd chosen the Christmas Ships, which sailed every night between December 1 and 24 all over the Seattle area. The Christmas Ship Parade had been enchanting the people of Seattle for over fifty years. Thousands gathered on the shoreline every night to enjoy a bonfire, drink hot chocolate, and sing along with holiday songs performed by the on-board choirs.

It was also possible to rent one of the ships for a party or get-together. Those rentals typically booked up fast, but when Seattle's pro football team asked for a Monday night rental, the local cruise company was overjoyed. The team and their guests would have a great time, especially since Tuesday was their league-mandated day off.

"It's all set. They're sending over the contract today, and you'll need to give them the half-down deposit when we sign and return the contract. The full balance is due five days before the event."

"Got it," Tom said. He pulled his wallet out of his pants pocket, fished out a credit card, and handed it to her. "This is for the deposit."

"I'm not sure they'll let me use your credit card."

"I'll verify the charge if they call my cell phone."

"Maybe we shouldn't give someone else your number, Tom."

"And I'll pay off the remaining balance before the party, Jillian," Zach said. "If you could remind me, I'd appreciate it."

"Are you guys sure? It's kind of a lot of money."

"We're sure," Tom said. He winked at her. "Have fun with my card."

"Maybe you shouldn't give this to me." She couldn't imagine putting a fifteen-thousand-dollar deposit on her own credit card for anything.

"Maybe you're right," he said. "Then again, my wife has to put it out in the yard to let it cool off after the Nordstrom Anniversary Sale each year." He winked at her. "Do your worst. My credit limit can handle it."

Zach let out a bark of laughter. "Don't tell her that, Reed. She's going to pass out or something. We're teasing you, Jillian."

Tom looked around on the desk. "How about we get those folks on the phone right now, I'll pay the damn thing, and then you won't be worried about it, will you?"

Two minutes later, Tom and Zach were sitting in the chairs in front of her desk. She dialed Argosy Cruise's offices, and she hit the speaker-phone button.

An employee answered the phone, and Tom said, "Hello. I'm Tom Reed of the Sharks, and I'd like to pay the deposit for our upcoming holiday party."

They all heard the sharp intake of breath. "Tom Reed? Is it really you?"

"It's really me. I'm going to be late for practice here, so let's charge my card. Will you also send me a paper receipt in the mail to the Sharks' offices? My accountant likes that stuff."

"I'd be happy to," the employee said. "Let me see how much you all owe."

Jillian wondered if she'd ever get used to the sheer amount of money these guys didn't flinch over spending. Their holiday party was the latest example. They wanted the best food, drinks, and a great DJ for dancing, but their white elephant gift exchange had a strict hundred-dollar limit. They also insisted on wearing ugly holiday sweaters to their parties. She couldn't imagine where a three-hundred-pound offensive lineman found a sweater that fit him, but it happened every year, according to other Sharks employees.

Tom grabbed a sticky note and a pen off Jillian's desk to write down the confirmation number for the deposit he'd just paid, thanked the employee, and hung up.

"So, Jill, are you coming to the party?" Zach said. "You know you're invited."

"I have to be there to make sure everything goes well."

"You have to be there to keep Taylor out of trouble," Tom said.

"Shit, yeah. Last year's gift exchange got a little out of hand," Zach said. "He's a bit overzealous."

"He'll listen to you," Tom said. He got to his feet and reached out to give Jillian a hug. "We appreciate all the help on this. Thank you so much."

"I'm happy to do it," she said. "Just let me know if there's something else you all need."

Zach gave her a hug too. "Are you going to be in your office for a little while?"

"Yeah. We're not starting the holiday decorating until after lunch."

They left her office. She glanced out into the cube area to see several Sharks employees shaking hands with them. The players didn't often venture into the admin side of the building, so it was always an occasion when they stopped by. She pulled up her latest to-do list on her desktop. She could get a few hours of work in before she handed out the stuff for decorating. Of course, her desk phone rang.

"Hi, Jillian, this is Mary Ann from Argosy Cruises. How are you doing?"

"I'm just fine. How are you?"

"Busy," she said and laughed a little. "I wanted to let you know that Tom Reed called up to pay the deposit for the Sharks' party earlier, so I'll send his receipt over in a separate envelope when the contract gets there."

"That would be great," Jillian said. "Thanks for doing that."

"We're happy to. You'll also find the menu information in the packet; we need a count of who wants each entrée five days before sailing. There's one more thing. I'm not sure what you're doing tonight, but you have been such a pleasure to work with that I wondered if you might enjoy a little extra holiday spirit. On us, of course."

"Sure," Jillian said. Maybe they were sending her a bottle of wine or something.

"We have to reposition one of the boats being used as part of the Christmas Ships parade. It's at the dock in Edmonds right now. We'll be returning it to Kirkland's dock this evening for our opening night. Would you and a guest like to ride along with our crew? We won't have a choir on board or anything like that, but I'm sure they could find some holiday music on the radio for you if you'd like."

"That sounds amazing," Jillian said. "I would love that. So, I'll need to take a cab or something to the dock?"

"Exactly. If you can get yourself and a guest to Edmonds, we'll take care of everything else. Plus, it's clear and cold tonight, which means a smooth ride to Kirkland."

"I'd love it," Jillian said. "Thank you so much for thinking of me."

"It's my pleasure," Mary Ann said. "Have a great time."

SETH GLANCED UP from changing a broken shoelace on one of his cleats to see Tom Reed and Zach Anderson standing in front of him.

"Jillian told us she needs to talk to you," Tom said.

"She said it's urgent," Zach chimed in.

"What's wrong?" Seth said.

"Hell if I know," Tom said.

"You know how women get," Zach said. "She might need some help with all the decorations in her office or something. They're really packed in there. I can't believe there's room for her to sit down at her desk right now."

"You'd better go talk to her. Now," Tom said.

"I'm a little busy—"

Zach and Tom each grabbed him by an elbow and stood him up. "Go talk to her."

Seth passed Derrick Collins on his way out of the locker room. "Jillian's looking for you," Derrick said.

"I heard."

He saw eleven of his teammates on his way to Jillian's office. They all told him she was looking for him, and oh, by the way, maybe he should move his ass. He wasn't sure why she didn't send him a text or whatever. Maybe something really was wrong. Or maybe his teammates were jerking his chain. It really didn't matter. Any excuse to talk to Jillian worked for him.

He took the last flight of stairs to the third floor at a sprint.

Jillian was sitting at her desk, tapping at her keyboard, when he rounded the corner into her office.

"I heard you're looking for me," he said.

"I am?"

"Reed and Anderson told me to get up here." He gestured at the stacks and stacks of decorations. "Is anyone helping you with this?"

"Yes," she said. She glanced up at him, and she swallowed hard. "Do you remember when we used to go on adventures together?"

"Of course I do."

She'd be stunned if she knew how many times a day he thought about her. He loved the memories of places they went and things they did together. Well, before she got scared and pulled back a little, and before he knew he had to let her set the pace of their relationship. It was the hardest thing he'd ever done.

"Are you busy this evening?" she said. "I understand if you are."

"Just laundry and some TV," he said. He'd be canceling his plans as soon as he got back to his locker and grabbed his phone. "What's on your mind?"

"Would you like to take a cruise on Lake Washington? The Christmas Ships people are taking a boat from Edmonds to Kirkland. We'll have to get a ride to Edmonds, but it should be really fun. Plus, it's free."

"Why don't I pick you up? We'll park in Kirkland, and we can go to Edmonds from there."

She picked up her cell phone. "I can get a reservation for us with Lyft. We need to be at the dock before seven PM," she said.

SETH SPRINTED OUT of the practice facility twenty minutes later and headed for his rig. He was due at Jillian's house at five thirty, but he had the biggest errand of his life to run first. She'd invited him out, which meant things between them were back on in a big way. He wasn't letting this chance go by.

He'd heard the other guys talk about shopping for an engagement ring before. Several brought the ring in to show their teammates before they officially popped the question. He wasn't going to be one of those guys. He knew what he was buying. After looking online and in person, he kept coming back to a simple diamond solitaire set in platinum. And he wanted her to say yes (and put the ring on her finger) before he told anyone else he was asking her to marry him.

The guys he played with wore one-carat diamond studs in their ears to practice. He was getting her a little bigger diamond as a result. Not too big, though. If the ring was too big, she'd take it back, pick out something smaller, and send the difference to Treehouse.

Maybe he should give them a donation today for the hell of it.

He strode into his one-stop-shopping choice jeweler's. Thirty seconds ago, he was calm and decisive. Butterflies were multiplying in his stomach with the quickness. His hands shook. He licked suddenly dry lips.

"May I help you?" a woman asked.

"I'd like to buy an…an engagement ring," he said. His voice sounded like a rusty hinge. He could hardly force it out past the dryness in his mouth.

"Follow me," she said.

She led him to a wall-length glass case of rings. He sank down on the padded bench in front of the cases. He shoved it back a little when his knees hit the counter. They must have sized the rings counter for short people or something.

"Do you have an idea of what you'd like to buy and how much you'd like to spend?" she said.

He clasped his hands together on the counter before he started fidgeting. He couldn't remember the last time he was this nervous. It wasn't buying a ring that scared the shit out of him; it was asking Jillian to marry him. What if she said no? He'd thought proposing in such a memorable setting was a great idea. He'd thought about the perfect place to ask her since the moment he realized he'd fallen in love with her, but nothing else seemed right.

Maybe it wasn't the best place to propose. Maybe he should wait a while. Waiting a while, however, would require that he stand up and walk out of the store. Right now, he wasn't sure he could do that. Maybe he should try some deep breathing or something.

"I know which type of ring I'm interested in."

"Would you like me to bring you a few to look at?"

He coughed a bit to clear his throat. "Sure. I'd like to see a solitaire set in platinum. Nothing under two carats, please."

Maybe he needed some water or something.

The saleswoman looked at him a bit quizzically. "Are you okay?"

"I'm nervous. I don't know why." He spread his hands out on the cool glass of the case. "May I have some water, if there's some available?"

"I'll get you a cup of water, and then I'll bring some rings," she said.

"That would be great. Thank you."

He stared at himself in the mirrored wall over the jewelry cases. He looked freaked out. Plus, he could feel cold sweat trickling down his back. He couldn't figure out why he was reacting like this. What was going to happen when he finally asked her? He'd better not pass out or whatever. He concentrated on his breathing.

The saleswoman returned a few minutes later. She sat down on the bench behind the counter and patted his hand.

"Does anyone else flip out over this, or am I just weird?"

She was probably his mom's age. She wore a black suit with a knee-length skirt. Her dark hair was cut close to her face. Her eyes were warm, like his mom's. She smiled at him.

"It's the biggest question you're going to ask in your life. Of course you're nervous." She put a velvet tray of rings down on the counter while she talked. "Why don't you tell me about your fiancée?"

"She hasn't said yes yet."

"She will. What's she like?"

Seth closed his eyes for a moment. He could talk all day, but his words could never convey what was in his heart. He felt his nervousness fading as he saw Jillian's smiling face in his mind.

"She's...she's...she's blonde. She has blue eyes. She's about this tall," he said. He gestured with one hand. "She smells like vanilla. Whenever she smiles at me, I feel like I'm home." He let out a long breath and met the salesperson's eyes. "She knows everything about me, and she loves me anyway." He took a gulp of water. "And I want to be her family."

He wanted to be that guy he'd pictured in his mind, looking on proudly as Jillian read a bedtime story to rosy-cheeked kids curled up next to her. He wanted their house to be a home, full of love and laughter.

The saleswoman nodded. "Then let's pick out the perfect ring for her."

Seth had the presence of mind a while ago to try on the little silver ring Jillian left on her bathroom counter before they went to bed that night. He still remembered how small her ring was on his hand. It barely cleared his fingernail. He pulled the most sparkly ring out of the tray and slid it over the third fingertip of his left hand. If his informal sizing efforts were correct, this would fit Jillian's finger.

"That's a two-and-a-half-carat brilliant cut, VVS1, E-color solitaire, Tiffany setting," the saleswoman said. "What do you think?"

Seth moved his hand around in the overhead lighting. The diamond's sparkle shimmered and arced off of every reflective surface. He wished he could buy something as beautiful as the sparkle in Jillian's eyes whenever she looked at him, but this would have to do. He slid the ring off his finger, held it for a moment in his fingertips, and looked up at the saleswoman.

"It's perfect. I'll take it."

JILLIAN CHANGED HER clothes three times while she waited for Seth to pick her up. They needed to dress warmly, but she still wanted to look nice. Her pretty turquoise fleece cardigan and a long-sleeved T-shirt under her wool pea coat would keep her warm. She confirmed the time and meeting place with the Lyft driver picking them up in Kirkland, and she fed CB, who tried to climb into her handbag.

"No, kitty, you can't go tonight."

CB let out a piteous meow.

"You stay here where it's warm."

CB redoubled her efforts to get in Jillian's bag. Seconds later, Jillian heard a knock at the door and Seth's voice.

"It's me."

CB ran to the door, got up on her hind legs, and pawed at it. "I know he's your favorite, kitty. Go take a nap." She grabbed the cat and pulled the front door open to let Seth inside the apartment.

Seth reached out for CB. "You get your stuff. I'll take care of this." He held the kitty up so he could look into her eyes. "Listen, girl. You can't come with us tonight. It's cold and it's wet out there, and I know you don't like wet."

She tried to head-butt him.

"I promise we'll play with you when we get home. Now scoot."

When Seth bent over to gently place her on the carpet, Jillian was amazed to see CB run away, hurl herself onto Jillian's bed, and curl up.

"Are you the cat whisperer? She obeys you!"

"She wants to rest up for later," Seth said. "Ready to go?"

He'd taken her suggestion to dress warmly to heart. He wore a heavy jacket with a sweater beneath, jeans, and boots. He'd pulled a knit cap on. He'd thrown a scarf around his neck too.

Seth and Jillian arrived at the dock in plenty of time to board the ship. The crew stood waiting for them on the dock. A taller man stepped forward and stuck out his hand to Jillian.

"Welcome to the Christmas Ship, Ms. Miller. I'm Captain Doug," he said.

Jillian shook his hand. "It's great to meet you. I'm Jillian, and this is Seth Taylor."

"Great to meet you, Mr. Taylor. We're big Sharks fans."

"I'm always happy to meet Sharks fans," Seth said.

"If you'd like to board, we'll get underway in a few minutes here. There are complimentary snacks and a beverage setup for your enjoyment. We'll also turn on the lights so you'll get the full effect," the captain said. "I hope you'll enjoy your evening."

"I'm sure we'll love it," Jillian said. "Thank you so much for doing all this for us."

"No problem," he assured her. "I hope you'll let my staff know if there's anything else we can do for you."

Jillian was helped onto the boat. Seth took her hand as they were shown to a huge interior salon featuring windows that framed the entire length of the ship. Two padded arm chairs were set up in the middle of the salon with a small table holding snacks, two champagne flutes, and an ice bucket with a chilling bottle of champagne. Anyone sitting in those chairs would have the perfect view of the lake.

"It's okay to go out on the deck if you'd like," the captain told them.

"This is wonderful. Thank you again," Jillian said.

A few minutes later, the ship moved through smooth water toward Kirkland. Both the interior and exterior of the ship were decorated in clear lights, and there was holiday music playing over the ship's sound system. Seth reached out for Jillian's hand again.

"Want to go out to the deck for a few minutes?"

"Sure," she said.

They leaned against the dock's railing, looking out at a crescent moon suspended in a cobalt sky and a thousand twinkling stars. Jillian could see boats tied up on docks nearer the shoreline that were already decorated for the holiday parade and waiting for their debut. Seth pulled her to his side. They stared down into water tinted navy blue by the night sky. The slight spray off of the water was freezing cold, but she didn't want to go inside. She knew she wanted to remember this night for the rest of her life.

"I'm so glad you came with me," she said. There were so many other things she needed to say, but right now, she wasn't sure where to start. Maybe she should try the most obvious. "I've missed you so much."

He hadn't gone anywhere. She'd been the one to step back, and he'd waited patiently while she figured things out. She missed the fact he was the only other person besides Kari she could pour her heart out to. To feel safe with another person was something she should never take for granted, or the fact he'd still be around when she worked through her own struggles in life. When they first met, his looks dazzled her, but she knew him well enough to know that he was so much more than a handsome face and a perfect body. She wanted to be his safe person too, someone he could confide in, someone who listened and understood.

Maybe he didn't want to give her the power to hurt him again or to deal with the insecurities she pulled like weeds growing on her soul, one at a time. She was a different woman than she'd been when they first met, but she was still working on herself. Maybe he wanted someone who didn't have so many flaws. She opened her mouth to say so, but nothing came out.

"I missed you too," he said. His arm tightened around her.

"Seth, I…I…" She struggled for words. "There's so many things I should say to you right now, and I—"

He leaned his forehead against hers. "I love you."

She snuggled against him as she wrapped her arms around his waist. "You do?"

"I have for a long time now, Jill. Do you love me too?"

"With all my heart," she said.

"You're sure about that?"

"I love you. Every minute of every day." She wished she had the words to tell him how much she loved him. Maybe she should try. "When I first met you, I thought you were so handsome, and I was so thrilled when you talked to me."

"So you thought I was hot."

She couldn't stop the laughter that bubbled up inside her. He loved her. She'd dreamed of this moment. Being able to tell him she loved him too was better than she'd ever imagined. Confessing her feelings to him made her heart sing with happiness.

"I know it's shallow," she said.

"It's not shallow if it's the truth."

She had to laugh again. "Is that so?"

"Absolutely." His eyes sparkled. "Tell me more."

"The more time I spent with you, the more I couldn't help my feelings. They grew and grew. I wasn't sure what you thought of me. I knew you wanted to be just friends."

"Until I showed up at your apartment one day and carried you off to bed."

She flushed at the memory. "Yes."

As they held each other, they glanced out at the lake and at the twinkling lights of homes on the shore. Husky Stadium was a beacon of light across the water. The snow-capped mountains that loomed over them were visible in the distance too. They'd be in Kirkland soon, but she knew she'd relive this night for the rest of her life.

"I fell in love with you because I couldn't resist you," he said. "I thought you were beautiful too, but the more I got to know you, the more I wanted to be around you. I love your sassy personality and your sense of humor. I love the way you care for other people. I want to spend every day with you. I want to be a better man for you. And I want to be your family." He pulled in a breath. "I guess that means I have something to ask you."

He was still fumbling in his pocket, but he sank to one knee on the deck, still holding her hand. The entire world telescoped to the two of them. The skyline of Seattle, the brightly lit ship, the water, and the sky illuminated with countless stars were a backdrop as Seth held up a ring box.

"Marry me, Jill."

She covered her mouth with one trembling hand. She didn't realize she was crying until she felt tears streaking down her cheeks. He pulled her other hand to his mouth and pressed a kiss into her knuckles.

"Are you sure?" she blurted out.

"I've never been so sure about anything in my life."

All she had to do was say that little word. She saw tears brimming in his eyes too. He squeezed her hand.

"Be mine," he whispered in the stillness. "Be my lover and my friend."

"Yes," she said.

## *Author's Note*

JILLIAN MILLER OF *Chasing Jillian* is a fictional character, but the struggles of foster children in the United States are all too real. Foster children end up in the system due to parents who are unable to care for their children for a variety of reasons. Once in the system, children are typically moved from placement to group home to another placement with no warning. An education is difficult at best to obtain. I was shocked to learn that less than half of foster children graduate from high school. Two-thirds of foster children don't go to college. Only 3 percent of foster children graduate from college. There is no security for those children—socially, emotionally, or financially. They grow up facing unthinkable challenges on a daily basis. They "age out" of the system at age eighteen in thirty-nine states, which means they must learn to survive on their own with little to no support.

These children did not ask for their circumstances. Their lives improve when they know someone cares about them.

My husband and I learned about Seattle's Treehouse many years ago. Treehouse's mission is to offer foster children a childhood and a future. They provide educational support, assistance with clothes/toiletries/books/toys, and some of the things that most other kids take for granted via "Little Wishes": music lessons, sports fees, or an ASB card are a few examples.

I'm donating a percentage of my share of the first week of *Chasing Jillian*'s sales to Treehouse. If you'd like to know more about Treehouse (or you'd like to help), please go to http://www.treehouseforkids.org/.

Don't drop the ball!
Be sure to score a copy of every
book in Julie Brannagh's
Love and Football series!

# BLITZING EMILY

## A Love and Football Novel

All's fair in Love and Football…

Emily Hamilton doesn't trust men. She's much more comfortable playing the romantic lead in front of a packed house onstage than in her own life. So when NFL star and alluring ladies' man Brandon McKenna acts as her personal white knight, she has no illusions that he'll stick around. However, a misunderstanding with the press throws them together in a fake engagement that yields unexpected (and breathtaking) benefits.

Every time Brandon calls her "Sugar," Emily almost believes he's playing for keeps—not just to score. Can she let down her defenses and get her own happily ever after?

# RUSHING AMY
## A Love and Football Novel

For Amy Hamilton, only three F's matter: Family, Football, and Flowers.

It might be nice to find someone to share Forever with too, but right now she's working double overtime while she gets her flower shop off the ground. The last thing she needs or wants is a distraction...or help, for that matter. Especially in the form of gorgeous and aggravatingly arrogant ex-NFL star Matt Stephens.

Matt lives by a playbook—his playbook. He never thought his toughest opponent would come in the form of a stunning florist with a stubborn streak to match his own. Since meeting her in the bar after her sister's wedding, he's known there's something between them. When she refuses, again and again, to go out with him, Matt will do anything to win her heart. But will Amy, who has everything to lose, let the clock run out on the one-yard line?

## CATCHING CAMERON
### A Love and Football Novel

Star sports reporter Cameron Ondine has one firm rule: she does not date football players. Ever. She tangled with one years ago, and it did not end well. Been there, done that.

But when Cameron comes face-to-face with the very man who shattered her heart—on camera, no less—her world is upended for a second time by recklessly handsome Seattle Shark Zach Anderson.

Zach has never been able to forget the gorgeous blonde who stole his breath away when he was still just a rookie. They've managed to give each other a wide berth for years, but when their jobs suddenly bring them together again and again, he knows he has to face his past once and for all.

Because as they spend more time together, he becomes less focused on the action on the field and more concerned with catching Cameron.

**COVERING KENDALL**

A Love and Football Novel

Kendall Tracy, general manager of the San Francisco Miners, is not one for rash decisions or one-night stands. But when she finds herself alone in a hotel room with a heart-stoppingly gorgeous man—who looks oddly familiar—Kendall throws her own rules out the window…and they blow right back into her face.

Drew McCoy should look familiar; he's a star player for her team's arch rival, the Seattle Sharks. Which would basically make Drew and Kendall the Romeo and Juliet of professional football…well, without all the dying.

Not that it's an issue. They agree to pretend their encounter never happened. Nothing good can come of it anyway, right?

Drew's not so sure. Kendall may be all wrong for him, but he can't stop thinking about her, and he finds that some risks are worth taking. Because the stakes are always highest when you're playing for keeps.

## HOLDING HOLLY
### A Love and Football Novella

Holly Reynolds has a secret. Make that two. The first involves upholding her grandmother's hobby answering Dear Santa letters from dozens of local school children. The second…well, he just came strolling in the door.

For the last two years, Holly has not been able to stop thinking about gorgeous Seattle Shark Derrick Collins. His on-field exploits induce nightmares in quarterbacks across the NFL, but she knows he has a heart of gold.

Derrick has never met a woman he wants to bring home to meet his family, mostly because he keeps picking the wrong ones—until he runs into sweet, shy Holly Reynolds. Different from anyone he's ever known, Derrick realizes she might just be everything he needs.

When he discovers her holiday letter-writing, he is determined to play Santa too. And as the pair team up to bring joy to one little boy very much in need, they discover the most precious Christmas gift of all: love.

## CHASING JILLIAN
### A Love and Football Novel

Score a touchdown with Julie Brannagh's
latest Love and Football novel about discovering
who you are and finding love along the way.

Jillian Miller likes her job working in the front office for
the Seattle Sharks, but lately, being surrounded by a con-
stant parade of perfection only seems to make her own
imperfections all the more obvious. She needs a change,
which takes her into foreign territory: the Sharks' workout facility after hours. The last thing she expects is a hot,
grumbly god among men to be there as a witness.

Star linebacker Seth Taylor has had a bad day—well, a
series of them recently. When he hits the Sharks' gym
to work out his frustration, he's startled to find someone
there—and even more surprised that it's Jillian, the team
owner's administrative assistant. When he learns of Jillian's mission to revamp her lifestyle, he finds himself
volunteering to help. Something about Jillian's beautiful
smile and quick wit makes him want to stick around. She
may not be like the swimsuit models he usually has on

his arm, but the more time Seth spends with Jillian, the harder he falls.

And as Jillian discovers that the new her is about so much more than what she sees in the mirror, can she discover that happiness and love are oh-so-much better than perfect?

## About the Author

---

**JULIE BRANNAGH** HAS been writing since she was old enough to hold a pencil. She lives in a small town near Seattle, where she once served as a city council member and owned a yarn shop. She shares her home with a wonderful husband, two uncivilized Maine Coons, and a rambunctious chocolate Lab.

When she's not writing, she's reading or armchair-quarterbacking her favorite NFL team from the comfort of the family room couch. Julie is a *USA Today* bestselling author, a Golden Heart finalist and the author of contemporary sports romances.

Discover great authors, exclusive offers, and more at hc.com.

Give in to your Impulses . . .
Continue reading for excerpts from
our newest Avon Impulse books.
Available now wherever e-books are sold.

HEART'S DESIRE
By T.J. Kline

DESIRE ME NOW
By Tiffany Clare

THE WEDDING GIFT
A SAVE THE DATE NOVELLA
By Cara Connelly

WHEN LOVE HAPPENS
RIBBON RIDGE BOOK THREE
By Darcy Burke

An Excerpt from

# HEART'S DESIRE
### by T.J. Kline

Jessie Hart has a soft spot for healing the broken, especially horses and children, but her business is failing. The one man who can save Heart Fire Ranch is the last man she wants to see, the man who broke her heart eight years ago . . .

Jessie heard the crunch of tires on the gravel driveway and stepped onto the porch of the enormous log home. Her parents had raised their family here, in the house her father had built just before her brother was born. The scent of pine surrounded her, warming her insides. Even after her brother and sister had built houses of their own on either end of the property, she'd remained here with her parents, helping them operate the dude ranch and training their horses. She inhaled deeply, wishing again that circumstances hadn't been so cruel as to leave her to figure out how to make the transition from dude ranch to horse rescue alone.

Leaning against the porch railing, she sipped her coffee and enjoyed the quiet of the morning. When a teen girl walked toward the barn to feed the horses, she lifted her hand in a wave. The poor girl was spending more time at the ranch than away from it these days, since her mother had violated parole again, but Jessie loved having her here. Aleta's foster mother, June, had been close friends with Jessie's own mother, and she understood the healing power horses had on kids who needed someone, or something, just to listen. Now that Aleta was living with June again, she was spending a lot of time at the ranch.

Jessie looked down the driveway as Bailey drove her truck closer to the house. She could just make out Nathan through the glare on the windshield. The resentment in her belly grew with each ticking second at the sight of him. Clenching her jaw and squaring her shoulders for the battle ahead, Jessie walked down the stairs to meet Justin's former best friend and the man who'd broken her heart.

The truck pulled to a stop in front of her, and Bailey jumped from the driver's seat wearing a shit-eating grin. Jessie narrowed her eyes, knowing exactly what that meant—she was in for a week of hell from this pain-in-the-ass, penny-pinching bean counter.

She didn't understand why he'd insisted on returning to the ranch. If Justin hadn't begged her to give Nathan a chance to help, she would have been perfectly content never to speak to his lying ass again.

She watched him turn his broad shoulders to her as he removed his luggage from the back seat. When he faced her, Jessie was barely able to contain her gasp of surprise. After he left, she'd avoided any mention of Nathan Kerrington like the plague, going as far as changing the channel when his name was mentioned on the news. She'd been praying that the past eight years had been cruel, that he'd gained a potbelly, or that he'd developed a receding hairline. She pictured him turning into a stereotypical computer geek.

This guy was perfection. Well, if she was into muscular men who looked like Hollywood actors and wore suits that cost several thousand dollars. Every strand of his dark brown hair was combed into place, even at six in the morning, after a flight from New York. There wasn't a wrinkle in his stiffly starched shirt.

His green eyes slid over her dirty jeans and T-shirt before climbing back up to focus on her face. Memories of stolen kisses and lingering caresses filled her mind before she could cast them aside. His slow perusal sent heat curling in her belly, spreading through her veins, making her feel uncomfortable. Was he just trying to be an ass? If so, it was working. She felt on edge immediately, but she wasn't about to let him know it. She crossed her arms over her chest and kicked her hip to the side.

"Nathan Kerrington. You've got some brass ones showing up here."

An Excerpt from

# DESIRE ME NOW

*by Tiffany Clare*

Amelia Grant has just escaped her lecherous
employer with nothing but the clothes on
her back. In the pre-dawn hours of London,
a horse and carriage comes barreling
down on her, and a stranger rushes to
her aid, sweeping her off her feet . . .

"Why did you kiss me?" She wasn't sure she wanted to hear the answer, but a part of her needed to know. And talking was safer right now.

"I have wanted to do that since you first stumbled into my path. Do you feel something growing between us?"

She'd been ignoring that feeling, thinking and hoping it would pass with time. She'd assumed she'd developed hero worship after Mr. Riley had rescued her and then taken care of her when she'd been at an ultimate low.

She couldn't deny the truth now. She did feel something for him; something not easily defined as mere lust but a deep desire to learn more about him and why he made her feel so out of sorts with what she thought was right.

Not that she would ever admit to that.

Who was she to garner the attention of this man? Women probably threw themselves at his feet and begged him to ruin them on a regular basis. That thought left her feeling cold. She eyed the door, longing for escape.

"Do not leave, Amelia." He stepped closer to her, near enough that she could kiss him again if she so desired. She ignored that desire. "Work for me as we planned. Just stay."

There was a kind of desolation in his voice at the thought

of her abandoning him. But that was impossible. And she was reading too much into his request. Logically, she knew she couldn't feel this sort of attachment to someone she had just met. Someone she didn't really know.

"I am afraid of what I will do," she admitted, more for herself than for him.

"Then do not think about it. Go with what your instincts tell you. If there is one thing I have always done, it is to follow my first inclination. I would not be in the position I am today, had I ignored those natural reflexes."

He caressed her cheek again. She nearly nestled into his palm before realizing what she was doing. With a heavy sigh, she pulled away from him before she made any more mistakes. This was not a good way to start her first official day as his secretary.

She couldn't help but ask. "And what do your instincts say about me?"

"I do not need my instincts to tell me where this is going. It is more base than that. I desire you. And there is nothing that can stop me from fulfilling and exploring what I want. You will be mine in the end, Amelia."

Her heart picked up speed at his admission. Her breathing grew more rapid as she assessed him. She desired him too. She, Amelia Marie Somerset, who wanted nothing more than to escape one vile man's sick craving to marry her and claim her, was willing to let the man in front of her ruin her, only because she felt different with him than she had with anyone else.

What would she lose of herself in the process of courting dangerous games with this man? Focusing on the hard angles of his face and the steady expression he wore, one thing was certain.

This man would ruin her.

And more startling was the realization that she would do nothing to stop him.

An Excerpt from

# THE WEDDING GIFT
## A Save the Date Novella
### *by Cara Connelly*

In the next Save the Date novella, mousey
Jan Marone finally allows herself to live,
laugh, and love . . . with a sexy fireman
during a weekend wedding in Key West!

"I'm sorry, ma'am, there's nothing I can do."

Jan Marone wrung her hands. "But I have a reservation."

"I know, I'm looking at it right here." The pretty blonde at the desk tapped her screen sympathetically. "I'll refund your deposit immediately."

"I don't want my deposit. I want a room. My cousin's getting married tomorrow, and I'm in the wedding."

The girl spread her hands. "The problem is, when one of the upstairs tubs overflowed this morning, the ceiling collapsed on your room. It's out of service for the weekend, and we're booked solid."

"I understand," Jan said, struggling to remain polite. Hearing the same excuse three times didn't make it easier to swallow. "How about a sister hotel?"

"We're independently owned. Paradise Inn is the oldest hotel on the island—"

Jan held up a hand. She knew the spiel. The large, rambling guesthouse was unique, and very Old Key West. Which was exactly why she'd booked it.

"Can you at least help me find a room somewhere else?"

"It's spring break. I'll make some calls, but . . ." A discouraging shrug and a gesture toward the coffeepot.

The girl didn't seem very concerned, but Jan smiled at her anyway. "Thanks, I appreciate you trying."

Parking her suitcase beside the coffee table, she surveyed the lobby wistfully. The windows and doors stood open, the wicker furniture and abundant potted plants blurring the line between indoors and out. The warm, humid breeze drifted through the airy space. Her parched Boston skin soaked it up like a sponge.

To a woman who'd never left New England before, it spelled tropical vacation. And it was slipping through her fingers like sand.

Growing ever gloomier, she wandered out through a side door and into a lush tropical garden—palm trees, hibiscus, a babbling waterfall.

Paradise.

And at its heart, a glittering pool, where six gorgeous feet of lean muscle and tanned skin drifted lazily on a float.

Ignoring everything else, Jan studied the man. Thick black hair, chiseled jaw, half smile curving full lips. And arms, perfect arms, draped over the sides, fingers trailing in the water.

He seemed utterly relaxed, the image of sensual decadence. Put him in an ad for Paradise Inn, and women would flock. Gay men would swarm.

As if sensing her attention, the hunk lifted his head and broke into a smile. "Hey Jan, getcha ass in the water!"

Mick McKenna. Her best and oldest friend.

He rolled off the float and jacked himself out of the pool. Water streamed from gray board shorts as he crossed the flagstones.

Stopping in front of her, he shook his hair like a Labrador.

"Geez! Don't you ever get tired of that?" She brushed droplets off her white cotton blouse.

He laughed his big, happy laugh. "Never have, never will. Get your suit on. The water's a perfect eighty-six degrees."

"I can't. They don't have a room for me."

The grin fell off his face. "What the hell?"

"Water damage." She shrugged like it wasn't tragic. Like she hadn't been anticipating this weekend for months.

"They must have another room." Mick started to go around her, no doubt to raise hell at the desk, McKenna-style.

She stopped him with a hand on his arm. "I tried everything. They're digging up a room for me somewhere else on the island."

He tunneled long fingers through his hair. "Take my room," he said.

An Excerpt from

# WHEN LOVE HAPPENS
## Ribbon Ridge Book Three
### *by Darcy Burke*

In the third Ribbon Ridge novel from
*USA Today* bestseller Darcy Burke,
Tori Archer is about to discover that even the
best kept secrets don't stay buried for long . . .

Tori Archer sipped her Nocktoberfest, Dad's signature beer for the annual Ribbon Ridge Oktoberfest, which was currently in full swing. She clung to the corner of the huge tent, defensively watching for her "date" or one of her annoying siblings that had forced her to go on this "date."

It wasn't really a date. He was a professional colleague, and the Archers had invited him to their signature event. For nine years, the family had sponsored the town's Oktoberfest. It featured Archer beer and this year, for the first time, a German feast overseen by her brother Kyle, who was an even more amazing chef than they'd all realized. Today was day three of the festival and she still wasn't tired of the fondue. But really, could one ever tire of cheese?

"Boo!"

Tori jumped, splashing a few drops of beer from her plastic mug onto her fingers. She turned her head and glared at Kyle. "Did you sneak through the flap in the corner behind me?"

"Guilty." He wore an apron tied around his waist and a custom Archer shirt, which read CHEF below the bow and arrow A-shaped logo. "How else was I supposed to talk to you? You've been avoiding everyone for the past hour and a half. Where's Cade?" He scanned the crowd looking for her not-date, the engineer they'd hired to work on The Alex, the hotel and restaurant venue they'd been renovating since last spring. With a special events space already completed, they'd turned their focus to the restaurant and would tackle the hotel next.

Tori took a drink of the dark amber Nocktoberfest and relished the hoppy flavor. "Don't know."

Kyle gave her a sidelong glance. "Didn't you come together?"

"No. Though it wasn't for your lack of trying. I met him here. We chatted. He saw someone he knew. I excused myself to get a beer." *An hour ago.*

Kyle turned toward her and frowned. "I don't get it. Lurking in corners isn't your style. You're typically the life of the party. You work a room better than anyone I know, except maybe Liam."

Tori narrowed her eyes. "I'm better at it than he is." Their brother Liam, a successful real estate magnate in Denver, possessed many of the same qualities she did: ambition, drive, and an absolute hatred of failure. Then again, who *wanted* to fail? But it was more than that for them. Failure was never an option.

Which didn't mean that it didn't occasionally come up and take a piece out of you when you were already down for the count.

Kyle snorted. "Yeah, whatever. You two can duke it out at Christmas or whenever Liam decides to deign us with his presence."

Tori touched his arm. "Hey, don't take his absence personally. He keeps his visits pretty few and far between, even before you moved back home. Which is more than I can say for you when you were in Florida."

Kyle's eyes clouded briefly with regret and he looked away. "Yeah, I know. And hopefully someday you'll stop giving me shit about it."

She laughed. "Too soon? I'm not mad at you for leaving anymore. I get why you had to go, but I'm your sister. I will always flip you shit about stuff like that. It's my job."

He returned his attention to her, his blue-green eyes—nearly identical to her own—narrowing. "Then it's my duty to harass you about Cade. He's totally into you. Why are you dogging him?"

It seemed that since Kyle and their sister Sara had both found their soul mates this year, they expected everyone else to do the same. Granted, their adopted brother Derek had also found his true love, and they'd gotten married in August. What none of them knew, however, was that Tori was already spoken for—at least on paper.